# THE IDEAL MAN

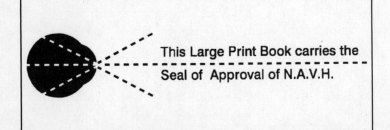

This Large Print Book carries the
Seal of Approval of N.A.V.H.

# THE IDEAL MAN

## JULIE GARWOOD

**THORNDIKE PRESS**
*A part of Gale, Cengage Learning*

GALE
CENGAGE Learning™

Detroit • New York • San Francisco • New Haven, Conn • Waterville, Maine • London

**GALE**
CENGAGE Learning

Copyright © 2011 by Julie Garwood.
Thorndike Press, a part of Gale, Cengage Learning.

Thorndike Press® Large Print Basic.
The text of this Large Print edition is unabridged.
Other aspects of the book may vary from the original edition.
Set in 16 pt. Plantin.

**LIBRARY OF CONGRESS CATALOGING-IN-PUBLICATION DATA**

Garwood, Julie.
   The ideal man / by Julie Garwood. — Large print ed.
   p. cm. — (Thorndike Press large print basic)
   ISBN-13: 978-1-4104-3868-3
   ISBN-10: 1-4104-3868-6
   1. Government investigators—Fiction. 2. Women detectives—Fiction. 3. Kidnapping—Fiction. 4. South Carolina—Fiction. 5. Large type books. I. Title.
   PS3557.A8427I34 2011
   813'.54—dc22                                                2011014340

Published in 2011 by arrangement with Dutton, a member of Penguin Group (USA), Inc.

Printed in the United States of America
1 2 3 4 5 6 7 15 14 13 12 11

AUG - 2011

To Macy Elyse and Kennedy Paige
for all the joy you've brought to my life.
Thank heaven for little girls.

# ONE

The first time she slit a man's throat she felt sick to her stomach. The second time? Not so much.

After she cut five or six more, the blade in her left hand began to feel like an extension of her body, and she started to take it all in stride. The exhilaration subsided, and so did the nausea. There was no longer a rush of anxiety, no longer a racing heartbeat. Blood didn't faze her. The thrill was gone, and that, in her line of work, was a very good thing.

Dr. Eleanor Kathleen Sullivan, or Ellie as she was called by her family and friends, was just four days shy of completing a grueling surgical fellowship in one of the busiest trauma centers in the Midwest. Since trauma was her specialty, she had certainly seen her share of mangled and brutalized bodies. It was her responsibility to put them back together, and as a senior fellow, she had the added duty of training the first- and second-year residents.

St. Vincent's emergency room had been full since 4:00 A.M. that morning, and Ellie was finishing what she hoped was her last surgery of the day, a repair of a splenic rupture. A teenager, barely old enough to have a driver's license, had decided to test the limits of the speedometer in his parents' Camry and had lost control, rolling the car over an embankment and landing upside down in an open field. Lucky for him, he had been wearing a seat belt, and luckier still, a man following some distance behind him had seen the whole thing and was able to call for an ambulance immediately. The boy made it to the emergency room just in time.

Ellie was observed by three second-year surgical residents, who hung on her every word. She was a natural teacher and, unlike 90 percent of the surgeons on staff at St. Vincent's Hospital, didn't have much of an ego. She was amazingly patient with the medical students and residents. While she worked, she explained — and explained again — until they finally understood what she was doing and why. No question was deemed too insignificant or foolish, which was one of the many reasons they idolized her, and for the male residents, the fact that she was drop-dead gorgeous didn't hurt. Because she was such a talented surgeon and supportive teacher, all these fledgling doctors fought to sign up for her rotation. Ironically, what they didn't know was that she was younger than most of them.

"You're off duty this weekend, aren't you, Ellie?"

Ellie glanced over at Dr. Kevin Andrews, the anesthesiologist, who had asked the question. He had joined the staff six months before and, since the day he'd met Ellie, had been hounding her to go out with him. He was an outrageous flirt and yet very sweet. Blond hair, blue eyes, tall and well built with an adorable smile, he could turn the head of almost every woman in the hospital, but for Ellie there just wasn't any spark.

"Yes, I am. I have the whole weekend off," she answered. "Charlie, would you like to close up for me?" she asked one of the hovering residents.

"Absolutely, Dr. Sullivan."

"You better hurry," Andrews said. "I'm waking him up."

The resident looked panic-stricken.

"Take your time, Charlie. He's just messing with you," she said, a smile in her voice.

"Tuesday's your last day at St. Vincent's, isn't it?" Andrews asked.

"That's right. Tuesday's my last official day. I might help out on a temporary basis later on, but I'm not promising anything yet."

"Then you *could* decide to come back permanently."

She didn't reply.

He persisted. "They'll give you anything you want. You could name your price, your hours . . . you should stay here, Ellie. You belong here."

She didn't agree or disagree. In truth, she didn't know where she belonged. It had been such a hard road to get this far, she hadn't had time to think about the future. At least that was the excuse she used for her indecision.

"Maybe," she finally conceded. "I just don't know yet."

She stood over Charlie, watching like a mother hen. "I want those stitches tight."

"Yes, Dr. Sullivan."

"So Monday night is my last chance to take you to heaven?" Andrews asked in a teasing drawl.

She laughed. "Heaven? Last week you were going to rock my world. Now you're going to take me to heaven?"

"I guarantee it. I've got testimonials if you want to see them."

"It's not going to happen, Kevin."

"I'm not giving up."

She sighed. "I know."

As she checked the last suture, she rolled her shoulders and stretched her neck to one side then the other to get the kinks out. She'd been in the OR since 5:00 A.M., which meant she had been bent over patients for eleven hours. Sad to say, that wasn't a record for her.

She felt wrung out and stiff and sore. A good run around the park would get those muscles moving, she decided, maybe even rev up her energy.

"You know what would help you get rid of a stiff neck?" Andrews said.

"Let me guess. A trip to heaven?"

One of the nurses snorted with laughter. "He's awfully persistent, Dr. Sullivan. Maybe you should give in."

Ellie removed her gloves and dropped them in the trash bag by the OR doors. "Thanks, Megan, but I think I'll just go for a run instead." As she pushed the doors wide, she untied her surgical mask and pulled off her cap, shaking her blond hair loose to fall to her shoulders.

Twenty minutes later she was officially off

duty. She changed into her workout clothes, a pair of faded red shorts and a white tank top. She double-tied her beat-up running shoes, grabbed a rubber band and swept her hair up in a ponytail, slipped her iPod into one pocket and her cell phone into the other, and she was ready. Walking a maze of corridors to get outside, she avoided the direct route through the ER for fear she'd get waylaid with another case.

There was never a lack of patients rolling through the doors. Along with the usual emergencies — the car accidents, the heart attacks, the work injuries — the ER saw a steady stream of victims of violent crimes. The vast majority were young men. Gangs roamed the area east of the highway, and shooting one another seemed to be a nightly sport. Since St. Vincent's was the largest trauma center in St. Louis, all the serious cases came to them. Weekends were a nightmare for the staff. There were times, especially during the hot summer months, when gurneys lined the halls of the ER with patients handcuffed to the railings while they waited to go into surgery. Additional police had to be routinely called in to monitor them to make certain one gang member hadn't been placed too close to a rival.

Ellie became a member of the One Hundred Club when she removed her one hundredth bullet. It wasn't a club she wanted to join, but she would always remember the case. The young man was only twenty years old, and it was the third time he'd been shot. She couldn't forget his insolence and his cold, empty eyes. They were almost as lifeless as the cadavers down in the morgue. Patching up these boys so that they could return to the streets and the same violence was heart wrenching, and she prayed, with every surgery, that this time they would learn something, that this time they would find a new life. It was a naive hope, but she clung to it anyway.

Like the other overworked and underpaid residents and fellows, Ellie operated on broken bodies, the consequence of violence. But she had never actually witnessed a crime . . . until today.

It was a hot and humid late afternoon. Two medical students had caught up with Ellie just as she began her run on the one-mile track in Cambridge Park, a vast area that sat adjacent to the hospital. Heavy rain clouds hung over them, and all three panted for air. After the first mile, both students dropped out, but Ellie was determined to get in at least one more mile before calling it quits. She made mental lists as she ran.

She had a million things to do before heading home to Winston Falls.

Dear God, it was muggy. The humidity was so thick, she felt as though she were running through a sauna. Sweat trickled down the back of her neck, and her drenched clothes clung to her body. Her friend Jennifer, a nurse in pediatrics, who was taking a shortcut across the track to get to the ER entrance, shouted to Ellie that she was crazy to run in this heat. Ellie waved and continued on. She probably was crazy, but getting any time to work out was such a luxury, she couldn't afford to be choosy about the weather.

Ellie could hear faint cheering coming from the new soccer field across the street to the north, and as she rounded the curve, she saw the players — high school–age girls — sprinting across the field. From the large number of fans in the bleachers, she guessed it was an important game.

The administrator of the hospital, the board, and a plethora of attorneys had fought the soccer field. They wanted to purchase the land to build another huge parking garage, and Ellie was happy they had lost their bid. Like the track and small playground to the south, the soccer field was far enough away from the hospital that, no matter how much noise the teams and fans made, the patients weren't disturbed.

Ellie was a football, basketball, and soccer fan, in that order. She loved to watch most sporting events. She admired the grace, skill, and finesse of the players, probably because she didn't possess any of those attributes herself. She had been such an awkward child, her mother had enrolled her in ballet classes, and she never got to play a sport. When she wasn't tripping over her own feet trying to do a plié, she was reading. She was much more comfortable with her books. Her aunt Vivien liked to call her a bookworm.

No time to watch any games today, she thought. She had way too much to do. She returned to her mental list of things to be accomplished before she could head home to her sister's wedding. Oh God, how she dreaded that. She wished she had another week to get ready for the ordeal; then admitted to herself that no amount of time would prepare her for the whispers and the sympathetic smiles from her friends and family. Who could blame them? After all, her sister Ava was marrying Ellie's ex-fiancé. It was going to be a week of mortification, she decided. But, hey, she was tough. She could handle it.

"Yeah, right," she whispered.

And then there was Evan Patterson. Just thinking about him made her stomach hurt. Would he dare show up in Winston Falls? God, she hoped not. But if he did, would she need to get another restraining order, even if she was going to be home for only a few days? She could feel herself getting worked up and had to force herself to calm down. She was an adult now, and she could handle anything that came her way. Even a maniac, she told herself. Besides, she was sure Evan wasn't back in Winston Falls. If he had returned, her father would have alerted her.

Ellie didn't want to worry about Patterson now or think about the wedding. Instead, she chose to focus on the task at hand. Just a little more than a half mile to go, then a lovely cold shower. She took her earphones from her pocket and was about to turn on her iPod to listen to a lecture on new thoracotomy procedures when she heard a loud pop.

Ellie stopped running. Lightning? She looked up at the ominous sky just as another pop echoed, then a third and a fourth in rapid succession. Had lightning hit a transformer? That would explain the bursts . . . except there hadn't been any lightning.

16

Gunshots? Had to be. As many bullets as Ellie had removed from gunshot victims, she'd never actually heard the sound of a gun firing. The noise came from somewhere up ahead. She glanced to the right toward the soccer field. No panic there. The game was still going on, so she had to be wrong. If not gunshots . . . then what?

Five or six seconds had passed since the first popping sound. Ellie reached for her earphones again. Okay, she'd been mistaken.

Then the screaming started.

Everything happened so fast. In the span of just a few more seconds, Ellie observed the chaotic scene unfold in front of her as though it were happening in slow motion.

In the distance, several men, wearing navy blue T-shirts and vests with FBI in bold yellow letters printed on the back, appeared almost out of nowhere and fanned out as they raced toward the trees in the center of the park. People were scattering every which way. Screams mingled with the cheers from the soccer field, the fans and players apparently oblivious to what was happening. A father ran from the playground toward the street with two little boys. The children weren't able to keep up, so the father scooped them into his arms and kept running. Several people who had been strolling through the park also scrambled to get away, as did three boys who had been tossing a Frisbee. One of the boys ran into the street, directly in front of an ambulance returning to the hospital. The vehicle came to a screeching halt, and the boy rushed around to the open window shouting something to the paramedic as he pointed toward the trees.

Suddenly, a man and a woman, linked arm in arm, drew her attention. They walked briskly toward her on the running path. There was something off about both of them. The man had a thick mustache. He wore dark glasses, a baseball cap pulled down over his forehead, and a brown, hooded windbreaker zipped up to his neck, a peculiar choice in the 90-degree weather. Was he all bundled up to keep his clothes dry when the storm broke? The man looked over his shoulder, his neck glistening with sweat. The woman looked directly at Ellie. Her bizarre appearance was startling. A short black wig sat slightly askew on her head with a few long hairs hanging down the side of her neck. Her eyes were such an intense, unnatural shade of green, she looked as though she were wearing novelty contacts, the ones you'd buy for a Halloween party. When the couple was about thirty feet away from Ellie, they veered toward the street.

Someone shouted a command. Then one of the FBI agents who had run into the trees appeared and headed straight for the pair. The woman let go of the man and began to run as he slowed and pulled something from his coat pocket. When he whirled around to face the agent shouting at him, Ellie saw the gun. Before she could react, he'd fired two shots. The first bullet struck the man in pursuit, the force so great it knocked him back before he crashed to the ground. The second bullet went wild. As Ellie dived to the grass, the shooter spun around and pointed the gun toward her. He didn't pull the trigger but instead ran to the street and jumped into a car that sped away.

The ambulance had just turned around to go in the direction the boys were pointing, but when the gunshots were fired, it changed course. Sirens on, the ambulance crossed over the curb and swerved to miss the hospital emergency entrance sign. It bounded across the park toward the gunshot victim, weaving in and out of the crowd that was scrambling toward the boulevard.

Ellie jumped to her feet and ran after it. Her mind was racing. Who were the surgeons on call tonight? Edmonds and Walmer, she remembered, and she'd seen both of them in the hospital. Good.

The target had been a good distance away from the shooter, but he'd taken a direct hit to the torso. Ellie had no idea how bad the wound was, but she thought, if she could stabilize him, he'd make it to the OR.

The ambulance crossed the grassy area of the park in no time and stopped a few feet away from the downed man. Two paramedics leapt to the ground. Ellie recognized them: Mary Lynn Scott and Russell Probst. Russell opened the back doors and pulled out the gurney while Mary Lynn reached for the large orange trauma bag and rushed forward, sliding to her knees beside the victim. By the time Ellie reached the scene, four armed agents had surrounded him. One knelt on the ground talking to the man, trying to keep him calm, while three others stood over him.

The tallest of the three agents who were standing blocked her view. He barely glanced at her as he brusquely ordered, "You don't need to see this. Go back to your soccer game."

Go back to your game? Was he serious? Ellie was about to protest when one of the paramedics looked up, spotted her, and shouted, "Oh thank God. Dr. Sullivan."

The agents looked at her skeptically and then slowly moved out of her way so that she could get past. Mary Lynn tossed her a pair of gloves, and Ellie pulled them on as she knelt down beside the man to assess the injury. Blood saturated the man's shirt. She gently lifted the compress Mary Lynn had pressed to his shoulder, saw the damage, and immediately sought to stem the bleeding. While she gave orders to Russell and Mary Lynn, she kept her voice steady. The patient was conscious, and she didn't want him to panic.

"How bad is it?" he asked.

She made it a point never to lie to a patient. That didn't mean she had to be brutally honest, however. "It's bad, but I've seen worse, much worse."

Russell handed her a clamp, and she found the source of the bleeding. The bullet hadn't gone through but had made quite an entrance.

Once Mary Lynn had gotten the IV line in, Ellie nodded to her to begin the drip.

"What's your name?" she asked as she began packing the wound.

"Sean . . . Sean . . . ah, hell, I can't remember my last name." His eyelids began to flutter as he struggled to stay conscious.

21

The agent kneeling beside him said, "Goodman."

"Yeah, that's right," Sean said, his voice growing weaker.

"Can you remember if you're allergic to anything?" Mary Lynn asked.

"Just bullets." Sean stared at Ellie through half-closed eyes. "Are you a doctor?"

"Yes," she said, flashing a reassuring smile. She finished packing the wound and leaned back on her heels.

"Dr. Sullivan's a trauma surgeon," Russell explained. "If you had to get shot, she's the one you want operating on you. She's the best there is."

"Okay, he's stable. You can take him," Ellie said as she peeled off her gloves and dropped them in the plastic container Mary Lynn opened for her.

Sean suddenly grabbed her arm, his grip surprisingly strong. "Wait . . ."

"Yes?"

"I want to marry Sara. Am I going to see her again?"

She leaned over him. "Yes, you will," she said. "But first you're going into the OR to get that bullet out. Now sleep. It's all good. The surgeon will take care of you."

"Who's on tonight?" Russell asked.

"Edmonds and Walmer," Mary Lynn answered.

Sean tightened his hold on Ellie's arm. "I want you." He didn't give her time to respond but held tight and forced himself to stay awake as he repeated, "He said you're the best. I want you to operate."

She put her hand on top of his and nodded. "Okay," she said. "Okay, I'll do it."

She stood and stepped back to get out of the way so that the paramedics could put Sean into the ambulance but was stopped by something solid. It felt as though she'd just backed into a slab of granite. The agent who had told her to go back to her soccer game was blocking her exit with his warm, hard chest. He put his hands on her shoulders to steady her, then let go. When he still didn't get out of her way, she stood her ground pressed against him.

"Dr. Sullivan, do you want to ride with us?" Russell called out.

"No, go ahead. He's stable now."

Russell swung the doors shut, jumped into the driver's seat, and the ambulance was on its way.

Ellie turned to the agent who had been kneeling with Sean. "Was anyone else hurt?"

The granite wall behind her answered.

"Not hurt, dead." He was very matter-of-fact.

"They weren't ours," another agent explained. "They were wanted men."

She turned around and came face to shoulders with the most intimidating man she'd ever seen, and that was saying something considering the monster chief of surgery she worked under. This man didn't look anything like him, though. The agent was tall, dark, and scary, with thick black hair and penetrating, steely gray eyes. His firm, square jaw was covered with at least one day's growth of beard, maybe two. He looked as though he hadn't slept in at least twenty-four hours, a look she knew all too well.

Ellie's heart skipped a beat. The man could scare the quills off a porcupine. But, oh God, was he sexy! Ellie gave herself a mental slap. An intimidating man who was built like a monument and could melt iron with his menacing glare — *this* was what she was attracted to?

The agent who had been kneeling stepped forward and put out his hand. "I'm Agent Tom Bradley. Sean Goodman's my partner." He introduced her to the two agents on his left and then to the man in front of her. "Agent Max Daniels."

24

She nodded. "If you'll excuse me, I need to get to the OR." She didn't wait for permission, but turned and ran back to the hospital.

Thirty minutes later she was dropping the bullet she'd retrieved from Sean's shoulder into a small metal pan. "Bag it and get it to one of the agents waiting outside. You know the drill."

Then the real work of repairing the damage began. Ellie had learned over the years that there was no such thing as a simple bullet wound. Bullets had a way of doing considerable damage before settling, but Agent Goodman was lucky. His bullet hadn't penetrated any major organs or nerves.

Once she'd closed, she followed the patient to recovery, wrote orders, and went to talk to the crowd gathered in the surgical waiting room. A dozen people with worried faces sat waiting for the news. Agent Daniels was standing, leaning against the wall with his arms across his chest. His gaze followed her as she entered the room, and her heart began to race. She knew she looked a mess. She pulled off her cap and threaded her fingers through her hair. Why in heaven's name she wanted to look good for him was beyond her comprehension, and yet she did.

"The surgeon's here," Daniels announced.

A petite young woman jumped up and rushed forward, followed by Agent Bradley and a crowd of worried relatives.

"The surgery went well," she began and then explained some of what she had repaired, trying not to be too technical. "I expect him to make a full recovery."

Sara, his fiancée, was crying as she stammered her thank-you. She shook Ellie's hand and held on to it.

"You can see him in about an hour," Ellie told her. "He's heavily sedated and he's not going to know you're there," she warned. "He'll be in recovery for a while, then they'll take him to ICU. Once the nurses in ICU have him settled, they'll send someone to get you. Any questions?"

A frazzled-looking nurse appeared in the doorway. "Dr. Sullivan?"

"Yes?"

"Would you mind looking at Mrs. Klein for us? She's Edmonds's patient, but he's in surgery."

"I'll be right there."

She patted Sara's hand and pulled free. "All right then. It's all good."

Out of the corner of her eye, she saw Agent Daniels smile as she turned to leave. She walked down the corridor and had just turned the corner when he caught up with her.

"Hey, Doctor."

She turned around. Her stupid heart went into overdrive again. "Yes?"

"We're going to need to talk to you about the shooting. You'll have to give a statement."

"When?"

"How about after you check on that patient?"

She couldn't resist. "Gee, I don't know. I hate to miss soccer practice."

She was laughing as she pushed the doors aside and disappeared into ICU.

Max Daniels stood there staring after her, a slight grin crossing his face.

"Damn," he whispered. "Damn."

# TWO

Agent Daniels waited for her in the hallway just outside the ICU doors. He was leaning with his back to the wall, one ankle crossed over the other, looking half asleep and thoroughly relaxed.

Ellie was impressed. It had taken her years of sleep deprivation to perfect the art of falling asleep on her feet. Never during surgery, of course — that was definitely frowned upon — but in between emergencies when she knew she had only a couple of minutes before she was paged again. Five minutes here, ten minutes there — it seemed to be enough to keep her refreshed and alert. She still didn't know how to relax, though, no matter how hard she tried. Daniels made it look easy.

Ellie was pleased she hadn't kept him waiting long. All she'd had to do for Mrs. Klein was adjust her medications. Mr. Klein was the real concern. Ellie had to once again order him to keep his hands off his wife's tubes and IVs and to stop trying to wake her up. The stubborn man couldn't quite grasp the notion of a medically induced coma, but he did understand that he would be banned from the ICU if he didn't behave himself. Janet Newman, the head nurse, was convinced Mr. Klein was attempting to kill his wife and blame it on the hospital. Janet pointed out that Mrs. Klein was twenty-nine years older than her husband, way too old to be considered a cougar, and she was also extremely wealthy. It was obvious to the nurse that the sneaky bastard — Janet's name for Mr. Klein — had married the poor woman for her fortune only.

Although Ellie didn't believe Mr. Klein wanted to harm his wife, she gave Janet new instructions: If there was another incident with the tubes, she was to call security and have Mr. Klein removed from the floor.

Dealing with the families took compassion, patience, and understanding; and on days like today, after working such a long shift, Ellie ran low on all three. It had been a grueling week with double shifts and very little sleep. She wondered if she looked as tired as she felt. The interview with the agent shouldn't take long, she thought, and then she could go home, take a hot shower, and fall into bed. That lovely thought made her sigh. Earlier, she had grabbed a few minutes to take a quick shower in the doctors' quarters, but it wasn't at all the same as showering in her own bathroom with her own apricot-scented shampoo, her body lotions, and her soft towels. She couldn't wait to get home.

Ellie should have known she wouldn't get out of the hospital that easily.

As she walked toward the agent, she said, "That didn't take any time at all, did it, Agent Daniels?"

"No, it didn't take long," he agreed. "Call me Max," he added.

She smiled. "And you may call me Ellie."

She had almost reached him when the ancient intercom crackled to life. "Dr. Blue to ICU. Dr. Blue to ICU." The summons was the not-too-subtle code for a patient crashing, a code blue. Everyone in the hospital knew what it meant, including every patient over the age of ten, but the administrator refused to give the code a different name.

Ellie stopped abruptly, took a deep breath, then turned to go back into the ICU.

She called over her shoulder, "Agent Daniels . . . I mean, Max . . . if you want, you could leave your number with recep-

30

tion, and I'll get hold of you just as soon as I'm finished here."

If he replied, she didn't hear him because the doors were closing behind her as she ran to the patient in trouble.

This time she was gone a little longer, but not much, just fifteen minutes, and when she once again stepped out into the hallway, she was surprised to see that Max was still there waiting for her. He was talking on his cell phone, but the second he spotted her, he ended the call and headed toward her.

It suddenly occurred to Ellie that the agent might be worried that his friend had been the patient who coded, and she hurried to reassure him.

"The code wasn't for Agent Goodman."

"Yeah, I know. I asked one of the nurses to go in and find out."

She nodded. "I just checked on him. He's resting comfortably."

"That's good," he replied. "The code?" he asked, curious. "How did that turn out?"

"The patient's back with us, so it's all good."

He smiled, and Ellie felt a flutter in her chest. How could anyone that tough looking have such a devastating smile? He was an imposing figure, tall and broad shouldered, with huge biceps and a wide chest that appeared to be all muscle. His jaw was hidden beneath a scruffy beard, but the slight dimple creasing his cheek was still noticeable. His thick hair needed a trim, and he looked as though he'd been to battle and back. There really wasn't anything "pretty boy" about him, nothing remotely gorgeous like Dr. Andrews; yet, cleaned up, this man had the potential to be a real heartthrob. But not for her. Been there. Almost done that.

Ellie forced herself to concentrate on the reason he was here, the shooting. She needed to explain that, if he wanted to question her, they would have to find someplace outside the hospital. As long as she was on the premises, the nurses and doctors would continue to page her. And the two older surgeons on call tonight would be happy to let her do their job while they watched ESPN in the doctors' lounge.

"I've got to get out of here," she began. "Otherwise, the interruptions . . . oh no." She groaned the last words. "Great," she whispered. "Just great."

Max turned to see a tall, round-shouldered man with a giant forehead and very little hair come barreling toward Ellie with a glare plastered on his face.

"Who is he?" he asked quietly. He could

32

have sworn he heard her whisper, "A dinosaur."

The man marching toward them was a doctor, an uptight one at that. He wore an immaculate white coat with a stethoscope dangling from one of the pockets. Pale blue, long-sleeved shirt, bold striped tie, black pants with perfect creases, and tasseled loafers that looked new — he was impeccably dressed. Max wondered if the man's personality was as starched as his appearance.

Dr. Brent Westfield was the chief of surgery at St. Vincent's. He had just rounded the corner. Spotting Ellie, he barked, "What are you doing here, Prod? Aren't you off this weekend? Of course you are. Do I have to remind you that, as of two weeks ago, we are all following new guidelines? No exceptions. You know that." He glanced at his Gucci sports watch and added, "You should have signed out two hours ago."

New guidelines. Right. Exasperated, Ellie simply nodded. It was true. According to the new hospital policy, residents and fellows could be on duty only a certain number of hours in a twenty-four-hour day; but there was a big loophole, one little phrase in the guidelines that made them useless: *unless* there was an emergency. And funny thing, there was always an emergency. Ellie

33

was certain the contingency was just a clever way for the hospital to appear to be following the guidelines while working the residents until they were dead on their feet. In reality, the new guidelines weren't that different from the old ones, and Westfield knew it. He was just in the mood to hassle her, she decided, probably because he was irritated that she hadn't signed a contract to stay with the hospital . . . at least not yet. She was still contemplating where she wanted to live and what she wanted to do — trauma center or general surgery. And she also had to take into account Evan Patterson. Where was he hiding? How could she make a decision without knowing where he was? Ellie was so tired now, nothing sounded good to her, but she knew she would have to make her decision soon because, even with all the scholarships and grants she had received, she owed a little over two hundred thousand.

"Do you want me to get in trouble with the board?" he demanded.

Was he kidding? The board of directors loved him. It was such a bogus question, she didn't bother to answer.

Westfield abruptly turned to Max. "And who is this?"

Ellie knew he had noticed the FBI badge

hooked to the left side of Max's belt and the gun holstered on the opposite side, but she didn't comment on it or mention that Max's navy blue T-shirt had big yellow FBI letters conspicuously printed across the back. Instead, she quickly made the introductions, and the two men shook hands. The chief had always been a commanding figure to Ellie because of his position of power, his aggressive tactics, and most important, his skill in the operating room, but standing next to the FBI agent who towered over him, Westfield suddenly didn't seem so intimidating. Max was more imposing. The agent radiated strength and confidence. She strongly doubted he was as contentious as the chief, though.

"I heard there was a shooting outside the hospital doors. Is that right?"

"Yes, it happened close to the hospital," Max answered.

Westfield waited for the agent to expound and was sorely disappointed. Usually, the chief's intense frown, pursed lips, and unnerving silence was enough to make the people he was interrogating so uneasy they would blurt out all sorts of information. His tactics weren't working on Max.

"Three men were killed?" he prodded.

"Yes, that's right."

Another ten seconds passed in silence. Then the chief asked, "An FBI agent was shot?"

"Yes."

Ellie was trying not to smile. Westfield had to be frustrated. By using his stern tone and his most serious scowl, he was doing his best to push the agent into giving an explanation, but it wasn't working. Apparently, Max couldn't be intimidated.

The chief abruptly turned to Ellie. "Who did the surgery on the agent?" And before she could answer, he added, "It couldn't have been you because you're off duty, aren't you? And you aren't on call this weekend. So who did the surgery? Was it Walmer?"

Westfield knew she had operated on the agent. The man knew everything that went on inside the hospital. He was just trying to exert his power and make her squirm. Four more days under his thumb, she reminded herself, just four more days and she was free. She needed to suck it up until then.

"No, sir, Dr. Walmer didn't do the surgery." Taking Max's lead, she didn't say another word.

"Edmonds?" he snapped.

"No, sir."

"Then who operated?"

36

"I did."

The glare was back in place. "Even though you were off duty?"

"Yes, sir, even though."

"Don't give me attitude, Sullivan," he said, pointing a finger at her.

Max kept expecting Ellie to tell Westfield that Agent Goodman had pleaded with her to do the surgery, but she didn't. She didn't offer any excuses. She simply stared Westfield in the eyes and waited.

"Help me understand," he began in his best sarcastic voice. "Why didn't you notify Walmer or Edmonds to hightail it to the OR?" And once again he didn't give her time to answer the question before posing another. "Do you think you're a better surgeon than they are?"

She didn't hesitate. "Yes, sir, I do. Absolutely."

Max could tell Westfield was pleased with her answer but trying not to let her know it.

"You're arrogant."

Ellie was about to say, "Thank you," but caught herself in time. "Yes, sir, I am."

And it was true. When it came to her work, she was arrogant, just like all the other surgeons in the hospital. It came with the territory and, in Ellie's opinion, was a necessary requirement. When a surgeon

37

held a scalpel in her hand and was about to cut open a patient, she had better have skill and almost superhuman confidence. Ellie honestly didn't think there was such a thing as a timid surgeon, and if there was, she certainly wouldn't want him cutting on her.

Unfortunately, none of her self-assuredness and arrogance spilled over into her personal life. During her last trip home, she had been told by her sister Ava that she was depressingly insecure. But, since Ava was the sister who was marrying Ellie's ex-fiancé, she wasn't inclined to listen to anything she had to say. Ava's twin, Annie, was living in San Diego and hadn't had a chance to weigh in on Ellie's faults. She would side with Ava, of course, but she would be much kinder about it. Despite her sisters' persistence, Ellie would disagree with both of them. She wasn't depressingly insecure. Just mildly so.

Ellie suddenly realized she was zoning out. Now wasn't the time to think about personal problems. She'd have plenty of time for that once she was home. *Focus,* she told herself. Westfield was chatting with Max again, probably telling him how to do his job. She took a deep breath in an attempt to get more oxygen to her befuddled brain.

Westfield turned back to her, his index

finger just inches from her face. "You. Get out of here. Now." He didn't snarl the order, but he came close.

Ellie watched him as he strode toward ICU. He shoved the doors out of his way, looked over his shoulder, and snapped, "And sign the contract."

The doors automatically closed behind him. She sighed and, in a faint Southern accent, said, "Isn't he sweet? We all just love him to pieces."

Max laughed. "How long have you been taking orders from him?"

"Forever."

"Why does he call you Prod?"

She shrugged. "He likes to."

She started walking down the long hallway with Max at her side.

"What does it mean?" he asked.

When she didn't immediately answer, he glanced down at her and saw her cheeks were flushed. She was embarrassed, and that only piqued his interest all the more. He let the question go for now. "Did I hear you call him a dinosaur? When I asked you who he was . . ."

She smiled. "You don't see the resemblance? Actually, I usually call him 'T. rex.' I think it's more personal. When he's on a roar — which is ninety percent of the time

— he does remind me of a gigantic, prehistoric beast."

She was moving at a fast clip.

"Ellie, hold up. Where are you going?"

"Upstairs to get my keys."

"We have to sit down and —"

"I know."

She kept right on going. Max was becoming frustrated. "Do you run everywhere you go?"

"Pretty much," she admitted. She slowed to a normal pace . . . normal for her, anyway. She noticed that Max had no trouble keeping up with her. In fact, with his long legs, he barely had to increase his stride beyond a stroll.

She glanced over at him. He was definitely out of her comfort zone. The man had so much testosterone, he made her nervous. He didn't scare her, though. When he smiled, the corners of his eyes creased, and there was a glint in them that made her shiver inside.

*Jeez, get a grip, Sullivan.* She was acting like a sex-starved teenager. Granted, it had been a long time since she had been with a man — a long, long time — but, still, her reaction to Max went beyond bizarre. It was completely contrary to her usual calm, rational nature. When she had time, she would figure out her weird behavior. There had to be some logical explanation. But then, maybe she didn't really have to worry about it at all because, as soon as Max questioned her about the shooting, he'd be on his way, and she would be sane again.

Max noticed that she kept looking at him with a puzzled expression on her face. "What is it?" he asked.

She shook her head. "Nothing important."

"Yeah?"

"I'm not going to be much help with descriptions I'm afraid," she said.

"We have to take your statement anyway."

"We?"

"Another agent, Ben MacBride, and I are working this together, and we have to question you."

"Okay," she agreed. "Where is he?"

"At the crime scene," he answered. *Where I should be,* he silently added.

"Why don't you start asking your questions while you walk with me."

"Doesn't work that way. I'm going to record what you say."

"Okay, then we need to find someplace quiet, right?"

"Right."

Ellie passed a bank of elevators and continued on to the stairs. "I'll grab my things, and we can get out of here. I stand a better chance of actually leaving if you're with me."

"How's that?"

She smiled. "You've got a gun."

Max kept pace as she ran up three flights. "You have a thing against elevators? A phobia?"

"This is the only exercise I get."

"You were running the track when the shooting started, weren't you?"

"How did you figure that out?" she asked, taking the steps a little slower while she waited for his answer.

"I'm an FBI agent, trained to be observant," he said.

"Oh, please. You thought I was one of the kids on that high school soccer team."

He laughed. "Yeah, I did," he admitted. "One of the other agents told me you were running the track."

He could laugh at himself. What an appealing trait, she thought. She liked that quality in a man . . . Seriously! What was happening to her? She really needed to get away from him as soon as possible.

"You haven't answered my question. Is it a phobia or just a quirk?" he wondered.

"I do the stairs and I run the track and I don't particularly like being crammed inside a little metal box with a bunch of other people."

He grinned. "So that's a yes. You do have a phobia."

Probably, she thought, but she wasn't going to admit it. She did ride in elevators with patients when she had to. She didn't like it, but she did it anyway.

"Where do you keep your things? On the roof?" he asked.

"Just here." Ellie entered the hallway on the fourth floor and opened the door to a dark room filled with lockers. She switched on a light and walked to the third one on the left. Had she been alone, she would have locked the door and changed into jeans and a T-shirt, but she wasn't alone, so she was going to have to stay in her scrubs. She didn't like wearing them outside the hospital, but she didn't have a choice now. She pulled out her backpack, put some of her clothes inside, grabbed her keys from the top shelf, and was ready to leave.

She followed him to the stairwell, appreciating the fact that he wasn't pushing the issue with the elevators. When his cell phone rang, he stopped on a landing to answer, and she stopped to wait for him.

Max's partner, Ben MacBride, was on the line and wanted help with a couple of

43

uncooperative witnesses.

"Yeah, okay, I'll be there in five."

"Hold on," Ben said. "Agent Hughes wants to talk to you."

While Max was waiting for Ben to get Hughes, he turned to Ellie. She stood on the step above him, and her eyes were level with his. He found it impossible not to stare at her. The woman was breathtaking. Her eyes were the most intense shade of blue. Her nose was dotted with freckles, which he found damn alluring, and her mouth . . . ah, man, he really needed to stop staring. He was already conjuring up all sorts of fantasies involving her full, luscious lips, and he was going to be in real trouble if he let his eyes wander lower.

Max didn't wait for Hughes to get on the line. He abruptly ended the call, turned, and continued down the stairs.

"Where are we going to do this?" she asked.

He smiled. Now, that was a leading question, considering where his thoughts had been.

"Go home." His voice was brisk.

"Really?"

"Yeah," he said, glancing back at her. "You can go home, and we'll come to you."

"Great," she said. "I can get out of these

44

scrubs. Let me give you my address . . ."

"I've got it."

"Cell phone?"

"Got that, too."

"But how —"

"You're a witness. I had all your information downloaded to my phone while I was waiting for you."

"You Googled me?"

"No, I didn't need to."

Ellie wondered what she would find if she Googled him. Under "occupation" would it say he was an FBI agent and give her the number of criminals he'd apprehended . . . and shot? No, of course not. His profile probably wouldn't tell her whether he was involved with anyone or whether he was married, either. She had taken the time to notice that he wasn't wearing a wedding band, and something told her that, if he was married, he would always wear it.

Now, why would she make that assumption? She wasn't clairvoyant, and the truth was, she didn't know anything about him other than he carried a badge, could be quite intimidating at times, and had a great smile. Was she making him admirable because she wanted him to be? From what she knew about the FBI — which was precious little — outsiders weren't privy to

45

personal information, but she might Google him anyway just to appease her curiosity.

Okay, she really needed a life outside of the OR. Then maybe she wouldn't have such a strong reaction to a man she barely knew.

They reached the main floor on the south side of the hospital. Ellie's ancient SUV was parked in the doctors' lot adjacent to the hospital. Max opened the exit door for her. She brushed against him as she walked outside and got a hint of his masculine scent and just a trace of aftershave. For a man who looked as though he hadn't picked up a razor in quite some time, he smelled really good.

She knew what she smelled like. Disinfectant. Unfortunately, that had been her perfume for the past several years. It could be worse, she thought. The pathology residents smelled like formaldehyde, even when they were off duty. The odor seemed to permeate their skin.

Max walked her to her car. It was a gentlemanly thing to do, but not at all necessary since it was light outside and there were police cars all over the campus. The crime scene team was still there, combing the park for additional evidence. Ellie didn't believe she could be any safer.

"Do you walk out here in the middle of the night?" Max asked as he looked around.

"Yes. Why?"

"I count only six lights, and this is a big parking lot with countless places to hide. Not good."

"If I'm leaving during the night, a guard walks me to my car."

"What happens when you get called to come in?"

*I park my car, then run like lightning to the doors with pepper spray in my hand,* she thought but didn't say.

"I try to park as close to the hospital doors as possible, and I'm vigilant," she stated with a nod.

"Vigilant, huh?"

His smile could stop traffic. She couldn't tell if he was teasing her or laughing at her.

Max opened her car door. "I'll see you later. It will probably be a couple of hours before we get to your place. Don't go anywhere. Stay home."

"Of course."

It wasn't until she had driven out of the lot and was on her way home that she glanced in the mirror. No makeup, hair a mess, and wearing scrubs that were two sizes too big for her — lovely. No wonder Max had escorted her to her car. He probably felt sorry for her. He wouldn't have given her a second glance under normal circumstances.

Oh well, what did it matter? After a brief interview, he would be history, and after next Tuesday, hopefully, she would be, too.

# THREE

The Landrys had escaped once again, but Max knew it was only a matter of time before the notorious couple would run out of luck. Since Dr. Ellie Sullivan was a potential witness to the shooting, it was his job to find out all he could about her before he added her to the witness list for the federal prosecutor.

He tried to be objective but found it impossible, for the more he learned about her, the less inclined he was to let anyone know she had witnessed anything, which was ludicrous considering the other agents in the park had watched her stabilize Sean Goodman, knew she had operated on him, and by now had heard that she had seen Calvin Landry shoot the agent.

While he had waited for Ellie in the hospital, Max had quickly pulled up all the superficial information on her: her phone numbers; addresses both in St. Louis and in Winston Falls, South Carolina; and her position and schedule at St. Vincent's Hospital. When he dug a little deeper, however, he uncovered something disturbing: court documents detailing five separate incidents involving Ellie and a teenager named Evan Patterson.

The first document was filed when Ellie was only eleven years old. According to the records, Evan, who was seventeen at the time, had become infatuated with the young girl after the two attended a science camp sponsored by the Winston Falls School District. His obsession grew, and when he physically assaulted her, Ellie's family brought charges against him. Since he was a juvenile with no previous record, he was given leniency.

The second time, Patterson became more aggressive. He tried to force her into his car. His statement to the police said he couldn't stop thinking about her, that they were kindred spirits, and once she was alone with him, he would be able to convince her that they belonged together. Patterson was given probation with court-ordered therapy.

Despite the strict rulings of the court, Patterson did not keep his distance, terrorizing the girl on two more occasions. His anger over her rejection had grown to an alarming intensity. For these offenses, he was ordered to undergo yet another psychological evaluation and a thirty-day hospitalization; however, with shrewd attorneys and plea bargains he bypassed judge and jury.

There was no plea bargain for the fifth offense of attempted murder.

Ellie was on her way home from school. She was with three girls who tried to protect her, but Patterson was big and strong. He grabbed Ellie and threw her into his car. The authorities found her two hours later, brutally beaten and left for dead in a ravine two miles out of town.

By the time she reached the emergency room, she had lost a lot of blood and her prognosis was bleak. She was flown to a trauma center, and the surgeons worked through the night to save her. She spent her twelfth birthday in the ICU.

"Ah, man," Max whispered as he read the last report. "That son of a bitch."

He was sitting in the local FBI office across from his partner, Ben MacBride, who had just hung up the phone.

"What are you reading?" Ben asked as Max was closing his laptop.

"Ellie Sullivan's background."

"Must be bad," Ben said. "The look on

your face when you were reading . . . like you wanted to kill someone."

Max nodded. "Then I nailed it."

Ben rubbed the back of his neck. "It's bad, huh?"

"Yes."

"Want me to read about her now?"

He shook his head. "No need."

Ben pushed his chair back. "Does Hughes expect us to file our reports tonight?"

Max said, "How long have you been an agent, Ben?"

His partner laughed. "Long enough to know that I just asked a dumb question. Still, I always hold out hope."

"Hope for what?"

"That we get finished at a normal time."

"Are you in a hurry to get back to the hotel?"

Ben was going through the drawers in the desk. "No. I'm in a hurry to eat. I'm starving."

"What are you looking for?"

"Candy, gum, anything." He shut the last drawer and shook his head. "Maybe we should move Sullivan's interview to tomorrow."

Max stood. "No, we need to talk to her tonight while it's still fresh in her mind."

"I'm betting she won't be forgetting what

happened for a long while."

"Doesn't matter. We need to do it to-night," he countered, walking to the door.

Ben trailed behind. "Okay, so here's what we do. We talk to her quick, grab something to eat, then come back here and finish our reports. Right?"

"Right."

"The interview *will* be quick, won't it? She's not one of those arrogant, obnoxious doctor types, is she? If she is, we could be there for hours before we get the information we need. You know what I'm talking about. Some of those older, crabby doctors have the superiority complexes, and they have to impress you with their knowledge before they'll answer questions. I hate that type. Is she one of those?"

Max remembered Ben hadn't met Ellie yet. He had been stationed on the other side of the park when the shooting started, and Max hadn't felt the need to tell him about her. It was going to be really interesting when he did meet her.

"Is she that type? Ah, hell, she is, isn't she? We'll be there till morning."

Max didn't answer but was smiling as he tossed the car keys to Ben.

# FOUR

Ellie's home was a sparsely furnished studio apartment a block west of Cranston and Glenwood. Just five miles from the hospital, it was an easy commute. Her apartment was on the second floor of a redbrick building that sat between two similar structures on a quiet, tree-lined street. Built in the 1940s, it still maintained some of the charm of a bygone era when even the smallest apartments were constructed with high ceilings and intricate moldings. For a studio, it was large and spacious, but it didn't offer much of a view. Her living room window overlooked the Dumpsters in the back alley.

There wasn't anything luxurious about the place, but it was home, and she was comfortable there. Each tenant needed a key to get into the front door of the building, and there were strong dead-bolt locks and peepholes on all the apartment doors. The super had keys to each apartment and each dead bolt, which meant he could walk into any apartment anytime, so without asking permission, her father had installed a second dead bolt that only she had the key to unlock.

If anyone were to ask her to describe her home, she could do it with one word: *safe.* Or better yet, two words: *minimalistic* and *safe.* Almost everything in the apartment was the uninteresting yet soothing color of cream. The walls, the down-filled, oversize sofa she'd purchased for forty dollars from a pampered housewife in Chesterfield who had grown tired of it just six months after she had bought it, the oversize chair she'd thrown in for free, the drapes, the blinds — all cream. The only break in Ellie's furniture color scheme came from a swivel chair a friend had given her. It was beige.

There were hardwood floors throughout, which was one of the reasons she had rented the place. The faded and worn-out floors were in desperate need of refinishing, but Ellie loved them because she felt the flaws gave them a lovely patina. They were also much easier than carpet to keep clean.

She did try to give her place a little personality. She bought a couple of brightly colored pillows from Macy's midnight madness sale, and she thought they added a little cheer. She would have loved to have covered the walls with beautiful contemporary paintings, but she couldn't afford them. She shopped at Goodwill, not Neiman Marcus.

The desk she had purchased from Goodwill had cost only fifteen dollars. One leg was considerably shorter than the other three, but a brick she found when she took the trash out was the exact size needed to balance the desk perfectly. She also purchased a pretty red lacquered tray for two dollars that was only slightly chipped on two corners, and a seriously battered coffee table that cost seven dollars. Added up, she spent less than a hundred dollars to furnish the living room and twice that much to have the sofa and chair cleaned.

She had no dining room, which was just as well since she had no dining room furniture. A wide, arched doorway separated the living room from the bedroom. Ellie splurged and bought a gorgeous dark cherry, queen-size sleigh bed and a new mattress and box springs. The bed took up most of the space in the tiny alcove disguised as a bedroom and faced the front door, and since it was the first thing a guest saw when he or she walked inside, Ellie decided to blow her budget on a beautiful duvet, a down comforter, and designer sheets. She found a sale and saved 60 percent on the bedding, including four pillows. Ellie thought it humorous that, because of the sale, the only color left on the shelf was cream. The bed did look gorgeous, though, and she loved slipping between the soft cotton sheets.

The bathroom was surprisingly large, but the galley kitchen was so narrow, only one adult could work in it. Ellie had to stand to one side of the burners to open the oven door. The appliances were new when she moved in, and there was enough counter space to suit her needs.

Max had told Ellie to stay home, and she planned to do just that after she stopped at Whole Foods to get groceries. She was in the mood for stir-fry with chicken and mounds of vegetables. Just thinking about food made her stomach grumble, and no wonder, she hadn't eaten anything since the PowerBar and orange juice she'd inhaled at breakfast.

She ended up with three large bags of groceries. She emptied the contents onto her kitchen counter and reached for an apple to eat while she checked her answering machine for messages. There were only two, neither of which required quick attention. Ellie hadn't wanted to spend money on a landline, but her father had insisted. He didn't trust cell phones. What if the charge was low and she got into trouble? How could she call for help? Ellie let her father win the argument because she wanted to give him peace of mind.

After she checked the time, she showered, blew her hair dry, and put on a pair of faded jeans, a pink T-shirt, and flip-flops. She even took the time to dab on some perfume and add a little lip gloss before starting dinner. She made enough for six meals, munching on salad while she worked. The two agents arrived just as she finished eating.

Ellie silently lectured herself on the way to the door. *Okay, you're not a teenager,* she reminded herself. This time she was going to take it all in stride or, rather, take *him* in stride. No heart palpitations, no breathlessness, just an ordinary "Hi, how are you doing?" Normal, she thought. She was going for normal.

The best-laid plans . . .

She opened the door, and *boom,* her heart started pounding. It really was the most amazing thing, having absolutely no control over her physical response to him.

His expression didn't give her a hint as to what he was thinking, yet she was certain he wasn't having the same crazy, heart-pounding reaction to her. But then, why would he? If she weren't a potential witness, he probably wouldn't have given her the time of day.

"Something smells good," Max remarked as he walked past her.

"I just made stir-fry."

"Yeah, that smells good, too."

Ben heard the comment and rolled his eyes as he followed Max into the apartment.

When Max turned around, Ben was staring at Ellie, spellbound. Ben shook his head and shot an accusatory look at Max, who responded with a satisfied grin. Maybe he should have told Ben about her, but seeing the expression on his partner's face was priceless. Ellie looked amazing with her hair down around her shoulders. The snug jeans and T-shirt hugged her slender body and long legs and showed the curves that had been hidden by the scrubs. The woman was just about perfect.

He glanced around her apartment and liked that, too. It was simply furnished, but there were a couple of bright touches that made it feel warm. He smiled when he spotted the brick wedged under one of the legs of the desk. A couple of packing boxes sat in the corner, and neat piles of papers were stacked on the desk and a chair.

Ellie shut the door and automatically flipped both dead bolts. She offered her hand as Ben MacBride introduced himself. He wasn't as tall or as muscular as Max, but he had an athletic build and a nice smile that instantly put her at ease.

Ben turned back to Max and shook his head.

"What?" Max said.

"You could have mentioned . . ."

"Mentioned what?" he asked innocently.

Ben decided to be blunt. "That she was frickin' beautiful." He quickly turned to Ellie to add, "You remind me of my wife. She's beautiful. At least I *think* she's still beautiful."

Ellie gave him a quizzical look. "You don't know?"

"Every time I see her, she's in the bathroom throwing up. But, yeah, I'm sure she's still beautiful."

She laughed. "She's pregnant."

He nodded. "Yes. Man, it does smell good in here."

"Stir-fry," she repeated. "There's plenty left, and it's still hot. Would you like —"

She didn't bother to finish her question because both Max and Ben were already in her kitchen. Max looked for plates as Ben sampled a piece of chicken. While they devoured every bit of the stir-fry, Ellie straightened up her living room. Her desk was covered with stacks of papers, and there was another stack on the swivel chair that she needed to go through and decide to either shred or pack for storage. She quickly moved the papers from the chair to form another stack on top of the desk. It looked a bit precarious, but as long as no one bumped the desk, the papers should stay put.

The two agents set their empty plates in the sink and joined her. When they were standing in her living room, the small area seemed even smaller. Ellie went to the sofa and sat down. Ben took the swivel chair and turned it to face her.

"Thanks, Ellie," he said. "The food was great. I didn't realize how hungry I was."

"I'm glad you enjoyed it," she replied.

Max moved around the room as though he were inspecting it. He seemed uptight, unlike the man she had met earlier who appeared to be so relaxed.

"Is there something you need, Agent Daniels?" she asked.

"Max," he reminded her. "No, I just noticed you don't have anything on your walls."

"No, I don't."

"How come?"

"Everything I like is too expensive, and I don't want to put up posters. I had enough of those in college."

"So you're poor," Ben said.

She laughed. "Yes."

"I thought doctors made a lot of money." Max made the comment.

"Some do," she agreed. "But, like many of my colleagues, I have substantial student loans."

"Don't they pay you at that hospital?" Max snapped the question.

"Yes, they do."

"Must not be much."

"No, it isn't."

He slowly circled her living room, acting like a caged animal searching for a way out. Ellie had the feeling he was angry about something and trying to keep it in check.

"What about photos? I know you have family. Don't you like them?" Max asked, frowning.

"I like some of them, and, yes, I do have photos. They're packed away."

"Why are they packed away?" he demanded.

"I'm finished at St. Vincent's Hospital on Tuesday."

The rapid-fire questions continued until

she began to feel like a suspect, not a witness. Irritated, she started to answer just as rapidly.

"Those boxes in the corner by the window have been sitting there a long time. There's dust on top of them. Why is that?"

"I'm a bad housekeeper," she said with a straight face.

"You never unpacked them?" He made the question sound like an accusation.

"No, I never did."

"Why not?"

"I like to be ready."

"Ready for what?"

"Ready to pick up and leave at a moment's notice," she snapped back.

"Where are you going?"

She shrugged. "I don't know."

He stopped pacing and was now standing over her, making her extremely nervous. How could she have ever thought he was relaxed? She was beginning to think she should confess something just to get him to stop interrogating her.

Ben was watching the exchange, astounded by Max's aggressive behavior. Had he been alone with his partner, he would have asked him what in God's name was wrong with him. He was acting as though he were about to pounce on her.

"You must have some idea where you'd like to go," Max challenged.

"No, I don't," she answered sharply. "Is there any other personal information you need?"

Seeing Ellie's indignation and suddenly realizing he'd sounded as though he were grilling her, he said, "I guess I'm not very good at small talk."

That was small talk?

"No kidding," Ben drawled.

Max could see the scowl deepening on Ellie's face, and he could almost feel the fire flashing from her eyes. He would have laughed had she not looked so annoyed. When he'd first met her, his opinion of her had been rather indifferent. Of course, he'd noticed that she was a beautiful, sexy woman he would love to take to bed. Nothing unusual about that. But then he'd watched how great she was with Sean Goodman. She was so calm and reassuring as she worked on him. Maybe it was all part of her job, but her kindness seemed genuine. Then, when she went back to the hospital to perform Sean's surgery, Max's impression of her expanded. Not only did he want to go to bed with her, he admired her as well. And when she gave him a little attitude in the stairwell and let him see her sense of humor, he realized he actually liked her . . . *and* wanted her. Nothing unusual about that.

He saw everything in a different light, however, when he'd checked into her background. Not quite everything, he qualified. He wanted her in bed — that didn't change — but he was filled with an overwhelming need to protect her. After reading her file, which was only a small portion of what she had gone through, Max felt great empathy for her. She had been powerless back then, with no control over what happened to her. He knew all about that, and that was why he wanted to help as much as he could. Ellie had been through enough. She didn't need more heartache. And if she testified . . .

Max didn't respond to Ellie's question. Instead, he surprised her by sitting down next to her on the sofa. He was so close, if she moved, she'd be glued to him. Ellie was confused. What was he doing? There was a perfectly good overstuffed chair he could have taken, and yet he chose the sofa. What did that mean? Ellie didn't know how to react. Should she move away? She didn't want to, but should she? Just as she was questioning his motives, Max took a digital recorder out of his pocket. Oh. Now she understood. He had to sit next to her so that the recorder could pick up the conversation. Bummer.

"Ben, are you ready to get started?" Max asked.

"Sure," he replied. "I'm the less experienced agent," he explained to Ellie. "By eleven months." He turned in the swivel chair and accidentally knocked the desk, starting an avalanche of papers to the floor.

Ellie rushed to help pick up. "It's a mess, I know, but I haven't had time to go through everything. Most of it can probably be thrown away."

"I've got this, Ellie. Go sit." He scooped up several papers, straightened them, and made a pile against the wall. "They can stay on the floor, right?"

She smiled. "Right."

Max grabbed another stack of papers that was headed to the floor and put a heavy anatomy book on top to keep them from falling again.

"What's this?" Ben held up several sheets that had been stapled together.

"What is it?" Max asked.

"Restraining order."

"Yeah?" Glancing at Ellie, Max walked around the desk and took the papers from Ben. Just as he expected, they were orders against Evan Patterson. He quickly flipped through them and handed them back to Ben.

Ben looked over the documents while Ellie remained silent, hoping he wouldn't read through them.

"Who is Evan Patterson?"

"Oh, those papers are old," she said.

"Uh-huh," Ben agreed. "Who is he?"

She had the feeling changing the subject wasn't going to work. Ben was FBI, which meant he was trained to get people to answer questions, but she wished he'd leave this alone. The subject of Evan Patterson was very difficult for her to talk about or even think about. She wanted the nightmare to stay in the past.

Ellie settled back on the sofa and pulled a pillow onto her lap. "I went to Sacred Heart High School for two years. He was there."

"Did he leave high school, or did you?" Ben asked, curious.

"I was the first to leave . . . it was a long time ago."

Ben glanced at Max, knowing that he had also picked up on Ellie's reticence.

"Where did you go after that?" Ben asked, thinking she had either transferred to another high school or perhaps been home-schooled to get away from Patterson.

Ellie hesitated before answering. "I was in college."

Ben tilted the chair back. He could see her embarrassment.

"So you're smart, huh?"

She smiled. "And poor."

"But real smart?" Ben asked.

"Prod," Max said. "Chief of surgery calls her Prod." He turned to her. "That's short for *prodigy,* isn't it?"

She didn't look happy that he had shared that information.

"Just one more question. Where's Evan Patterson now?" Ben asked.

"I don't know. If he was to come back to Winston Falls where my family lives, my father would let me know." She lifted the pillow and squeezed it to her chest.

Max could tell she hated talking about Patterson. That was obvious. "I'll find out where he is now," he said.

Frowning, she asked, "Why? Why would you do that?"

*Because I know what he did to you,* he thought. "It will give you a little peace of mind knowing exactly where he is, won't it?" he asked.

"Yes, of course, but . . ."

"But what?"

"My father has friends in the FBI. Neither

68

one of them could find Patterson. Why do you think you can? Do you think you're better at it than they are?"

Did she realize she was repeating the same question the chief of surgery had asked her?

He decided to answer in kind. "Absolutely. I am better."

She suddenly got it. "You're as arrogant as I am."

"When it comes to the job, yeah, I am." He continued to stare into her gorgeous eyes as he asked, "Do you want me to find him or not?"

"Yes, please, but . . ." She started to say something more then changed her mind. "Thank you."

"Hold on," Ben began. "Catch me up. Did Patterson just decide to leave your hometown, or did something happen?"

She sighed. And here she thought the conversation was finished. "Yes, something happened, and he was committed to the Stockton Institute, for a time anyway."

"What's the Stockton Institute?"

Max answered. "A state-run facility for the criminally insane. Patterson attacked her, damn near killed her. Read the reports. That will answer some of your questions."

Ellie frowned at Max when she said, "You knew all about Patterson before Ben saw the restraining order, didn't you?" Before he could answer, she continued, "Of course, you did. My God, it's only been what? Four? Five hours since we met?"

"Longer than that."

"How did you get all that information so quickly?"

"It's in your file."

Her hand went to her throat. "For anyone to read?" She sounded appalled.

"No, not for just anyone." Then, frowning, he asked, "What did you mean, Patterson went to Stockton for a time?"

"That wasn't in the file?" she asked.

"No. Now tell me." He sounded as though he were grilling her again.

"Patterson's family is very wealthy, and they were able to get him transferred to a private facility. And guess what? Eventually he was given weekend passes to go home."

"After he tried to kill you?" Ben asked.

Oh God, she was going to have to dredge it all up again. She took a deep breath. "After Patterson left me for dead . . . actually, I was told he thought he had killed me . . ."

"Yes?" Ben urged when she hesitated. His tone was softer this time.

"He ran, and the police and FBI couldn't find him right away. So my father, with the

70

help of the two FBI agents who had become friends, decided I needed to go into hiding."

Max filled in the blanks for Ben. "The son of a bitch had been terrorizing her for over a year. He'd even grabbed her a couple of times, but she was able to get away. He wasn't going to give up until he killed her."

Ellie continued. "As soon as I was ready to leave the hospital, my father drove me here. One of his friends introduced him to a couple, the Wheatleys. They took me in. They're both teachers and very kind people. They had no children of their own, and they opened their home to me." For the first time since the topic had come up, she smiled. "They didn't know what to do with me."

She didn't expound, and neither Ben nor Max pressed.

"They took good care of me," she said. "I stayed with them while I finished college and all the way through medical school and part of residency."

"And you're finishing your residency now," Ben concluded.

"No, I've already finished my residency. Now I'm finishing my fellowship in trauma. Are we done talking about Patterson?"

Ben nodded. "Almost. One last question, and we'll move on. Just tell me, when did

Patterson get released?"

"He's been in and out for the past ten years. About six months ago, my father heard he'd gotten out and vanished. The attorneys were supposed to keep watch, and so were my father's friends, but none of them were informed of his release. It was by chance that my father heard about him." She clasped her hands together emphatically and said, "Now I'm done talking about this. You're here to interview me about the shooting, remember? So why don't you get to it."

Max nodded to Ben, who pulled his chair closer to the coffee table and said, "Okay, let's start. Go ahead and turn the recorder on, Max."

Ben stated the date, time, location, and the names of the people in the room for the recorder, then asked, "Dr. Sullivan, did you see Agent Sean Goodman get shot?"

"Yes, I did."

"Tell us what happened from the time you left the hospital. It's my understanding you were going for a run. Isn't that right? Why don't you start there."

Now that the subject of Patterson was off the table, Ellie could take a deep breath without feeling as though her chest was trying to crush her. She tried to be as accurate as possible as she told what she had seen, and then she patiently answered a myriad of questions. She didn't have as much trouble describing the man who shot Agent Goodman as she did the strange woman, but she stressed that she didn't think she would be able to point either of them out in a courtroom.

"He looked directly at me, but he had sunglasses on. I could see the sweat on his face. The sunglasses slipped down his nose, and I saw his eyes, but only for a second, then he swung the gun around, and I dropped to the ground."

"Describe him for me," Ben requested.

"He was around six feet tall. He wore a brown windbreaker and black pants."

"And the woman?"

"She was dressed all in black. Black slacks, black top. She was shorter than he was, around five seven, and I'd guess her weight to be about one hundred thirty."

"What else did you notice about her?"

"She was freaky looking. She was wearing a black wig, but it was askew. And her eyes didn't look real."

"What do you mean, not real?"

"They sort of . . . glowed. Definitely contacts," she added quickly so he wouldn't think she was nuts. "It all happened so fast, and they had their heads turned away from me most of the time."

Ben calmly led her through more questions. He seemed laid-back about it all, but Ellie was certain it was all an act to put her at ease. She knew from past experience that when a policeman or federal agent was harmed, the city went into lockdown mode until the culprit or culprits were apprehended. Sean Goodman was not only a friend, he was also a fellow agent. Taking it all in stride? Not possible.

"What about Agent Goodman? He saw them," she said.

Ben nodded. "Yes, he did."

"Sean saw a man and a woman moving fast toward the street. We're not sure if he saw their faces before he was shot, and like you said, they obviously tried to change their appearance," Max explained.

"If he had gotten closer . . . ," Ben began.

Ellie shook her head, stopping him. "Had he gotten closer, the bullet would have done a lot more damage, especially if he was hit in the chest. Those wounds are . . . messy."

"Why wasn't he wearing a vest?" Ben asked Max. "Do you know?"

"He was supposed to stay in the van, but the second he got out, he should have put the vest on. Farber and Stanley had taken their vests off," he added. "They thought it was all over. Maybe Sean thought that, too."

"Yeah, maybe he did," Ben allowed.

"What about those kids who ran into the street to flag down the ambulance? They must have seen the couple running away," Ellie said.

"They didn't see their faces." Max sounded irritated again.

"There were people all over the park. Could someone else have gotten a better —"

"We've checked," he barked and turned the recorder off.

She frowned at him. "Are you always this grumpy?"

Surprised by her question, he repeated, "Grumpy?"

"Yeah, he is kind of grumpy today," Ben interjected.

"The hell I am."

Laughing, Ellie moved the pillow out of her way and stood. "I'm getting a Diet Coke. You two want anything?"

"Sure, I'll take a Coke," Ben said.

She turned to Max. "I shouldn't have called you grumpy. You've had a bad day. Your friend was shot, and from what you've told me, the plan to apprehend these people fell apart." She headed toward the kitchen and added, "So it's okay to be grumpy."

"Yeah, he's usually real cheery." Ben laughed as he told the lie. His cell phone vibrated, and he quickly read the text.

"Hey, Ellie, could I ask you a medical question?"

She peeked around the corner. "Sure. What do you want to know?"

"What does it mean when a pregnant woman has all the symptoms of indigestion?"

She thought he was joking until he looked up from his text, and she saw the concern in his eyes.

"It means she has indigestion."

He wasn't convinced. He read his wife's symptoms aloud, told Ellie that she was four months along, and that she had miscarried their first child at exactly four months.

Ellie reached for her cell phone. "What's her name?"

"Addison."

"Give me her cell phone number."

Leaning against the doorway she began to text, her thumbs tapping out her message with lightning speed.

Ben was impressed. "You're fast."

She smiled. "I've been doing this for a while."

Ellie gave Ben's wife suggestions to help

with the indigestion and ended the message by telling Addison she could text her with other questions when she needed to.

"Thanks," Ben said when she had finished. "She worries."

Ellie gave him her cell phone number. "If you have concerns, you can text me, too."

When Ellie returned with the Cokes, she handed one to Ben and took her seat next to Max.

"Will Sean get into trouble because he didn't wear his vest?"

Max answered. "He did get into trouble. He got shot, remember?"

That wasn't what she meant, but she didn't pursue the matter.

Max turned the recorder back on. "Ben, do you have any other questions you want to ask Ellie?"

"No, I think we're done for now," he replied. "You're going to be around, though, aren't you? You aren't taking off for Europe?"

"Did you forget the 'I'm poor' part of the interview?" she asked.

He laughed. "Right. So no Europe."

"I will be going to Winston Falls for a wedding next week, but until then I'll be here, and you can always get me on my cell phone."

Once again, Max hit the button to turn the recorder off just as Ben asked, "Where is Winston Falls?'

"South Carolina."

"Ellie's family lives there. It's her hometown," Max volunteered.

"How often do you get back home?"

"Not often."

"Are you going anywhere after the wedding?"

"No, I'll come back here . . . for a while."

"I guess we're finished," Max announced and started to stand. Ellie put her hand on his knee to stop him.

"Now it's my turn to ask questions," she told him.

"That's not how it works," he replied.

She ignored his comment. "Why were they in the park?"

Ben answered her. "The FBI has been following them since the last case didn't make it to court, and when we heard about the buy, we set a trap. Max and I wanted in on it."

"What was the buy? Drugs?"

"Weapons," he said. "Very sophisticated weapons."

Before she could ask him another question, his cell phone rang. He saw who was calling and said, "I've got to take this."

He disappeared into her kitchen for some privacy before he answered his phone. Ellie turned to Max, realized then that her hand was still resting on his leg, and pulled back. "What did he mean, the last case didn't make it to court?"

"Witnesses couldn't testify."

"Couldn't or wouldn't."

"Couldn't."

She didn't push him to explain, but said, "What went wrong in the park?"

"A lot of things."

It was as much as he was going to tell her, she realized after waiting several seconds. She tried another question. "Ben said the FBI has been following them, so you know who they are?"

"Yes."

"And?"

When he didn't immediately answer, she gave him a good nudge with her foot. He was so surprised, he smiled. "Did you just kick a federal agent?"

"No, I nudged a federal agent. I'm getting ready to kick."

"Calvin and Erika Landry."

"Now, was that so hard?"

He laughed and she was happy to see the tension ease from his face for a second.

"I've never heard of them," she said.

"I didn't think you had. They don't usually do business here. We've had other dealings with them. Fact is, we've been chasing them for some time. We knew about the deal that was going down at the park, and we were hoping we could catch them in the act. Unfortunately, they got away before anyone could identify them. That's why eyewitnesses to the shooting are so important. Too many agents have been working on this for too long."

"What about you?"

"What about me?"

"Do you live in St. Louis? I'm just curious about who's involved in this case," she hastened to add so he wouldn't think she was being too personal.

Max stood, slipped the recorder into his pocket, and said, "For the past six years I've lived in Honolulu."

She didn't know why she was so bummed out by the news, but she was. She hardly knew the man, and he definitely was all wrong for her. Yet there was just something about him . . . The truth was, she had never had such an immediate attraction to any other man before, not even her ex-fiancé, though she'd be loath to admit it.

It was all so confusing. She didn't want a relationship with Max, but she wanted the possibility of one? She wasn't making any sense.

Her brain chemistry was all messed up, she decided, and that was why her physical reaction to him was so intense. That was it exactly. Her endorphins were going haywire. Sleep deprivation was probably one reason for the imbalance, and being a workaholic with no social outlets was probably another.

There was one other theory: She was crazy, just plain crazy.

Ben finished his call and was leaning against the door frame, drinking his Diet Coke. He pulled away when Max said, "Let's go."

"Is Ellie going on the witness list?" he asked.

Max shook his head. "Agent Hughes is running this, remember? If Ellie's name goes on that list, you know what will happen."

"Yeah, but you and I could stop it."

"From Honolulu? Not possible."

Stop what, Ellie wondered. She waited for Max or Ben to explain, but neither did.

"I'm telling you Hughes will want —"

Max cut him off. "I said no." He walked to the door and unbolted the locks.

Ben turned to put his drink on the kitchen counter and headed to the door that Max was holding open.

"I'm sorry I couldn't be more helpful," Ellie said, a bit puzzled by their brusque departure.

"It's okay." Max started to pull the door closed but stopped abruptly. He stood for a second as though weighing his thoughts before saying, "Are there any good restaurants around here?"

"If you like Italian, you should go to the Hill. There's a great restaurant called the Trellis. You'll love it. It's casual dress. You'll see everything from suits to shorts."

"Okay. I'll pick you up at seven tomorrow night."

He shut the door before she had time to react.

"Wait . . . what?"

# FIVE

Finding out who the blond runner was on the track turned out to be surprisingly easy.

A shoot-out on hospital grounds with FBI agents swarming all over the park was big news. Every local station led the evening broadcast with a report about the downed agent and the hunt for the perpetrators. The hospital was still buzzing about the incident. The staff, the volunteers, even the patients wanted to rehash the event. Some even did a bit of embellishing.

Willis Cogburn knew how the gossip grapevine worked and used it to his advantage. Dressed as a deliveryman for a local florist, he carried a potted plant with Agent Sean Goodman's name on it into the hospital. It was late afternoon when he made the delivery, and the lobby was empty except for a few volunteers milling around behind the reception desk waiting to help anyone who wanted assistance.

An older, white-haired gentleman, wearing the name tag "Roland," looked up the number of the patient's room, marked it on a Post-It, and stuck it to the bright red bow attached to the plant before setting it on a cart with other floral arrangements ready for delivery.

Willis didn't have to ask where Sean Goodman was. All he had to do was engage the volunteer in conversation while he leaned over the counter and read the room number.

"How's that FBI agent doing? I sure hope he's going to make it," Willis asked sympathetically.

"He's almost as good as new," Roland said. "One of the aides told me they already moved him out of ICU into a private room. He might even get to go home as early as the day after tomorrow."

"That's good to hear," Willis said. Shaking his head, he added, "You all had quite a commotion here, didn't you? Were you on duty?"

Roland vigorously nodded. "I sure was, but I didn't see any of it happen, thank goodness. I didn't even hear the gunshots."

"What exactly did happen?"

Roland was eager to recount what he had heard, and when he had finished, another volunteer named Bill added a few facts.

"The way I heard it," Bill began, "a man and a woman were running away from the federal agents, and then suddenly the man turned around and shot the agent closing in on them."

Roland plopped down in a swivel chair and rested his elbows on the arms. "That's how I heard it, too," he agreed.

"Did they catch the man and woman yet?" Willis asked, knowing full well they hadn't.

"No," Bill said.

"But they will," Roland interjected. "And when they do, that pair will be put away for a long time. You don't get off with a light sentence when you shoot a federal agent."

"Have you heard why the FBI was after them?" Willis asked, leaning on the counter as though he had all the time in the world to chat.

"I heard it was a sting operation," Bill answered eagerly. "They were selling guns or drugs or something."

Roland shook his head. "That's not what I heard. One of the secretaries in admissions told me the security guard said they were passing government secrets."

Before the two men could get into an argument, Willis steered the conversation in another direction. "Does the FBI know who they're looking for?"

"FBI agents and cops have been crawlin' all over the place trying to get information, looking for witnesses," Roland said.

"Miles down in X-ray told me the agent was close enough he could identify them if he had to."

"That's great," Willis replied. "You know what I heard?"

"What's that?" Roland asked.

"There was a girl on the track who might have seen the whole thing. Someone said she was a high school kid running laps."

Roland snorted. "There wasn't any girl on the track," he scoffed. "It's our own Dr. Sullivan. Does she look like she's in high school to you, Bill?"

"No, of course she doesn't. More like college age."

"What kind of doctor is she?" Willis asked.

"Surgeon," Bill answered. "She's the one who took the bullet out of the agent. Lucky for him she was there when he got shot."

"Sure is," Willis said. "Any other witnesses that you know of?"

"I'm sure if anyone else got close enough to see the man and woman, the FBI will find them. They've been talking to everyone around here."

"That's right," Roland agreed. "They

stopped me on my way in this afternoon to ask me questions."

After a few more minutes of conversation, Willis Cogburn was on his way to his car. He'd parked in the back lot so no one would see he wasn't driving a florist van. Once he was inside, he made a call.

He didn't waste time on a greeting but said, "Goodman will be going home at the earliest the day after tomorrow. He's in room four twelve, so you can keep tabs on him in case they let him go sooner. Remember, George, we don't do anything until Cal gives us the go-ahead. Just be ready."

"Did you find out who the girl is?"

"Yes."

"Okay, then, let's get this done. The sooner the better to my way of thinking."

"That's not your call. You know the instructions. I get her at the same time you get Goodman. Cal doesn't want any deviations from his plan. He wants it to happen simultaneously."

"Cal doesn't even know for certain if Goodman or the girl can ID him or Erika," George pointed out.

"He's a careful man," Willis replied. "He doesn't take chances, and he's paying us a lot of money."

"That's right," George said. "But we don't

get the rest of the money until the job's done, and like I said, the sooner the better."

"How many times do I have to say it? We wait for the go-ahead." Willis all but shouted into the phone. "You were in the army, for God's sake. Show a little discipline. You should be used to taking orders. You don't want to get on Cal's bad side. I brought you in because you're my little brother, George, but my neck is on the line here. Don't screw this up. If you do the job right, he'll want to use you again, and each time you'll make more money until you're a regular like me. Be patient."

Unfortunately, George was not the patient kind.

# Six

It wasn't the worst invitation Ellie had ever received. The fact was, it didn't even make the top ten. Still, it was strange, and the question remained: Had Max actually asked her out? She replayed the conversation in her mind several times and decided, no, he hadn't asked. He'd told.

Maybe it wasn't even a real date. Ben would probably be with him. The two of them were in town for only a short while, and they needed someone who was familiar with the city to take them to a good restaurant. Yes, that was it . . . maybe.

Every time she thought about it, she laughed. Max had left his card on the coffee table with his cell phone number. She could have called and canceled, but she didn't. Instead, she spent an hour the next afternoon going through her pitiful wardrobe, trying on one outfit after another, and finally settling on a black-and-white sundress with a full skirt and a boatneck. The fit through the waist was snug, and the length reached mid-knee. She decided to wear her new-last-year black ballet flats. It was either those or her flip-flops, unless she wanted to wear tennis shoes. The heels she'd worn to the hospital banquet last month were out of the question. Her feet had ached for a week afterward.

She would have put on some cool jewelry, but she didn't own any. She did have a silver heart her grandmother had given her for her eighteenth birthday, but the chain was broken, and she hadn't had time to get it fixed.

Hair brushed and down around her shoulders; makeup, perfume, and body lotion applied — she was good to go.

She was ready at seven and he was on time. He looked surprised when he saw her, as though he expected someone else.

"You look nice," he said.

So did he. He'd gotten a haircut and shaved. He still looked intimidating, she thought, but then he stood well over six feet and was built like a rock. He couldn't really look any other way. Black pants, light blue shirt with the sleeves rolled back at the wrists, open collar, and the gun . . . the ever-present gun at his side.

He pulled the door closed and waited as she used her keys to lock both dead bolts. She dropped her keys into her purse and headed down the stairs.

"Is Ben joining us?" she asked.

He smiled. "Do you usually go out with two guys at the same time?"

She turned to him. "Then this is a date?"

They reached his rental car, a new SUV. He opened the door for her and said, "Sort of."

Before she could ask him to explain, he changed the subject. "I made the reservation for seven thirty, but I got busy and didn't download directions. Do you know the way? Or should I pull up the GPS?"

"I know the way. What's a 'sort of' date?"

"How about no business talk until after dinner?"

Business? What kind of business? So it wasn't a date. That realization led to the question: Okay, what did he want? And since it was business of a sort, why wasn't Ben included?

Might as well find out, she decided. "What's your partner doing tonight?"

"Working," he answered. "You did a good thing for his wife. Addison worries."

She smiled. "Yes, I know she does. I got three texts from her."

"That's not bad. Three texts in what? Twenty-four hours?"

"No, three texts in one hour," she corrected. "By eleven o'clock Friday night we were BFFs. She's very nice. A little neurotic about the baby, but I understand why."

"You'd like her if you met her."

"I do like her. I talked to her for about an hour this afternoon."

She crossed one leg over the other and noticed he was noticing. They were at a stop sign, but he didn't seem to be in a hurry to move on.

"When you're finished checking out my legs, turn left."

He wasn't at all embarrassed. "They're great-looking legs," he told her. "I'm hungry. How much farther is it?"

"Not far," she answered, turning toward him. He had a beautiful profile. Square jaw, great bone structure. Everything about him emanated strength and made her feel safe, but then a gun and a badge would do that. However, Ellie felt there was much more to him than his outward appearance revealed, and she was eager to find out what was behind those intense eyes.

"What's Honolulu like?"

"Beautiful. It's always beautiful there, but the city's crowded. Why don't you come see for yourself."

"I don't know how to surf," she teased.

"It's not a requirement."

"Do you?"

"Surf? No."

"It looks fun," she remarked. "I would like to visit Honolulu someday. The climate appeals to me, especially in January with the ice storms and snow here. You told me you've lived there for six years?"

"That's right."

"Where did you grow up? Certainly not Hawaii."

"Yeah? Why not?" he asked, glancing at her.

"You're too . . ." She started to say, "uptight," then changed her mind. "Rugged," she finished. "Oh, we're here. Restaurant's right around the corner. Parking's in back."

A car pulled away from the curb and Max pulled his car into the spot. He opened her door and waited for her to explain her evaluation of him, but she just smiled as she stepped onto the sidewalk and headed toward the awning over the restaurant's front door. He couldn't help but notice how her hips moved as she walked away from him.

He caught up with her. "Rugged, huh?"

93

"Not exactly rugged," she said. "There's just something about you . . ."

"Yeah? What if I told you I grew up in Los Angeles?"

"No, I don't think so."

He laughed. "You're nuts. You know that?"

"Oh? Did you grow up in Los Angeles?"

"No, but —"

"Of course you didn't. The people there are much more laid-back."

"Ellie, these sweeping statements of yours . . ."

They entered the restaurant, and he muttered, "I hate crowds." He took her arm and led her to the podium, where an elegantly dressed woman stood with a reservation book in front of her.

"Your table will be ready momentarily, Mr. Daniels," she said with a gracious smile. "If you'd like to wait in the bar, I'll call you."

Max rounded the corner and saw that the bar area was packed as well. He spotted one empty stool at the end of the bar and had just put his hand on the small of her back to guide her toward it when a large man with a jovial face called to Ellie from across the room. After threading his way around the tables to get to them, the man threw his massive arms around Ellie and kissed her on both cheeks.

The owner of the Trellis, Tommy Greco, was a former boxer whose nose had been broken more than once. Word had it that he was ruthless in the ring, but outside he was a gentle man, kind and soft-spoken. Nothing much ever riled him, except maybe putting too much garlic in his famous chicken spiedini.

He released Ellie from his grip and said, "Your boyfriend has a gun."

"It goes with the badge," she replied.

She stepped back and quickly introduced the two men.

"I heard about that shooting," he said to Max. Turning to Ellie, he added, "And I heard you operated on the agent who took the bullet."

"Tommy, how did you know I did the surgery?" she asked. She knew the shooting had been on the news, of course, and in the papers, but the surgeon's name wasn't mentioned.

"Come on, kid, you know I hear everything that happens in this town."

He led them to a table secluded from the others in a quiet niche. "You two get the executive table tonight," he said. Wiggling his eyebrows, he added, "Lots of privacy."

He unfolded her napkin and dropped it into her lap. "It was nice meeting you, Agent

Daniels. You take good care of my girl, you hear me. Has she told you how we met?"

"No," Max answered.

"Make her tell you about the golfer who came in with his friends a while back. It happened just after I opened the restaurant." Tommy suddenly spotted someone else he knew across the room and was off with his arms spread wide to greet them.

Alone again, Ellie was intent on asking Max why he had asked her out, but a waiter appeared to take their drink order. When he walked away, she turned back to Max.

Before she could get her question out, he said, "Butte."

"Pardon me?"

"Butte, Montana. That's where I was born and where I grew up."

She slapped the tabletop. "Ah, of course. Now you make sense."

"Now you don't make any sense," he countered.

How could she explain it so that he understood? Not possible, she decided. He did make sense to her now, though. There was an unbridled energy about him, and to her he seemed a maverick and a little on the wild side. Yes, that was it. As wild and untamed as the Montana landscape.

Max was looking at her as if she'd lost her

mind, and Ellie realized she needed to curb her imagination. "I'm pretty sure you didn't ask me out so that I'd show you a nice restaurant. What did you want to talk to me about?"

"Let's have dinner first. What sounds good to you?"

"Uh-oh. You're avoiding the subject, which means it's bad."

He was as good at switching topics as she was. "How come Tommy calls you 'kid'?"

"He introduced me to some of his father's friends who all happened to be in their eighties, and to them I was a kid, I guess. He called me the kid doctor, which, by the way, I didn't like. I told him so, and he stopped. So don't you try it."

He laughed. "I won't. And for the record, I don't think of you as a kid. I barely glanced at you when we first met. All I saw were shorts and a ponytail." And legs, he admitted to himself, long, perfect legs. "When I look at you now," he said, his eyes looking deeply into hers, "the last thing I see is a kid."

Ellie could feel the blood rushing to her head and her heart pounding again. She quickly picked up a menu and pretended to study it. When she glimpsed at him a few seconds later, he was still staring at her, but this time there was a concerned look on his face.

"It's time you told me why we're here," she said, laying the menu on the table.

"You're right," he admitted. He leaned forward. "This isn't something I would normally do . . ."

Seeing his hesitation, Ellie became anxious. "Just tell me," she insisted.

"This stays between you and me, okay?"

"Yes, okay," she said.

"Don't change your story," he said finally.

"What story?"

"Your account of the shooting," he explained. "Don't change any of it."

"Why would I change it?" she asked, perplexed.

"As this investigation progresses, you might be questioned again, either by the police or by the FBI, especially Agent Hughes. He may try to lead you or even coerce you to remember details you couldn't recall before. Don't tell him or anyone else more than you told Ben and me, that you didn't see the couple well enough to recognize them."

Max had become so serious and his tone so persistent, Ellie wondered why he was telling her this. Her thoughts went back to the conversations they'd had in her apartment.

"You haven't told me much about this case or the people you've been chasing. You said their name was Landry, right?"

"That's right."

"And you said you've been trying to catch them for a long time."

"When the Landrys moved to Honolulu and started doing business there, Ben and I were brought in. They were arrested, and the case was solid. We had three witnesses, but as I already mentioned, the case never made it to court."

"You didn't tell me why it didn't make it to court."

"Two of the witnesses disappeared. We're still looking for them, but no luck so far."

"What about the third witness?"

"Killed in a hit-and-run."

Ellie felt a shiver run down her arms.

Max let her absorb the information before continuing. "We need eyewitnesses who will testify against them, people who can positively connect them to a crime. But if those eyewitnesses come forward, we'll have to guarantee their safety. And that's why, if you have enough information to testify, you'll probably end up in witness protection."

"Oh no, I won't," she replied.

"I know how your life was turned upside down by Evan Patterson. You had to leave your home and your family for all those years. If you have to go into witness protection . . ."

"No, I would never allow that to happen. Max, I've spent half my life in hiding," she whispered. "I think I've reached my breaking point. Lately, I've felt frozen. I can't seem to make decisions as to where I want to live, and the idea of signing a contract, even for one year, scares me."

"You're waiting to find out where Patterson is, aren't you?"

Time to admit the truth, she decided. "Yes, I am. Even now he's controlling my life. I hate that. And now you're suggesting I might have to hide from the Landrys. Enough," she snapped. "I've really had enough. I told you and Ben that I don't think I can identify either one of the Landrys. Shouldn't that keep me safe from them?"

He nodded. "Maybe. Just be careful . . . and stick to your story."

"I will," she answered. She studied him for a minute, thinking how thoughtful it was of him to try to protect her; then she asked, "Could you get into trouble for telling me about the other investigation that fell apart and about those witnesses?"

"No, I'm not giving away confidential information. You would have to spend a little time on the Internet searching for articles, but you could find out all about that case. It was in the newspapers."

"Do you think those two witnesses who disappeared are still alive?"

"I don't know," he said, shaking his head. "I think they may have gotten spooked when they heard about the hit-and-run, and they took off."

Who could blame them? she thought. She took a breath and said, "Thanks for telling me."

"Just promise you'll be careful."

"I will."

He picked up his menu. "Are you ready to order?"

"I'm not very hungry."

Max read through the menu, and when he glanced up at Ellie again, she was staring into space, lost in thought, absentmindedly turning her spoon over and over on the table. He should have stuck to his guns and waited until after dinner to tell her about the Landrys, but she'd been too perceptive and forced him to give her the news sooner than he'd planned. *Way to go, Daniels,* he chided himself. Here he was, sitting across from a gorgeous, sexy woman, and all she could think about was the danger that threatened to uproot her life.

Determined to change her mood, he said, "Tell me something."

"Yes?"

"On a scale of one to ten, how's the date going so far?"

# SEVEN

As soon as the waiter had taken their orders and left, Max said, "I think every man in here is staring at you."

The comment surprised her, and she looked around. "You're exaggerating."

He wasn't. Ellie was stunning, and even he, as cynical as he had become, was a bit in awe of her. After spending a short time with her, however, he'd come to realize her appearance didn't define her.

Ellie said, "Do you know, when I walked out of ICU and saw you waiting in the hall, I thought you looked so relaxed. I almost envied you."

"I was relaxed."

She didn't argue, yet the look she gave him indicated she didn't believe him.

"Okay, I was worried about Goodman," he admitted. "And I was angry."

"About the shooting." It was a statement, not a question.

"Yes, of course the shooting, but I was also furious that the Landrys got away. We should have had them." And with what was supposed to be an airtight case this time, he thought.

"What did Agent Hughes have to do with the investigation?" To clarify, she said, "You and Ben were talking about him when you were at my apartment."

"Hughes flew down from Omaha to take charge when he heard the Landrys were involved. He's been chasing them for about four years now."

"You don't like him much, do you?"

He shrugged. "Our methods are different."

Tommy strolled over to their table, refilled their glasses, and handed the pitcher of ice water to a hovering waiter.

"Did you tell Max about the golfers yet?" he asked Ellie.

"No, I didn't."

"Come on, it's a good story. She's humble," he told Max. "She won't tell you how it really went down, but I will."

"What happened?"

Both Tommy and Max turned to her. There was no getting out of it, she knew.

"It turns out I have a bit of a temper when

I'm pushed," she began. "I'm not proud of that."

"No, you kept your cool," Tommy insisted. "It was that jerk you were with who lost his temper. The guy had an ego the size of Nevada." To Max he said, "And all she did was try not to embarrass him."

"Up to a point," she interjected.

"See, here's what happened," Tommy continued. "There were four men, all of them in their fifties, I'm guessing, sitting at a table across my restaurant from where Ellie and the deadhead were sitting. The golfers were a loud bunch but not offensive. They were just having some fun, and they weren't bothering any of my other customers. They'd had a lot to drink before they got here. Who could blame them? It was a real pisser out there that day, over ninety degrees." He turned to Ellie. "Are you gonna help me tell it?"

She laughed. "All of them had ordered steaks," she explained.

"Grade A prime. Meat that will melt in your mouth," Tommy crooned. "I only serve the best."

"I happened to look over just as one of the golfers took a bite of his steak."

"It was a twenty-one-ounce porterhouse," Tommy interjected. "One of the customers' favorites."

"The man stuffed a piece the size of a small roast into his mouth. I couldn't believe it," she added. "I watched him, hoping he'd keep chewing."

"But he didn't," Tommy said, grinning.

"I'm guessing it didn't melt in his mouth," Max said.

"No, it didn't." Ellie continued, "He swallowed and, of course, began to choke. He tried to stand, then crashed to the floor."

"I didn't get to see any of this," Tommy said. "I was busy in the front, but I heard the guy's friends shouting for help and yelling that their friend was having a heart attack. I ran over to see for myself, and I saw him on the floor. The guy's face was getting red." Turning to Ellie again, he said, "Go ahead, you tell what happened next." Tommy's enthusiasm was comical.

"My date, Dr. Dwight Parish, said, 'I've got this,' and ran over to the golfer, whose name I later found out was Chuck," she said.

"Chuck the Choker is what I dubbed him," Tommy added.

"What did you do?" Max asked Ellie.

"I started the clock the second Chuck tried to swallow the meat —"

He interrupted. "What do you mean, you

started the clock?"

"Oxygen deprivation," she explained. "There was plenty of time, but I always start the clock, which means I note the time down to the second."

"The deadhead announces he's a doctor," Tommy said, "and he kneels down beside Chuck and starts pushing his chest, giving him CPR. He, too, believed Chuck was having a heart attack. The jerk acted like he was running a seminar or something, talking to the crowd while he pumped Chuck's chest."

"Then what happened?" Max wondered.

"I tried to explain to Dwight that the man was choking," Ellie said.

"Yeah, she did," Tommy agreed. "I stood beside her. She was real nice about it, but the deadhead wouldn't listen, even after she told him she'd seen Chuck try to swallow a hunk of meat. Deadhead was too busy dazzling the crowd to pay attention. And all that pumping didn't dislodge the meat, did it?"

"No, it didn't," Ellie said.

"And I'm watching, getting real worried. It's bad for business when a customer dies in your restaurant."

Max had to agree. "Yeah, that would be bad."

"I didn't know the kid was a doctor then," he added. "But she was trying to convince deadhead that Chuck wasn't having a heart problem —"

"Had anyone called nine-one-one?"

"Oh yeah, of course. So tell him what happened next," Tommy urged.

"I was watching the time," she said. "And I politely asked Dwight to get out of my way."

Max raised an eyebrow. There was something about the way she made the comment that told him she wasn't quite telling the truth. "Politely, huh?"

"*I* thought so."

"Before you go on, tell me, what kind of doctor is Dwight?"

"He just finished his residency."

"In what field?"

"Psychiatry."

"Ah," he said, smiling.

"It's an important and difficult residency," she told him. "However, Dwight has a Superman complex and was determined to revive the golfer. If he had had paddles, he would have tried to shock him. I say 'try' because I wouldn't have let him."

"Dwight sounds like a jackass," he commented.

Tommy nodded vigorously.

"Okay, so go on," he urged, caught up in the story, but before she could continue, he asked, "Weren't you a little worried? What if you couldn't get the meat out?"

She looked astonished, as though she couldn't understand why he'd ask such a silly question.

"There was still plenty of time, and I had a backup plan. Clean steak knife, alcohol. If I had to, I'd open his throat. I wasn't going to let him die. All of what Tommy and I have told you took less than a minute," she added. "It sounds like a lot was going on, but it happened really fast. I explained that the man was choking, but Dwight continued to argue that I was wrong, that it was a heart attack. He said he knew the symptoms. He was once again talking more to the crowd than to me, and it was difficult to get a word in.

"I'm a trauma surgeon," she reminded Max. "And we are trained to take charge. We're . . . aggressive when we need to be. I tried to explain to Dwight . . . but he just wouldn't listen, so I did what I had to do . . ."

Tommy finished for her, "She used her foot and knocked Dwight out of the way. He landed halfway across the room."

"Tommy helped me get Chuck upright,

then I dislodged the meat and pulled it out of his throat. All the while I'm checking the clock. It was all good," she said. "I still had plenty of time."

"I wanted to throw the meat at Dwight, but she wouldn't let me," Tommy grumbled.

"And Chuck?" Max asked.

"No worse for the wear," Tommy said. He stepped aside to let the waiter set plates in front of them. "You kids go ahead and eat your salads now, and I'll check on your dinners."

As soon as he left, Max asked, "Did good old Dwight ask you out on another date?"

"Like I would go?" She shook her head. "Since I had had my fingers down Chuck's throat, I went to the ladies' room to wash my hands, and when I came back to the table, Dwight had taken off."

"What a gentleman."

As the evening wore on, Max asked questions about her work. It was obvious that she had a real passion for helping people, and he loved the way her eyes lit up when she talked about them.

"It must be stressful at times," he commented.

"It is," she answered. "But what about you? Your job has to be riddled with stress."

"Sometimes," he admitted. He smiled and

added, "And then there are those criminals who all but capture themselves. One of my first cases as an agent I barely had to investigate."

"What do you mean?" she asked.

He put down his fork and leaned back in his chair. "It was a robbery of a neighborhood bank, a one-man job. I don't think the robber had much experience, though. When he walked into the bank with a cap pulled down over his eyes and a gun concealed in his pocket, he found the lobby crowded with customers. He was so nervous, he decided he should wait until they had cleared out before going up to the teller to make his demands. But he didn't want to look suspicious just milling around the bank doing nothing, so he went to a table with some forms stacked on top.

"In the surveillance tapes, you could see him pick up the pen and start writing on one of the forms. He must have been pretty distracted because, after he finally made it to the teller and got away with the cash, he didn't think to pick up the forms he had been filling out."

"What were they?" Ellie asked.

"Applications for a job."

"No," she said incredulously.

"Yep," he said. "He wrote down his name,

address . . . everything we needed to drive to his house and pick him up."

"I can't believe anyone would be that stupid."

He nodded agreement. "A friend of mine who's on the police force in Honolulu told me about a crime he covered where this man went into a convenience store to rob it. He got the money from the cash register and then demanded the clerk hand over a bottle of whiskey, too. Out of habit, the clerk asked to see some form of ID, and . . ."

"He gave him his ID," she finished.

"That's right."

"Tell me another one," she pleaded, laughing.

"I've got a hundred of them, but just one more," he said. "It's my favorite. There was this one guy who tried to rob a bank. He carried a grocery bag to use as a mask to conceal his identity. His ingenious plan was to put it over his head, then throw the front door of the bank open and rush in. He'd cut holes in the bag for his eyes but evidently hadn't tried it out because, when he put it on, the holes lined up with his forehead. On the tape, you see the guy come barging into the bank with a bag over his head, waving his gun and turning in circles, trying to get the tellers to give him the cash. He was threatening a potted plant."

Max liked the way Ellie's eyes sparkled when she laughed. The waiter appeared with the bill, and he knew it was almost time for them to leave. He was sorry to see the evening end.

"Ellie, if Dwight left you here, how did you get home?"

"I was going to take a cab, but Tommy's wife, Mary, was on her way out the door, and she drove me home. She's not here tonight, or Tommy would have brought her over to our table to introduce her. He's very proud of her. They've been married for almost thirty years."

"That makes them unique."

"You sound cynical."

"When it comes to marriage, I guess I am. I've had friends whose happily-ever-after lasted about three years."

"My parents have been married a long time, and they're not an anomaly."

He didn't comment. "Are you ready to go?"

He surprised her by taking her hand as they walked through the restaurant. It wasn't until they were once again in the car and on their way back to her apartment that she returned to the subject of his cynicism. She wanted to know what had happened to make him so sour.

"I take it your parents are divorced?"

"No. They're not. They've been married a long time, too."

"But they're miserable."

He laughed. "No, they're happy together."

"Then it's just you, unless . . ."

"Unless what?"

"How many ex-wives do you have?"

"None," he assured her. "I've never been married."

"Any long-term relationships?"

He glanced at her. "Define long-term."

"More than three months."

He had to think about it. "No," he said. "I like women, Ellie, and the women I take to bed know there isn't going be a long-term anything."

Was it a different woman every night? She didn't have the nerve to ask.

"What about you?" he asked. "Are you involved with anyone?"

"No."

"How come?"

"No time," she said. *And no desire in a long while. . . . until you came along,* she silently added.

"That's an excuse, not a reason," he told her. "What about friends with benefits . . . you know . . . casual sex?"

The question surprised her. "No, so far not interested. Some of my friends have sex with friends, and they tell me it releases a lot of stress. It just seems a little too cold and clinical to me."

The rest of the ride home was quiet, but she wasn't uncomfortable with the silence. Ellie kept thinking about her answers to his questions. No sex, no friends with benefits, no involvement . . . My God, she'd made herself sound like a female eunuch. And a bore.

Max parked in front of her building and walked inside with her. He insisted on checking her apartment to make sure it was safe, which Ellie appreciated. It took as long as a hiccup. She waited by her door as he looked around. Soft light from a single lamp illuminated the living room.

"Would you like something to drink?" she asked as he walked toward her.

"No, I'm good."

He was inches away. She swallowed and said, "I have to tell you . . ."

"What?" he asked as he planted his hands against the door on either side of her.

"I liked the date portion of the evening much better than the serious talk."

"The date portion isn't over yet."

And with that he leaned down and kissed

her. His lips on hers felt sweet. It was a soft kiss until her mouth opened under his and she moved into him. She sighed when his tongue swept inside and rubbed against hers. His touch was electrifying.

And that was only the beginning.

He wrapped his arms around her and pulled her up against him as his mouth slanted over hers again and again.

"Damn, you taste good." His voice was raspy. He kissed the side of her neck and felt her shiver.

She put her arms around his neck and her fingers tugged on his hair to get him to kiss her again. She had wondered what it would feel like to be kissed by him, but no fantasy could match the reality. He overwhelmed her, and it was wonderful. He kissed her again, a hot, wet, openmouthed kiss that made her want much, much more, and when he pulled back she felt dazed.

"Do you want me to stay or leave?" he asked.

She kissed the pulse at the base of his neck. "I guess I can try casual," she whispered, shocked by how ragged her own voice sounded.

"Sweetheart, if I stay, it isn't gonna be casual."

He tilted her chin up with his thumb,

116

needing to see her eyes and hear her say the words before he started tearing his clothes off and then hers.

His cell phone rang a scant second before Ellie's phone beeped.

Max took a deep breath, then reluctantly pulled away from her to answer the call. Ellie found her phone in her purse and read the text.

"I'm on my way," he said into his phone. He ended the call and looked up to see Ellie opening the door.

"There's been a shooting at the hospital."

At the same time she said, "I've been called in to surgery."

# EIGHT

Ellie thought she should drive herself to the hospital, but Max disagreed. He wasn't going to let her out of his sight until he knew what in thunder was going on. Ignoring her protests, he grabbed her keys, locked the dead bolts, and pulled her along to his car.

"I could be in surgery all night," she pointed out.

"I'll wait and drive you home."

"But that could be hours . . ."

"I'll wait."

She stopped arguing. The set of his jaw indicated he was going to be stubborn. She gave him directions to a shortcut crossing over the highway, and then she called Wendy, the ER nurse, to find out what she was going to be walking into.

"It's another pileup on I-70," Wendy said. "We've got mangled bodies on their way in. Dr. Westfield wants you here now."

"I'm on my way," she said. "I heard there

was a shooting."

"Yes, there was, and right inside the emergency room doors. Gangs are becoming more accommodating. They're shooting each other right where they know they can get help. Pretty soon they'll be shooting it out in front of the OR doors. Cuts out the middleman, you know — the ambulance driver, the paramedic. I'm telling you, Ellie, it's a war zone in the ER now."

"I'll be there soon."

She disconnected the call and turned to Max to repeat what Wendy had told her.

"It's a little surprising it hasn't happened before now," she said. "Even with security, the number of weapons confiscated from gangs when they're brought into the hospital is shocking. It was only a matter of time before one of those weapons was overlooked."

"The hospital should spring for more security. Triple it," he said. "Only way to control it."

She agreed. "Who called you about the shooting?"

"Ben."

"He was at the hospital this late?"

"He was heading back to check on Sean when he heard there were shots in the hospital. He should be there by now. We need to find out what's going on, to make sure Sean wasn't the target. We've got an agent watching out for him."

"Do you think the Landrys would send someone to . . ."

"Better safe than sorry."

Max took the entrance to the hospital on two wheels and screeched to a stop near the emergency room doors.

"If you can't find me on the surgical floor, look in Sean's room," he told her.

The emergency room looked like a set for a disaster movie. Each bay was packed. Doctors and nurses rushed from one to the other tending to victims of the highway accident. Mixed in among them were a few gang members, some handcuffed to their gurneys, also waiting to be treated for their wounds. Policemen were stationed around the area.

Most of the accident victims were dazed and quiet, but the gang members were not so compliant. Some were screaming for drugs while others shouted obscenities and threats because they weren't getting priority attention. It was loud and chaotic.

Ben was waiting just inside the doors. "It's bedlam in here."

He was right. They had to shout to be heard.

Ellie realized she was gripping her phone and didn't have her purse or a pocket to put it in. Without a thought as to what she was doing, she handed the phone to Max. He already had her keys. He might as well hold her phone, too.

Max and Ben stayed right behind her as she made her way around gurneys and supply carts.

"How's Sean?" Max asked immediately.

"He's doing okay. There's someone with him now."

"What's the word on the shooting?"

"From what I've gathered, a rookie cop was watching the ER doors. A guy walked in, and when his jacket fell open, the cop spotted a gun in his pocket. The cop pulled his weapon and told the guy to hand over his gun, but he drew on him. The rookie had no choice but to fire, shot him in the chest. There were enough witnesses to prove it was self-defense. The doctors tried to resuscitate the shooter, but it was too late. The police claim there's a gang war going on."

Ellie heard him. "It seems there always is," she said.

"One of the officers told me there was a real bloodbath tonight at some deserted warehouse. An ambush," he added. "Two

121

dead, six injured. Most are thinking the shooter was here on a vendetta, but a couple of people I talked to said he didn't fit the gangbanger profile."

"No ID?" Max asked.

"No," Ben answered. "Probably wouldn't be a bad idea for us to follow up on this."

"We don't usually see this crowd until the middle of the night," Ellie remarked as she pushed a gurney aside so they could pass.

Max noticed that she was oblivious to the catcalls and the crude compliments shouted at her from various gurneys. One skinhead yelled something so obscene Max wanted to grab him by the neck, but Ellie didn't seem the least affected.

"Hey, wait up, Ellie," Ben said. "You passed the elevators."

"We're taking the stairs," Max told him.

"Okay," he said, not comprehending why anyone would run up three flights when there were perfectly good elevators just steps away.

Max climbed the stairs ahead of them and opened the door on the fourth floor. With a parting nod, Ellie ran to the locker room to change into scrubs. A seventy-year-old man was waiting on the operating table for her. His car had been sandwiched between a semi and a moving van on the highway, and he had suffered a ruptured kidney. It would take her the next few hours to complete the partial nephrectomy.

She didn't see Max again until almost one in the morning. Just as he had said, he was in Sean's room. He was sprawled in a chair watching one of the news channels. The sound was so low she didn't know how he could hear it. Ben was there, too. He was sound asleep in a chair on the other side the bed. There was an agent sitting in a chair outside of Sean's door.

Ben woke up when she brushed past him. Startled, he jumped to his feet, realized where he was, and stepped back so Ellie could get to Sean.

Yawning, he whispered, "Good night," and quietly left the room.

Ellie had already changed back into street clothes. Since she was in his room, she decided to check Sean's incision. She slipped on a pair of gloves and gently pulled the hospital gown down. Sean slept through her inspection. When she turned around, Max was waiting for her by the door. His hair was tousled, and she thought he looked incredibly sexy.

Can anyone be too tired for sex? She was dead on her feet, but she still wanted to jump his bones. Good thing he wasn't a

123

mind reader.

As they walked down the corridor, he commented, "It's the middle of the night. How come you look so good?"

She had glanced at herself in the mirror when she was changing, and she knew she looked like hell. "You need glasses."

He smiled. "No, I don't."

They took their time descending the stairs. Ellie was used to running everywhere, but she didn't mind the slow pace. In fact, she fought the urge to lean into him.

"So what happens now?" she asked.

"I take you home," he answered.

"I mean with the Landry case."

"Tomorrow — or rather, today — after you've had some sleep, you'll need to go to the police station and look at some photos. Agent Hughes will be there."

"And you?"

"Ben and I will be doing some paperwork, and then we fly back to Honolulu."

All thoughts of tearing his clothes off and having mind-blowing sex came to a screeching halt. It would have been an amazing night, she knew, but it would have been just one night. Recreational sex came with a price . . . especially for her. She wasn't the sophisticated and experienced sort who could have sex with a man and forget about him the next morning. Max was leaving for good, and she would never see him again, so it would be best if they said their good-byes and went their separate ways.

Decision made, she relaxed.

Max's cell phone rang. Ben was on the line.

"I thought you were on your way back to the hotel," Max said.

"I'm in the ER," Ben said. "We've got a situation here. A police officer requested some help with a kid, and I suggested you. Mind stopping by?"

"Yeah, all right."

As Ellie and Max cut through the emergency room area, they noticed how quiet it was compared with the earlier scene. The hallways were empty, and they didn't have to zigzag around the gurneys.

Then they turned the corner and spotted Ben. He stood in front of a door with his arms folded, blocking access. A young policeman, a middle-aged man, and a hospital aide were standing in front of him arguing. The aide had a set of keys and wanted Ben to move so he could unlock the door. Ben wasn't budging.

"Get out of the way and I'll just shoot the lock," the older man suggested. He pulled a small handgun from his pocket. "Move out of my way. I'll —"

Ben reacted with lightning speed. Before the man could blink, he'd confiscated the gun. He handed it to the officer.

The policeman glared at the man. "How did you get in the hospital with that gun, Gorman? And what are you doing with it anyway? You're a social worker — and a damned poor one at that. You should find another line of work."

"I've got a permit to carry," Gorman boasted. "I work in a bad part of town. I need protection. Now give me my gun back."

"Security here sucks," the officer muttered to Ben.

"I want to see your permit," Ben demanded.

"It's in my glove compartment."

"What's going on?' Max asked.

Ben nodded to the social worker and said, "Things got out of hand."

"Yeah? What's the problem?"

Ellie knew all about Gorman. He was mean and liked to throw his weight around.

Gorman started to explain, but Max put his hand up, nodded to the officer, and said, "You tell me."

"A boy was being dragged out of the ER by Gorman."

"I'm a social worker. I have every right —" Gorman began. He quickly shut his mouth when he saw Max's dark expression.

Max read the officer's name and said, "Go on, Officer Lane."

"The boy was screaming while Gorman dragged him," he said again. "The aide," he continued with a nod toward the young man holding the keys, "had the boy's other arm. They were hurting him."

"I was using necessary force," Gorman defended.

"He told me to grab him," the aide said.

"Anyway," the officer said in a loud voice to get the others to be quiet, "the boy broke free. He ran through an open exam room where a doctor was sewing up a patient, and he got hold of a scalpel. He locked himself in this private exam room."

"How old is this boy?"

"Nine or ten."

Jeez. "And you want to pull a gun on him?" Max quietly asked the social worker.

Gorman shrank at the anger in Max's eyes. He took a step back and decided to bluster his way through the situation.

"I'm putting this boy in lockup. Resisting and fighting me . . ."

Turning to the aide, Max said, "Unlock the door and don't leave. You and I aren't finished."

The aide's hands shook as he tried three keys before finally opening the door. He hastily stepped away.

"Officer Lane, escort these two men into the waiting room and wait for me," Max ordered. He turned to Ellie. "I won't be long."

He entered the room and quietly shut the door behind him.

Ellie went to the nurse's station to find out who the boy belonged to. She knew the nurse on duty. Her name was Mary, and she was a sweet older woman who was on a perpetual diet.

"What can you tell me about —"

"That sweet boy Gorman terrorized?"

Ellie nodded. Mary moved closer to the counter so she wouldn't be overheard.

"I don't know who called social services. The boy and his brother were in a car accident. The older brother just got out of surgery. Broken leg," she explained. "The little guy has some cuts, but he checked out all right. He said his aunt is coming to get him, but she won't be here until tomorrow. That's all he would say. Then Gorman came charging in. I thought about calling security, but then Officer Lane came on duty and he helped."

Ben joined Ellie at the counter. He could see she was becoming anxious. She kept glancing at the door.

"It's okay," he said. "Max knows what he's doing. A nine-year-old with a scalpel won't be a problem for him. He's gone into much trickier situations."

That news didn't comfort her. "Why didn't you or Officer Lane go in? Why did you ask Max?"

"Because he's better at this sort of crisis than I am. He knows what's going on inside that boy's head. Max can help him, and pretty soon the boy will know he can trust him." He went on, "There was this case about a year ago. An uncle was using his nephew as a punching bag, and one day the kid had had enough. He got hold of his uncle's gun and was going to kill him. The two of them were locked in the boy's bedroom. I remember the walls were green, and there were posters of superheroes all over."

"What happened?"

"There was a standoff, and the boy held the uncle at gunpoint. It took some convincing for the boy to let Max come in. He found out that the uncle had tried to sexually assault the boy, and that was when the boy went for the gun. Max understood that the boy wanted his uncle to suffer, and so he described in detail what was going to happen to the uncle when he was sent to prison. It was pretty gross stuff, but it placated the boy, and he gave Max the gun.

"The uncle started screaming at the kid then, so Max walked over and coldcocked him. By the time I was there putting the cuffs on him, the pervert had come around and was blubbering. I guess what Max had told the kid scared him. The prick," he added, almost as an afterthought.

"What if that boy had turned the gun on Max?" she asked.

"He was prepared for that. He knows how to handle these situations."

Ellie kept watching the closed door. "Scalpels are sharp," she said. "If the boy slashes an artery or —"

"Max won't let him hurt him."

And he was right. The door opened and Max walked out. He had one hand on the shoulder of the little boy, who was glued to his side, and he held the scalpel in his other hand.

The boy seemed too little to be nine or ten, Ellie thought, and he looked so scared. She wanted to find Gorman and sock him. As she walked toward them, the child's eyes got big and he shuffled to get behind Max.

Max looked down and said, "It's okay.

She's with me. Let's let her look at your arms, okay? Then we'll find you some food and a bed. You're staying here tonight."

The boy's name was Kyle, and both of his arms had red streaks from being wrenched. Max lifted him onto an exam table.

When Kyle saw Ellie putting on gloves, he said, "No shots."

"No shots," she agreed. "I just want to examine you."

She helped him remove his T-shirt.

"The other doctor said the seat belt saved me," Kyle whispered. "See? There's the bruise where it held me. I was in the backseat."

Ellie was more interested in his left shoulder and his arms. The skin was red and inflamed from his wrist to his elbows, and the left wrist was sprained. The right arm wasn't as bad.

"Where are your parents, Kyle?" Ellie asked.

"My mom died, and I don't know my dad," he answered.

"Any other family?"

"Just my brother. I live with him. My aunt lives in Chicago, and she said she'll come tomorrow and get me."

Ellie looked at Max. "I'm going to admit him," she said.

"What does that mean?" Kyle asked with a frantic look in his eyes.

"It means you're going to sleep here tonight."

"With my brother?"

"When your brother gets out of recovery, I'll make sure he's on the same floor. All right?" Ellie asked.

"What about that man? He said he was going to put me in jail."

"I'll take care of him, like I promised," Max said.

"I'm sorry I took that knife. I thought they'd leave me alone if I could scare them."

Ellie went back to the nurse's station to start the admission process. She called the office and explained that an aide employed by the hospital had inflicted some of the injury to the child and that there was a possibility of a lawsuit. Since she was the admitting physician, she would determine when the child could be released. By the time the paperwork was completed, Kyle was sound asleep.

"It's a bad sprain in his wrist," she told Max. "I'm surprised Gorman didn't pull his arm out of the socket. He'll need ice packs on the shoulder, too."

She waited at the nurse's station while Max and Ben went into the waiting room to talk to Gorman and the aide.

She heard Officer Lane say in a raised voice, "You have the right to remain silent . . ." She couldn't hear the rest because Gorman was shouting.

A minute later Max returned to her. "You ready?"

She turned back to the nurse. "Thanks, Mary."

"Don't worry. I know the night crew on three. They'll watch out for that boy," Mary assured.

Nodding, Ellie followed Max out into the night air. Ben called good night as he headed to his car.

"How did you get Kyle to calm down?" she asked.

"I didn't say anything. I just let him talk. The poor kid was scared out of his mind. When he was ready to listen to me, I promised him no one was going to lock him up and that I would keep that social worker away from him."

"He obviously believed you. You were good with him."

They reached the car, and Max opened the door. "You'll check on him in the morning?"

"Of course I will, and I'll make sure someone stays with him until his aunt arrives. You don't need to worry."

"With you looking out for him, I won't worry at all."

Ellie slipped into the passenger seat, clipped on the seat belt, and closed her eyes. They hadn't even pulled out of the parking lot before she was asleep. Had Max not been watching, he wouldn't have believed it. Her deep, even breathing indicated she had drifted off into a sound slumber. As he drove, he thought about her. She was a woman who was used to being in control, and yet she felt comfortable with him. She wouldn't have let herself sleep if she didn't feel safe.

He remembered the route she had shown him, and it didn't take any time at all to get her home. He parked the car in front of her building, turned the motor off, then unhooked his seat belt and hers.

"Come on, sweetheart. You need to get to bed."

The second he touched her arm she was alert. "You don't need to walk in with me."

"Yes, I do."

When he opened her car door, he took her hand.

Neither one of them said another word until they were inside her apartment. He did a quick check, pulled her phone out of his pocket, and handed it to her. Then he bent down and kissed her. She leaned into him and that was all the permission he needed. He wrapped his arms around her and deepened the kiss. She followed his lead and used her tongue to drive him as wild as he was driving her.

What was the harm in a few kisses . . . farewell kisses . . . she thought, as her arms curled around his neck.

Max pulled back, looked into her eyes, and with a low growl kissed her again. He loved the taste of her, like sugar and mint, and the feel of her soft, luscious body pressed against him. Most of all he loved the way she responded to him.

How could he resist her? The kiss was hot, wet, thoroughly arousing, and when Max realized it was getting out of control and he didn't want to stop, he forced himself to end it. He couldn't seem to let go of her, though. Holding her tight, he took a couple of deep, shaky breaths, trying to regain some semblance of control. He knew he shouldn't have started this. He should let go of her and walk out the door. Yeah, that's what he should do. Ellie wasn't the one-night-only kind of girl. She wasn't a hookup or a throwaway, as some of the guys in the office called their one-night stands.

*Let go and walk out the door.* He silently chanted the command and still didn't move. How could he? Ellie was kissing the pulse at the base of his neck, making his heart rate accelerate. She kissed the side of his neck, then moved up to his ear. Her mouth was soft against his skin, and her tongue was driving him nuts.

He tightened his hold on her. "We need to stop this," he began, realizing his words contradicted his actions, since he couldn't make himself let go.

"I know," she whispered, kissing him again.

"I've got to get back to Honolulu, and I don't want to . . ." He was losing his train of thought, and all he could think about was kissing her.

"You don't want to what?" she asked. Her fingers splayed into his hair as she leaned up to kiss his jaw.

He had to think about the question for several seconds, then said, "Hurt you. Yeah, that's it. Sex tonight, gone tomorrow, I don't think you could handle that."

The truth was, he wasn't sure he could handle it either. Ellie was going to be real hard to walk away from, almost impossible. He didn't question why he felt that way, just knew it in his heart. She was so differ-

136

ent from the other women he had known. She wouldn't be forgettable.

"Ellie, it would be easy for me to get you into bed . . . ," he began.

Easy? She felt her spine stiffen. How egotistical! A couple of seconds passed before honesty kicked in. He was telling the truth. It would be easy for him, but it would be just as easy for her to get him into bed. And hadn't she decided that was a bad idea?

Her lips brushed his jaw when she said, "And I'd end up getting hurt?"

"Yes." His voice shook. "I think you would."

Ellie pulled away. "You're right," she said with a sigh. "You need a more experienced woman, someone who knows what she's doing." God, he was arrogant, but oh was he sexy. It took all she had not to throw herself into his arms again, but instead, she opened the door. "Have a nice flight home."

# NINE

Ben surprised Ellie early Sunday afternoon when he knocked on her door and told her he would drive her to the police station to look at some photos. If he had arrived fifteen minutes later, he would have missed her. Dressed casually in jeans, a white T-shirt, and tennis shoes, Ellie was throwing her phone into her purse with her lipstick, brush, wallet, latex gloves — she had learned never to be without them — a pack of tissues, and a small plastic bottle of disinfectant. She never left home without that item either.

She didn't ask Ben where Max was, but he volunteered the information anyway. "Rob — that would be Agent Hughes," he explained, "wanted Max's help interviewing another possible witness. A young man was cutting through the park and says he saw the Landrys."

"He can identify them?"

"We'll see," Ben said, unwilling to say more.

"So he won't be at the station?" she asked as she slid into the passenger seat of Ben's car.

"Who? Max? No."

"I meant Agent Hughes," she explained. "I thought he wanted to be there when I looked at the photos."

Ben shook his head. "He's so anxious for you to identify the Landrys, it's been suggested that he might inadvertently steer you toward those photos, so he's going to stay away."

She nodded. "That's fine."

"Agent Wahlberg will be there to observe," he said. "He's local."

Ellie's cell phone rang. She looked at the screen and said, "Excuse me. It's the hospital." After a brief conversation, she put the phone back in her purse. "I just dismissed Kyle. His aunt is there to pick him up. He'll be staying with her," she announced.

"That's good," Ben said. "I'd hate to think he'd have to deal with another Gorman."

"He's not a typical social worker. Most are very competent and understanding," she said. "Hopefully, Gorman's replacement will be more compassionate."

A few blocks later Ellie said, "Tell me

about the Landrys."

"They're a piece of . . ." He didn't finish the sentence, although he thought of several choice words he could have used to describe the pair. "They started out in Omaha," he began. "That's where they lived until about five years ago." He rubbed the back of his neck as he added, "They sell weapons to anyone who can pay. Untraceable weapons. They started small — handguns, every make and model, then moved up to semi-automatic, then moved up again. . . ."

He pulled onto the highway and cut over to the center lane. "There are guns on the street now with bullets that can cut through steel. Bulletproof vests don't stand a chance."

"I know. I've seen the damage they can do. We call them spinners."

"We?"

"The other surgeons and I," she said. "The bullets spin around inside the body, shredding arteries and organs. Last winter I tried to repair the damage one did to a ten-year-old boy. His mother told me he was walking across the street when the shooting started."

"Did he make it?"

"No, he was gone before we could get it out. I promised his mother I would never forget him, and I won't. He was such a beautiful little boy. His name was Joel Watkins." She turned to look out the side window as she said, "I know the Landrys didn't sell that specific gun to the man who killed Joel, but to me they're just as responsible. Anyone who puts guns on the street should be held accountable for every death."

He didn't disagree. "There are hundreds of other dealers, but the Landrys . . . well, they're going to get a special place in hell."

"No doubt," she said.

"They moved to Honolulu a couple of years ago when they got into bigger and better weapons."

"They must have had something very big going on to bring them all the way here."

"Yes," he said. "Unfortunately, the men they were meeting were killed in the park. It would have been nice if we could have turned one of them."

They reached the station, and Ben found a parking spot in the lot around the corner.

Ellie followed him through a set of double doors and asked, "How long do you think it will take before you catch them?"

"Hard to say, but I'm sure they'll eventually show up. If not here, then in Honolulu. They're used to getting pulled in."

"And they'll see what evidence you have?"

"And witnesses."

She felt a shiver. She had been warned how they worked. Witnesses disappeared, and if there was no clear evidence to indict them, the Landrys went back to business as usual.

Agent Wahlberg was waiting for them at the front desk and escorted them up to the second floor to a long, spacious room. The walls were industrial beige, and the desks were all but on top of one another. Every desk had a computer monitor on it and a chair sitting adjacent to it. Most of them were empty, but it was Sunday and still early in the day. Tonight, she guessed, would be another story if the station was anything like the ER.

Ellie passed a large, slouch-shouldered Hispanic man wearing a tank top and jeans. He was handcuffed to his chair and sat next to a detective who was typing a report into his computer. She noticed a woman and a little boy anxiously watching the proceedings from a bench across the room and assumed they were related. The man's head was bent as he grumbled answers to the detective's questions.

Ellie walked by the man and paused momentarily. She also noticed something else, backtracked to get a better look, then continued on to the back of the room where Wahlberg and Ben waited. Wahlberg courteously pulled a chair out while Ben placed two binders on the desk in front of her. He opened one to a page of mug shots. After getting instructions from Wahlberg, Ellie proceeded to study the faces on each page.

Every few minutes she looked up to see what was happening with the man sitting with the detective. There wasn't any question what she had to do. When she saw the detective unlock the handcuffs, she pushed her chair back, stood, and said, "Excuse me a minute."

Ben started to follow her, but she raised her hand. "I'll be right back."

"What's she doing?" Wahlberg asked.

"I don't know," Ben replied.

Ellie didn't have any idea how the man would react, but it was her responsibility to talk to him.

"This is your lucky day, Carlos Garcia," the detective was saying as she approached. "I'm gonna let you go, but I won't be so lenient next time."

As soon as Carlos stood, so did his wife and child. Ellie walked around the desk to face the man.

"I'd like to have a word with you in private."

Carlos looked wary at first, then angry at the request. The detective stood and asked, "What do you need with him? Maybe I could help you?"

"No," she answered. She thrust her hand out to Carlos, all but grabbing his to shake it.

"Who are you?" he asked, glancing at his wife and then back to her. "Did I do something to you?"

"No," she assured him. "Would you mind following me? It will only take a minute."

She didn't wait for his response but walked toward the corner of the room. Carlos followed.

"Look, lady, I don't know what you think —"

She interrupted. "My name is Dr. Sullivan," she began.

And that was all the detective who had been working with Carlos heard. The rest of the conversation was spoken in such a low voice he couldn't catch a word. A few moments later Carlos called his wife over, and she was included in the conversation. She nodded as she listened to what Ellie was saying, looking more and more worried.

"What is she doing?" Wahlberg asked the question again.

Ben shrugged. He watched Ellie lean over

144

the desk, grab a piece of paper, and write on it before handing it to Carlos.

Ellie put her hand on Carlos's shoulder. "This isn't going to cost you anything. I promise. The doctor owes me. Just promise me you'll go soon. I'll make sure he works you in. My cell phone number is on the bottom," she added, looking at his wife. "If there is any problem, you call me."

Both Carlos and his wife shook her hand. Ellie even shook the little boy's hand.

"Okay then," Ben heard her say as she walked back to him.

Without a word of explanation, she resumed her inspection of the photos.

"Ellie?"

She looked up. "Yes?"

"Did you know that man?"

"No, I didn't," she replied as she turned the page.

"Why did you talk to him?" Wahlberg wondered.

"I needed to," she answered, but she didn't say another word about the matter.

She wasn't going to explain that, as she walked past Carlos, she had noticed the mole on the back of his neck and, upon closer inspection, was 95 percent certain it was a melanoma. It needed to be checked as soon as possible.

Carlos's wife had told Ellie she, too, had noticed it, and that she was sure it hadn't been there long. That was a good sign. Hopefully, if it was melanoma, it would be caught before it spread throughout the body. Ellie wanted her diagnosis to be wrong, but she doubted it was.

Both agents let the matter drop. Ben pulled up a chair and began to answer some texts as he waited.

Ellie turned a page and continued to examine the pictures of some of the homeliest and most terrifying men and women she'd ever seen. And that was saying something considering the number of gangbangers she'd put back together.

Her phone beeped that she had a text, and she paused to respond to it. When she was finished, she turned to Ben. "Your wife says hello."

He grinned. "What's she worried about today?"

"Diet," she answered. "And just for the record, I like hearing from her, so don't tease her when you get home."

"I won't," he promised.

Ellie turned back to the photos.

"Look who's here," Wahlberg said. "I knew Hughes couldn't stay away. And that must be the guy who was in the park and says he saw the Landrys."

She looked up to see two men coming toward her. The one leading the way appeared to be in his early forties, but his hair was prematurely gray and his face was creased with deep frown lines that suggested he was not used to smiling often. He carried himself with authority, so she suspected he was Hughes, the agent she'd been warned about. With him was a younger man with a lanky build. His long hair was combed forward, concealing his forehead and nearly covering his eyes. And right behind them was Max.

Her heart skipped a beat. Damn it, she thought she wouldn't see him after last night. Now she had to go through the angst again?

Oh no, she wouldn't, she decided. She would choose not to be affected by him.

Great plan, lousy follow-through. Her stupid heart was racing by the time he reached her. It didn't help that he was dressed in a pair of jeans and a gray T-shirt that showed off the muscles in his chest and upper arms.

*Stop noticing,* she told herself. She said hello and quickly returned to the mug shots. She would rather have stared at Max, but then who wouldn't? *Ignore him,* her better judgment told her. That was the key to averting a heart attack. A heart attack? The possibility of such a thing happening was so absurd she couldn't help but smile.

"What are you smiling about?" Ben asked.

"These lovely photos."

Agent Hughes came around the desk to face her. "We haven't been introduced," he said. "Don't get up," he added as he extended his hand.

He was a polite but extremely stiff man, Ellie decided. The job showed on his face, but he seemed pleasant enough and not as overbearing as Max had suggested.

"Have you looked through that book yet? Did you really examine each picture?" Hughes asked her.

"She just got started," Ben said.

"You should probably back off," Max added with some irritation in his tone. "Let her look at the mug shots without any pressure."

"Introduce me to the lady," the young man standing next to Max requested. "My name's Greg," he said as his eyes scanned her body from head to toe.

She started to say, "Ellie," but Max was quicker. "She's Dr. Sullivan."

"What kind of a doctor are you?" Greg asked.

"Why don't you go sit at that desk over there and start looking through the binder," Max suggested. He stood directly behind Ellie and casually placed his hands on her shoulders. "Or you could look at the photos on the computer. Your choice."

"I'll do what she's doing," Greg said. "In fact, why don't I sit next to her, and we can go through the pictures together."

"That's not how this is gonna work," Max said. "Go sit."

"Ellie, have you looked through this entire binder?" Hughes asked. And before she could answer, he said, "Maybe you ought to start over."

"Why don't you go sit with Greg," Ben said, "and let Ellie look without any prodding."

Hughes raised a hand. "Okay, okay. Just make sure she —"

"Enough already," Max snapped.

"Do you want to tell her what page the Landrys are on?" Ben asked.

Hughes shook his head and crossed the room to get some coffee but turned back to say, "Maybe we should just put six or seven photos on the table like we usually do . . . maybe . . ."

"You can't change the set now. Let her look."

Ellie felt as though she were in the middle of some macho competition. Hughes's demeanor had become so intense, she was glad he was going to give her some space, but she did start over on the first page. She paused halfway through and tapped a photo. "I remember him. He came through the OR last year. Switchblade nicked the lateral thoracic artery. It was a tough surgery."

"Don't nicks in arteries bleed out quickly?" Ben asked.

"Not when the surgeon has her finger on it holding it together."

"You did that?"

She nodded as she studied more faces. Three pages later she tapped another photo. "Two bullets in the stomach. Horrible recovery."

And on it went. Twice more she pointed to photos and described the surgeries.

Max leaned against the desk. He watched her look at both Cal and Erika Landry's photos, which Hughes had inserted among the other mug shots, and there was absolutely no recognition on her part.

He went to Hughes and gave him the bad news, that Ellie hadn't been able to identify the Landrys.

Hughes couldn't hide his disappointment. "Have her look again," he insisted. "Maybe she was distracted when she —"

"She's gone through them twice now. She's not gonna be a witness, so she doesn't go on the list."

Ellie wasn't paying any attention to the raised voices. She received two texts back to back. She read the first and decided to ignore it, but the second text was more insistent. Dr. Westfield wanted to make a deal. If she would come in and do a colon resection for him, he would let today be her last day at the hospital. The offer was too good to resist. Since Westfield didn't need her in the OR until five o'clock and the patient was stable, she texted to say she would do it.

"Okay, Ellie, you're done here," Agent Hughes reluctantly told her.

She stood, slipped her phone into her purse and, trying to ignore Max, said, "It's been a pleasure, gentlemen."

She turned to leave but stopped, realizing she hadn't driven her car to the station.

"I need a ride home."

Every man in the room immediately offered to take her. Greg was the most vocal and leapt to his feet. "I'll drive you, and maybe we could stop for lunch."

Max shoved him back in the chair. "She's not going anywhere with you."

Ben was intrigued by Max's behavior. He apparently had decided he didn't like or trust Greg, and that didn't make any sense at all. Then he noticed the way Max was looking at Ellie. Ah, now he understood. Damn, he was slow today. He should have picked up on the signal much earlier. He stood and fished the keys out of his pocket and started toward Ellie, but Max stopped him.

"I've got this," Max muttered. He took Ellie's arm and practically pulled her across the room toward the stairs.

"It's amazing," Ellie whispered so only he could hear.

"What?"

"One minute you're this aloof federal agent, and the next you're Neanderthal man."

He flashed a smile. "I just want to get you out of here before Hughes shoves the Landry photos in your face."

Once they were in his car and on their way, she said, "Maybe Greg will be able to identify the Landrys."

"Yeah, maybe. He says he got a good look at Cal before he put on the sunglasses."

"Are you going to tell him witnesses have a way of disappearing?"

"Hughes will talk to him."

"When does your flight leave?"

"In a day or two. It depends on how much we need to do here."

She hated that she was going to have to say good-bye again. No kisses this time, she vowed, and no angst.

"I forgot to say good-bye to Ben," she remarked.

"I'll tell him. Listen, Ellie . . ."

"Yes?"

"I'm not forgetting about Evan Patterson. I will find him, and as soon as I do, I'll call you."

"Maybe he's back in a mental ward somewhere," she suggested.

"I'm checking," he promised.

He pulled up to her building.

"I'm not going inside," she told him as she unhooked her seat belt. She fished her car keys from her purse and got out before he turned off the motor.

"You be careful," she said in farewell. She was able to stop herself before she added, "Chasing bad guys." How lame would that have been?

He didn't say good-bye to her. At least she didn't think he did, but then she practically dived into her car and drove away. She forced herself not to look in the rearview mirror, and after she'd turned the corner,

she sighed. Not too awkward, she decided.
But in the back of her mind an unwanted
thought nagged at her. She should have
slept with him.

# TEN

Greg Roper was a dream come true. Agent Hughes was overjoyed to have found such a strong witness to testify against the Landrys. The twenty-six-year-old had come forward the day after the shooting and had told Hughes he had seen both Cal and Erika Landry in the park.

When Hughes met Roper at the police station to look at the photos Sunday afternoon, the agent had his suspicions that Roper was a bit of a flake because of the way he kept hitting on Ellie Sullivan, but as soon as she left the station, Roper got down to business and quickly pointed out the suspects.

As far as Hughes was concerned, Roper was an ideal witness. He had never had any trouble with the police, had never even gotten a speeding ticket, and he had held down a good job for more than four years. Most important to Hughes was the fact that Roper wasn't at all ambivalent about what he saw. He explained that he was crossing the park and was taking a shortcut through a thicket of shrubbery to get to his car when he saw Erika Landry. She was sitting in the passenger seat of a big Mercedes that was driving slowly down the street.

"What was she doing?" Hughes asked.

"She pulled down the visor to look at herself in the mirror, and then she tugged on her hair, and it all moved at once. It was a wig, and I think she was trying to fix the thing."

"And Cal Landry?"

"I didn't see his face yet, but when he parked the car at the end of the block and got out, I saw him. He stood there surveying the street, but he turned as he was bringing up his sunglasses. I was close enough to see the scar on his cheek."

"Why did you stay where you were? Why didn't you keep going?"

"I was curious. At first I thought maybe the woman was going through chemo or something and didn't have any hair, but when she adjusted the wig, her long red hair fell loose, and she pushed it back in. She had pretty red hair. Why was she hiding it under a wig? Then I saw the man reach into his pocket and look down at something, like he was checking on it. I couldn't see what it was, but it made me even more curious. I could tell they were up to something, and I had time, so I decided to follow them and see what it was. I guess you could say I was being nosy. They didn't know I was there. They walked into the area of the park where the trees are pretty dense, and then suddenly they turned around and started walking really fast in the opposite direction. That's when I saw the FBI agent running after them."

"Did you see Landry shoot Agent Goodman?"

"I sure did. I saw him fire his gun in that direction where the agent was, and I saw the agent drop down, so, yes, I saw him shoot him."

Roper insisted that the Landrys never saw him. "Never even looked my way, but the bushes hid me. I don't think they would have seen me if they had looked."

Hughes suggested strongly that Roper not discuss what he had seen with his family or friends.

There was a BOLO on the Landrys, but Hughes fully expected the couple to appear at a police station somewhere with their attorneys flanking them. They'd say they'd heard the feds were looking for them. Even though they'd accuse the FBI of harassment, they'd cooperate and answer questions. They might even admit they were in the park, but they'd confess their innocence, and they'd have a couple of witnesses to back them up.

Greg Roper was going to be their downfall . . . if Hughes could keep him alive long enough to testify.

# ELEVEN

Ellie drove directly to the hospital and was finished with her surgery by five thirty. She was walking out the door when she was called back in. A bus filled with teenagers returning to St. Louis from a football camp had been broadsided by a semi, and there were four life-threatening injuries. Ellie did two more surgeries and didn't get home until after three in the morning. She crawled into bed and slept twelve straight hours.

When she awoke, she felt restless and didn't want to be alone, which was a rare feeling for her. She decided to go to her home away from home. She called Uncle Oliver and Aunt Millie Wheatley, the dear people who had taken her in when she was twelve years old. They loved her, nurtured and protected her, and she suddenly missed them horribly.

It wasn't as though she hadn't seen them in a while. She talked to them at least twice a week, sometimes more, and ate dinner at their house every other Sunday, depending on her schedule. But she had the sudden urge to spend some time with them before she left town.

Aunt Millie answered the phone when she called.

"May I spend the night?" Ellie asked. What was wrong with her? She sounded so pathetic.

"Of course," Millie answered. "Your room is always ready for you."

"I'll be there in twenty."

Ellie immediately felt better. Just hearing the voice of someone who loved her made a difference.

An hour later she was sitting in the Wheatley kitchen, drinking hot tea. Uncle Oliver wanted to know about her latest surgeries and, of course, wanted the details about the incident outside the hospital. She talked about the surgery but didn't tell him she had seen the shooting. If he knew that she had been so close to the gunshots, he would have been very upset.

When her uncle had gone to bed, she and Millie discussed the upcoming wedding in Winston Falls.

"You're nervous about going home, aren't you?" Millie asked.

"Yes. I'm afraid," she admitted.

"Your father would know if that monster is back in town," she said, referring to Patterson.

"That's not it. I'm nervous about . . . them. I want to fit in the family . . ." She shook her head. "I don't think I will."

"It will be all right. Just don't push it," she suggested. She reached across the table and patted Ellie's hand.

Anxious to change the subject, Ellie blurted, "I met someone."

"Oh?" Millie began to smile. "It's about time."

Ellie told her about Max and what a bizarre reaction she'd had when she met him.

"He's all wrong for me," she said. "He's abrupt and gruff, and at times he can be downright rude. For a living, he carries a gun and chases bad guys. His life is the antithesis of mine. Definitely not the ideal man . . . and yet, there was instant attraction . . . almost animalistic," she admitted. "I couldn't control it."

"That's how it was with your uncle and me. Instant attraction. Want to know a secret? We're old now. He's balding. I've gained twenty pounds and have more wrinkles than a weary bloodhound, but the attraction is still there, and it's just as strong. If you think you might have feelings for this man, don't fight them."

"There's a problem."

"What is it?"

"He lives in Honolulu."

Millie drummed her fingers on the table. "Honolulu, huh?"

Ellie nodded. "A world away."

# TWELVE

At first, Ellie was nervous about going home. Now she dreaded it.

She lay awake staring at the shadows that were cast on the wall by the streetlight outside her bedroom window. She had stayed up late talking to Millie, and now she couldn't get to sleep.

Her room was just as she had left it. Her favorite books were still lined up on the shelf above her desk. Her bed still had the light pink comforter. The bureau still had the colorful porcelain lamp that she and Millie had found at a flea market. And there were clothes in the closet that she hadn't worn in years but couldn't bring herself to discard. This room was her safe haven.

It hadn't been that way at first. When she was brought to the Wheatleys all those years ago, she was terrified and uncertain of her future; but Oliver and Millie gave her what she needed most, a secure, loving environment and time to adjust. They opened up their home and their hearts to her, and she would never be able to repay them for their generosity and kindness. When she was in their house, she felt protected.

Winston Falls, however, would always be her real home. Her visits had been infrequent over the years, and she usually couldn't wait to get back to see her family. This time was different.

It had been almost eighteen months since her last trip to Winston Falls, and that had ended in disaster. She had brought her fiancé, John Noble, home to meet her parents and her sister Ava. They all seemed to like John very much — especially Ava — and everything was going well until the second day, the day that Ellie abruptly broke off her engagement and flew back to her apartment alone.

Her parents knew what had happened — they were in the living room when Ellie went upstairs and opened the wrong door — and they were duly horrified and mortified. Ava had insisted she never meant to hurt anyone, but it was too late for apologies.

Their mother didn't know what to do about the situation. After pacing about the house for several hours, she made the decision to never ever discuss the unpleasant event. Their father didn't want to be put in the position of having to take sides, so he decided to let his daughters work it out between them. He had a long talk with Ava and then let it go.

Ellie felt devastated and hurt, but by the time she was back and settled in her apartment again, she had forgiven her parents for not throwing Ava out of the house. Once she'd calmed down, Ellie realized it was wrong of her to expect them to choose one daughter over another. She had great sympathy for them, especially her father. The poor man had put up with so much because of her. She once told him she knew that she was a perpetual thorn in his side almost from the day she was born, and he had a good laugh.

"You, young lady, make life so much more interesting," he'd told her.

She wasn't so certain about that. She knew he had his hands full with her. At age three, she was reading and doing simple math, and her vocabulary was more advanced than most adults. By age five, she was deemed a prodigy. With that realization came the responsibility for her father to protect her from being exploited. Because he was a professor in the math department at the local university, he was able to keep Ellie from being bored by scheduling individual sessions with other professors in history, sociology, English literature, anatomy, and any other subject that caught her interest.

Her parents tried to make Ellie's life as normal as possible, but it was difficult. She was only ten when she entered Sacred Heart High School. The social aspect of high school was difficult for her because she was so much younger than the other students, but the older boys especially looked out for her.

Her father believed he had done a fair job of helping her live a happy and somewhat normal life until Evan Patterson came along. Patterson turned their lives upside down and dragged them through hell.

From the moment he saw her at a summer camp for advanced science students, the seventeen-year-old Patterson became obsessed. She wasn't aware of his interest, though, until he began walking back and forth in front of her house. Shortly after that, she started to receive photos of him and love letters. When she showed them to her father, he grew concerned that a boy so much older than Ellie was showing interest. He called Evan's parents to voice his misgivings but was told that the boy was quiet and shy and, because he was a gifted student like Ellie, was probably showing only how much he admired her academic accomplishments. Despite their glowing praise for their son, Ellie's father wasn't pacified. He responded by asking two seniors to walk her to and from school.

The first time Patterson made personal contact with Ellie was during the lunch hour at her school. She had gone outside and was sitting on a bench near the fountain eating an apple. Patterson came out of nowhere. He told her he needed to talk to her because she hadn't responded to his letters. He seemed very agitated. Ellie tried not to let him see that she was afraid as she told him he should stop writing to her, but her rejection only made him angrier. When Patterson grabbed her, she screamed. A teacher monitoring the school yard immediately tried to stop him, but Patterson was big for his age and very strong. He knocked her to the ground and tried to drag Ellie away with him.

Help came from the most surprising person — Spike Bennett, or the town terror, as the nuns called him. He was a troublemaker and proud of it. Sacred Heart kept him as a student because his father had donated quite a bit of money and also because the sisters liked lost causes. They were determined to rehabilitate him, but they weren't having much success. He cursed and constantly got into fights, usually starting them just for the fun of it. But on that day, Spike became Ellie's hero. He tackled Patterson and got Ellie away from him. While Patterson was pummeling him, Spike was yelling for Ellie to run.

Ellie wouldn't leave. She threw herself on top of Patterson and hit him with her fists. Other students came running, and it took three big boys to hold Patterson down until the police arrived. Spike was taken to the hospital for stitches.

Since Patterson had never caused any trouble before, the judge was lenient. He ordered a psychiatric evaluation and mandatory therapy for six months. Ellie's father, however, wasn't satisfied. He went to the authorities and obtained a restraining order. The following week, Ellie's schedule changed and she left Sacred Heart to attend classes at the university, so Evan never had contact with her at school again, but her nightmare was only beginning.

The restraining order did little good. Patterson continued to stalk her. His adoration turned into harassment, and his harassment turned into threats. Despite all the precautions her parents took to protect her, Ellie was still vulnerable, and Patterson found ways to get close enough to assault her. The authorities were able to bring him up on charges, but each time, his attorneys worked a deal to send him for help. Beyond the restraining order, the police were powerless to do much about him. Ellie's parents did everything they could to protect her, making sure she was never alone when she was away from home. But even that didn't help on the terrible day he finally got her away from her protectors and beat her to within an inch of her life.

Patterson was finally locked up, but her parents were advised that there was a strong possibility that he would be moved to a private mental institution — his parents would bear the costs — and he could gain his freedom much sooner. So Ellie's mother and father made the most difficult decision of their lives, to send their daughter away, to hide her from the maniac. A friend in the FBI helped them by finding the Wheatleys, who lived eight hundred miles away. Ellie's father was pleased because they were both teachers. They were good, loving people and a godsend for Ellie.

When Ellie was discharged from the

hospital, her mother went with her to the Wheatleys and stayed until Ellie had regained some of her strength and had become comfortable with her new guardians. Over the next couple of years Ellie was allowed to come home for brief visits, but that happened only after her parents were assured that Patterson was not free. Although the cost of the flights was a financial burden, it was well worth having their daughter with them. Things changed dramatically, however, when Patterson was moved to yet another private institution and given weekend passes. That meant Ellie had to stay away.

Her father didn't want her to feel isolated from the family, and for several years he made it a point to talk to her every single day. So did her mother. Ava and Annie kept in contact by e-mail and text.

Eventually, life and education got in the way. Ellie chose trauma medicine as her vocation, which meant endless hours at the hospital. It wasn't possible to have long chats anymore. Just a quick hello, love you, and good-bye. For Ellie, that was enough.

She loved her family and normally would jump at the chance to be with them again, but going home was going to feel different this time. After the debacle of her last visit, she didn't know what she would be facing. Would they expect her to be cheerful and excited to be celebrating the happiest day in her sister's life?

And what about Patterson? He was always in the back of her mind. Was he looking for her? Would he show up one day? Now that he had vanished, Ellie's fear was magnified. Where was he? And what was he planning?

# THIRTEEN

Ellie called her parents to let them know she would be home Tuesday evening. Her father wanted to pick her up at the airport, but she insisted on renting a car so she wouldn't be dependent on anyone for rides. She didn't tell him she also wanted to be able to get away in a hurry if she needed to.

Because she was able to catch an earlier flight, she landed ahead of schedule and was in her rental car and on her way to Winston Falls shortly after noon. It was a pretty drive. Two-thirds of it was on a four-lane highway, and she made quick time. The rest of the trip was on a paved two-lane road that curved through the countryside. There were several steep turns as the road wound through the hills, and very few signs. On either side of the road were thick shrubs and trees, and in some spots wilting but still colorful wildflowers.

Ellie made sure her rental car had GPS

because she didn't know the route all that well. Although she had been home many times, her father had done all the driving, and she really hadn't paid much attention to roads and turns.

At times she felt as though she were driving through a forest. Branches from some of the trees reached over the road, blocking the sun. It was a bit eerie, she thought, and foreboding. She opened her window to let some fresh air in and immediately felt the thick humidity pour over her face. With it came the heavy smell of the earth and a tinge of claustrophobia. She recognized the side road that led to the waterfall and was tempted to turn off, but she quickly rejected the idea. As she recalled, the natural phenomenon that gave her town its name was about a half mile off the beaten path, and she would have to walk that distance to get to it. Maybe another day, she thought.

The town came into view, and the first sign she saw was the one pointing the way to the Winston Falls Hospital. A shiver caught her by surprise. The memory of that hospital was so vivid. After Patterson had finished with her and had left her for dead, she was taken there to be stabilized and then airlifted to a trauma center. It was a long time ago, but coming home brought it all back. *Put it aside,* she told herself.

Winston Falls was a typical Southern town. The wide, tree-lined streets oozed charm. She pulled off Main Street, went two blocks over, passed Sacred Heart High School, and turned down Birch Street, where her parents lived. Nearly all the houses in this older part of town had wide front porches, and the residents liked to relax outside in the late afternoons with their newspaper and their sweet tea. She remembered sitting on the painted wooden boards of the large wraparound porch of her own house, playing board games with her sisters.

A block away she spotted her home. The two-story house had recently been painted a pale yellow, and the front door and shutters were now black. Black wicker chairs sat on the porch, and their new red cushions matched the potted geraniums flanking each of the wide porch steps.

Her father must have been looking out the window because, as soon as she pulled into the driveway, he opened the front door and motioned to her, shouting, "Park behind the garage, Ellie."

The paved area to the rear of the garage was originally intended as a basketball court, but her family often used it for parking when people came to visit. At the edge of the court were steps that led up to an apartment above the garage. It had been recently painted as well, and she noticed there were blinds in each of the upstairs windows now. Her parents had really spruced up the place, she thought.

She had barely turned off her car engine when her father came out the back door and down the steps. He opened his arms wide and she rushed into them. No matter how old she became, she would never grow tired of her father's bear hugs. When he finally let go, he took her by the shoulders and held her at arm's length.

"Are you okay? Did you have any trouble getting here?" he asked anxiously.

"I'm fine, Daddy," she assured him.

Southern girls grew up calling their fathers "Daddy," and Ellie wasn't the exception, though occasionally the Midwestern influence kicked in and she'd call him "Dad."

Ellie opened the car trunk, and her father lifted out her bag.

"This is light as a feather. Did you put anything inside?"

She followed him into the house, and he set the bag in the back hall before going into the large country kitchen.

"Where's Mom?" she asked.

"Doing some grocery shopping. She'll be home soon. We didn't think you'd be here until late."

Ellie was glad it was just the two of them so they could talk.

"How about a nice glass of iced sweet tea?" he asked, opening the refrigerator.

"I'm afraid I don't like sweet tea," she admitted, feeling terribly disloyal to her Southern heritage. "I'll make some plain."

"No, no, your mother made both."

Ellie got the glasses out and filled them with ice while her father poured the tea. She took a drink of hers and grimaced. They switched glasses, and she headed to the living room.

"Want to sit on the porch?" she asked.

"No, no," he said a little too quickly. "Let's sit inside. It's cooler in here."

She understood his motives. "But we could sit outside after it gets dark?"

"Yes, we could if you want to. It will be cooler then."

"And it would be more difficult for anyone walking past to see us, right? Or, rather, see me?"

"Now, Ellie . . ."

"Dad, I don't want to hide inside this house all the while I'm here."

"I just want you to be cautious. Your

mother worries."

He walked to the bay window overlooking the front yard and the street beyond and stood there staring out. It had been more than a year and a half since she'd been with her father, and there was a distinct difference in his appearance. He didn't look well. His complexion had a gray tinge, and he'd put on a little weight in his belly.

"It's going to be a hectic week before the wedding . . . ," he said.

"Yes, I know."

". . . and we don't know where he is."

"Evan Patterson."

He turned to her. "Yes, of course Patterson. I would rest easier if I knew where he was hiding."

"We can't let him run our lives . . . ruin our lives," she corrected. "He shouldn't have that kind of power over us."

He didn't answer. The strain of worrying was there on his face. Her father was a distinguished-looking man with thick silver hair and handsome facial features. His shoulders were broad and straight, and she knew he tried to take care of himself, but stress could do so much damage, and he'd lived with it for years. All because of Patterson and his sick obsession with her.

She was beginning to wonder whether

coming home was a mistake.

Changing the subject to something more pleasant, she said, "You painted the house since I was last here. I like the color."

"We painted it last month," he replied, smiling now. "Your mother has been on a cleaning frenzy because of the wedding. I'll take you to see the apartment above the garage. We finally cleaned it out. It didn't take much to spruce it up. The two bedrooms and the bath were in good shape, but we refinished the floors. All we had to do with the tiny kitchen was replace the stove and fix a pipe under the kitchen sink. Except for the plumbing and the electrical, your mother and I did most of the work," he said proudly.

"What made you decide to do it now?"

"We have so many relatives coming in for the wedding, and not all of them will want to stay in the motels or the one fancy hotel we have here in town."

"You should consider renting it out after the wedding," she suggested. "I'm sure there are students at the university who would love to have the space."

Her father shook his head and sat down on the sofa facing her. "Finishing the apartment adds to the value of the property," he explained. "I don't want any college kids tearing it up. This home is an asset, and that includes the apartment when it comes time to sell."

She laughed. "Oh, Daddy, you love this house. You'll never sell it."

"I don't know about that. I'm getting old, and all those stairs . . ."

"Mother loves this house, too," she reminded him.

"I'm just saying sometime in the future."

The conversation ended when the back door opened and her mother called out, "I need help carrying in the groceries."

Ellie jumped up and ran to the kitchen. "I'll help."

Her mother was so surprised to see her, she nearly dropped one of the bags on the floor. She quickly turned to set them on the kitchen counter and then grabbed Ellie for a long embrace. "You're early," she exclaimed.

After Ellie had carried in the remaining groceries, her mother made her stand in front of her for an inspection. "Have you grown? I swear you look taller. Maybe you're just thinner. Have you been eating? With those horrible long hours at the hospital, I'll bet you've been skipping meals. Are you hungry, Ellie? I'm defrosting a chicken casserole. It should be ready to pop in the oven. What about something to drink? I could fix you —"

"Mother, I'm fine, and I'm not a guest," she said.

Her mother smiled. "I'm just so happy to see you."

Ellie pulled a chair out at the kitchen table, told her mother to sit while she put the groceries away, and to please catch her up on all the news.

"Ava will be dropping by tomorrow or the day after. She's got so much to do still before the wedding. She and John just purchased the cutest little house about two miles from here. John's taken a position at the Winston Falls Clinic," she added.

Ellie put the milk in the refrigerator and folded the grocery bags.

"He'll be working next to the hospital," her mother went on. "Ava told me that dermatologists have set hours. That will be nice, won't it? To get home for supper each night?"

Her mother was looking expectantly at her. She wanted some kind of a response or acknowledgment about Ava and John. Ellie refused to discuss either one of them, and so she stayed silent.

"Your father and I are thrilled that John decided to move here. It will be nice to have them so close."

"When will Annie get here?" she asked, ignoring her mother's comments about Ava.

"She can't leave San Diego until Thursday, but she'll be here for an entire week."

Ellie pulled a chair out and sat down across from her mother. "You and Dad should go to San Diego sometime to visit her. It would be a great vacation for you."

"Oh heavens, no. That would cost a fortune."

"Are you worried about finances?" she asked.

It was a foolish question, she decided. Her mother and father were always worried about money. Just the expense of having her live so far away all those years had been a drain on them. The flights alone had been exorbitant.

"No, we're not. We're frugal," she explained. "And we live on a budget."

"The house looks wonderful, and Dad said the apartment is finished."

"It was time we cleaned up this old house and fixed up the apartment."

"You look great, Mom."

It was a sincere compliment. Her mother was a beautiful woman. She still had the same figure as the day she was married. Ava and Annie shared their mother's bone structure and coloring. All three were slender and had honey blond hair and blue eyes.

"It's the new makeup. It's supposed to make you look rested."

Ellie laughed. "That's a new one. I'll have to buy some."

"Listen, I know I didn't want to discuss this before, but I've decided we need to talk about Ava, to clear the air before —"

Ellie cut her off. She wasn't in the mood to hear about her sister. "I'd like to talk about Dad."

"What about him?"

"When did he have his last physical? He doesn't look good, Mom."

"Don't let him hear you say that. You'll hurt his feelings."

"Mother —"

"He's tired, that's all."

"Maybe he should use some of your miracle makeup," she said, her irritation obvious in her voice.

"Don't you take that tone with me, young lady," she said. "Your father is fine. He saw the doctor just last week."

Her mother was defensive, and Ellie couldn't understand why. She wasn't attacking her father. She was concerned about him.

She decided to let that subject go, too. The list of what she couldn't discuss was growing. Money and health and Ava. What was next?

Her mother reached across the table and took Ellie's hand. "I'm so happy you're home, and I'm sorry if I'm a little short. There's just so much more to do."

"What can I do to help?"

"Your father wants to paint all the bedrooms before the relatives arrive. He's finished our room and the study across the hall from us, and he's also done two of the bedrooms upstairs. He still has Annie's old room. You could help with that."

"I'll be happy to," she said.

Her father walked into the kitchen and put his hands on Ellie's shoulders.

"Ellie's going to help you paint," her mother told him.

"Great. After I get home from the university, we'll tackle Annie's old room together."

"You can have your room tonight, Ellie," her mother said. "But after painting, I don't want you upstairs until the fumes are gone."

"Who's going to be sleeping in the garage apartment?"

"Perhaps Aunt Vivien and Aunt Cecilia," her father suggested.

"Those steps are too steep for Vivien," her

mother said.

"She would have to go upstairs to get to the bedrooms in here," Ellie pointed out.

"Yes, but these steps aren't as steep. They're much wider, and there aren't as many of them."

"If Aunt Cecilia hasn't lost any weight, she won't be able to get up these stairs either. Besides, the aunts will want to be in the house with you and Dad."

"I imagine they would," she agreed. "They like to be in the thick of things."

"Why don't I stay in the garage apartment? And the aunts can stay here in the house."

"I don't know about that. You'll be all alone," her father said.

"Dad, it's ten feet from the house," she exaggerated. "If I get in trouble, I'll shout. You'll hear me."

Her father thought for a second. "I suppose I could get another dead bolt and put it in . . . just to be on the safe side."

"It would solve another problem, William," her mother said.

"Now, Claire, you don't need to be bringing that up until we have time to sit and talk to Ellie."

"Aren't we talking now?" Ellie asked.

"A serious talk," her father qualified.

She didn't like the sound of that. The last time they had a serious talk, they told her she couldn't come home for Christmas.

She turned to her mother. "Solve what other problem?" she asked suspiciously.

"Since you brought it up, you might as well go ahead and tell her," her father said.

"Ava might be spending the night here, the night before the wedding. She doesn't want John to see her. She said it's bad luck."

Ellie couldn't resist a bit of sarcasm. "Is she wearing black? Or red for —"

"She's wearing a white gown," her mother said.

"That's a stretch," Ellie replied. "Isn't she worried she'll be struck by lightning when she goes into the church?"

"You stop that right now," her mother snapped. "What happened is in the past, and we have to find a way to move on."

Ellie didn't respond. Her father sat down at the round table between the two women. "Go ahead and tell her the rest. Get it out in the open now."

"Ava still wants you to be in the wedding."

"No," Ellie answered vehemently. "I haven't spoken to her since the last time I was here, and that was eighteen months ago. Why in God's name would she insist I be in the wedding? Mom, if you'll recall, she wanted you to ask me months ago, and I told you to tell her no. I haven't changed my mind. I only came back here because you and Dad insisted, and I will try to attend the wedding, but that's it." Shaking her head, she added, "I don't know why she won't let it drop."

"There are terrible rumors about what happened, and Ava believes that if you are in the wedding, people will know it was all a misunderstanding."

"Rumors? Not rumors . . . the truth, Mom. She can't rewrite history."

"She thinks she'll be humiliated if you don't —"

"Is that why you insisted I come home for the wedding? So Ava won't be humiliated?"

"Of course not," her mother said. "It's just that people talk, and —"

"I'm not going to be in the wedding. I'm not even sure I can make myself go."

"You don't have to worry about finding a bridesmaid dress," her mother continued. "They're all wearing long black dresses, and each one is different. Any black dress will do."

"Mother, you need to listen to me. I am not going to be in that wedding."

Her father stopped the argument. "Come on, Ellie. We'll go to the hardware store to get a dead bolt, and then the grocery store to get you set up in the apartment."

"I'll have dinner on the table in an hour and a half," her mother said. She was shaking her head at Ellie and looking pitiful. Ellie expected her to dab at her eyes next.

"See you later, Mom," Ellie said as she dutifully kissed her on the cheek. Then she whispered, "Guilt doesn't work on me, Mom. I'm not going to change my mind."

Her mother whispered back, "We'll see."

# FOURTEEN

Max and Ben had one last meeting with
Agent Hughes to go over the details of the
Landry case before they headed home to
Honolulu.

"Greg Roper pointed right at them,"
Hughes told Max. He sounded giddy. "No
one helped or guided him to their photos.
Isn't that right, Ben?"

"Yes, that's right," he agreed.

"So we've got an honest-to-God real witness," Hughes said. "I won't put him on the
list yet. This stays with us now, all right?"

Max nodded. Hughes was getting smart.
As soon as he gave the name to the prosecutor, a whole lot of people would have access
to the information.

"Maybe we should get some protection
for him," Ben suggested.

"Once he's been identified as a witness,
we will," Hughes assured.

"What about Sean Goodman? The Landrys don't know whether he got a good look at them. Will you keep someone with him?"

"As long as he's in the hospital," Hughes answered. "There are too many people coming and going there, and security isn't the tightest. Just look at what happened with that gangbanger the other night."

"The police claim he didn't fit the profile of a gangbanger," Max said. "Has he been identified yet?"

Ben shook his head. "There wasn't any identification on him, and no one at the hospital admitted to knowing him. I talked to the detectives this morning. They're looking at all the hospital surveillance tapes, trying to see if someone dropped him off or if he had a car."

Max was not ready to dismiss the shooting as gang related just yet. "Maybe we ought to be sure before we head to the airport."

"Be sure of what?" Hughes asked.

"That he was a gangbanger —"

"He was," Hughes interrupted.

"But if he wasn't," Max continued as though he hadn't been interrupted. "Then I've got to ask . . ."

"Uh-oh, he's doing the what-if's," Ben said.

"Yeah, I am," Max replied. "And I'm asking, what if he wasn't there to take out a rival gang? What if Sean Goodman was the target, and that rookie policeman stopped him before he could get to his floor?"

Ben took his cell phone from his pocket. "Let me give the detective I talked to a call. See if they've found anything yet."

The conversation was brief, and when Ben ended his call, he turned to Max. "The cameras showed him getting out of his car. It was parked in the hospital's back corner lot. Nebraska plates. When they pulled up the plates, they found it registered to a George Cogburn."

Max looked at Hughes. "You know the name Cogburn, don't you?"

Hughes nodded. "Yes, I do, though I haven't heard it in a long while. When the Landrys lived in Omaha, there was a Willis Cogburn who did some dirty work for them."

Ben went to a computer and, after typing his ID and password into the database, entered Willis Cogburn's name. A mug shot appeared on the screen. "Willis just got out of prison," he told them. "Looks like he could be back in action."

"The car was registered to a George Cogburn, though," Hughes reminded.

Ben did a search and pulled up George's

driver's license. "Same address. He resembles Willis, too. I'd guess they're brothers or maybe cousins."

Max nodded. "The question now is, where's Willis? If his brother was working for the Landrys, too, then he was at the hospital to go after witnesses. Maybe Willis doesn't want to go back to prison, and he sent his little brother to do the job for him."

Hughes had not been listening to their last exchange. He was busy on his cell phone. With the phone still to his ear, he told them, "Willis checked in with his probation officer last Thursday. He doesn't see him again for a month. That's plenty of time for him to do some side work."

Ben said, "Okay, so we now know that George Cogburn was after Sean Goodman. If that rookie hadn't seen the gun —"

Max interjected, "Maybe it wasn't just Sean he was after." His jaw tightened as he thought about what this meant. "It looks like the Landrys aren't going to wait for an indictment this time. It's pretty obvious, they're looking for witnesses now."

"The only reliable witness we have is Greg Roper, and if we keep him under wraps, they won't get to him," Hughes assured.

"What about Ellie Sullivan?" Max asked. "They were feet away from her on that track. They could be going after her, too."

"She isn't going to be listed as a witness," Hughes insisted. "They don't even know who she is."

Max's temper was rising. "Don't know who she is? Are you serious? One trip to the hospital, and they'd know. Everyone's still talking about what happened. Ten minutes, Hughes. That's all it would take to get Ellie's name. George Cogburn went into that hospital to take out a witness, and Willis Cogburn could go after her next. I'll be damned if I'll let that happen."

Hughes put his hands up. "Look, I hear you. I'll see that someone warns her and that the hospital security is advised to be on the alert."

"She's not at the hospital," Max said. "She's gone back to her hometown in South Carolina to see her family."

"That's good, then," Hughes said.

"That's not good," Ben countered. "You know as well as we do that the Landrys will stop at nothing to save themselves. Right now, we don't know where they are, and we don't know where Willis Cogburn is."

Max was adamant. "Ellie Sullivan needs protection."

Hughes started to argue, "But if she's not —"

"And she needs it now," Max demanded. "You're the lead agent on this case, but if you won't order it, I will."

Hughes relented. "Okay, I'll call the field office in South Carolina and see what I can do."

A couple of hours later, Ben and Max were on their way to the airport to catch their flight back to Honolulu. Despite Hughes's assurance that Ellie would be guarded, there was a gnawing apprehension in the pit of Max's stomach.

He was about to go through security when his cell phone rang. It was Agent Hughes.

He didn't waste time on pleasantries.

"Just got word from Omaha that Willis Cogburn hasn't been showing up at his apartment. They got inside for a search and found a note in his trash can with the names Sean Goodman and Dr. Ellie Sullivan on it."

"Tell me you've got someone on the way to her now," Max demanded.

"I did what I could, but we can't get anyone to Winston Falls for a couple of days, maybe even a week. Everyone at the nearest field office is tied up with cases, and they're understaffed. I'll talk to the locals down there. See if they can watch over her until she leaves."

"They weren't any help in the past when Ellie's family needed them. I don't trust them to do more than send a car by a couple of times a day. I'm guessing they're a pretty small operation."

Hughes's frustration came through loud and clear. "Look, I'll find someone. It's just going to take some time. Dr. Sullivan needs to be warned. I'll call her and caution her to be careful until we can get her some protection or until we've got a handle on where all the players are."

Max immediately thought of the stress Ellie and her family were already feeling from the Patterson threat. "Don't call her," he said.

"There's not much choice here. She needs to be warned," Hughes argued.

"I'll go," Max blurted.

"What?" Hughes asked, surprised. "You can't go. You have to be back in Honolulu to work on the case there."

"I'll take personal leave," Max said. "Just for a week, until Ellie gets back home. Ben's got our end of the case under control. He can consult with me by phone. I'll make all the arrangements with the Honolulu office."

He ended the call before Hughes could say another word.

# FIFTEEN

She wasn't happy to see him. In fact, she nearly had heart failure when Max pulled into the driveway. She was painting Annie's old bedroom on the second floor, and she happened to look out the window just as Max was getting out of his car.

She was so rattled, she dropped the paintbrush. Fortunately, it landed on the tarp she'd put down on the hardwood floors.

What was he doing here? Had something happened? Of course something had happened, she decided, answering her own question. He wouldn't be here otherwise.

Maybe he found out where Evan Patterson was hiding and wanted to tell her. No, no, if that was true, he would have picked up the phone and called her.

Oh Lord, her father was home. He was probably sitting on the front porch reading the news on his laptop. He was already stressed out. A federal agent stopping by could send him right over the edge.

Dressed in a pair of old shorts, a sleeveless blouse spotted with lavender paint, and flip-flops, she dashed down the stairs, flew through the living room, and ran outside. She passed her father without saying a word and came to a screeching halt about a foot in front of Max.

She couldn't seem to catch her breath, but it wasn't because she was out of shape. It was because of him. When he saw her, a huge smile spread across his face. That dimple in his cheek could cause foolish women to go weak in the knees. She wasn't a foolish woman, she reminded herself.

He looked sexy as sin. Damn it.

Her greeting wasn't polite. "What are you doing here?"

Max was looking past her. "Is that your father? He looks like he's going to pass out. Ah . . ."

"Ah, what?" she asked, frowning.

"He's staring at my gun."

"Great," she whispered. "Just great."

"Meaning?"

"I'm so happy you could make it," she said loud enough for her father to hear. She then leaned up and kissed Max on his cheek.

He couldn't resist. He pulled her into his arms, told her she had paint in her hair, and kissed her on her mouth. It was quick but amazingly thorough. "That should put some color back in his face," he said.

She put her arms around his neck and whispered into his ear, "I haven't told my parents about the shooting in the park . . . or about Sean Goodman . . . you know . . ."

"Got it."

Side by side they walked up the porch steps to where her father waited, and Ellie made the introductions.

"Dad, this is my friend Max Daniels."

"William Sullivan," her father said, stepping forward to shake his hand.

"It's good to meet you, sir."

Never one to mince words, William said, "I notice you carry a gun."

"Yes, sir, I do."

"And a badge," Ellie nervously interjected. "He carries a badge, too. Max is an agent with the FBI."

Frowning intently now, her father asked how the two had met. It was obvious he was suspicious.

"The hospital," she rushed to answer before Max could say a word. "We met in the hospital. His friend needed surgery." She added nonchalantly, "Routine stuff."

She was nodding vigorously, even as she tried to calm down. This wasn't the Inquisition. Why was she so nervous? She knew the answer to that one. She was a frickin' basket case because Max had astounded her, showing up the way he did.

Max could see the worry in her father's eyes, so he casually took hold of Ellie's hand and pulled her into his side. "Ellie did the surgery," he said proudly.

She nodded again. She was beginning to feel like a bobble-head doll. "Yes, I did, and Max and I started seeing each other."

She felt terrible lying to her father, but she justified her actions by reasoning that her motives were good. If she told him the truth, he would dwell on all the possibilities of what could have happened to her.

Her father visibly relaxed. "I'm very happy to meet one of Ellie's friends. Why don't we go inside and get something cool to drink. You must be parched." He motioned for them to go in ahead of him.

Ellie's mother came out of the kitchen, wiping her hands on a frilly apron. "William, dinner will be ready in —" She stopped mid-sentence as soon as she saw Max, and her reaction was almost identical to her husband's when he'd first noticed the gun.

"Claire, this is Max Daniels," William said. "He's a friend of Ellie's."

"A friend?"

"Yes, Mother," Ellie said. "A friend."

"Oh," she said as she nervously patted her hair. Her gaze bounced back and forth between the pair.

Max smiled as he took her hand. "It's a pleasure to meet you."

"My goodness, you're handsome." She laughed after making the comment. "You're staying for dinner, of course."

"I'd love to."

Her mother beamed with pleasure. What had come over her? Ellie wondered.

"Why don't we sit in our hearth room just off the kitchen," her father suggested.

Where they could grill him, Ellie thought. And she was right. The questions began, one on top of the other.

Ellie didn't know whether Max liked sweet tea or not, but the glass was offered, and he accepted. She stood by the kitchen island, watching, and had the most amazing revelation: Max could be charming. And her mother? She was so excited and flustered, she was blushing. Was her behavior because her daughter had finally found another man? That possibility riled. Or was her mother acting strange because Max was so adorable . . . with her, anyway.

"Ellie, why don't you go upstairs and

change before dinner," her mother suggested.

"I'm almost finished painting the room. I just have the trim to do." *And one wall,* she silently added. "When is dinner?"

"In an hour."

"I'll help paint," Max said.

Ellie was all for that. She couldn't wait to get him alone and find out why he had come all this way.

"No, you're a guest," her father said.

"He likes to paint," Ellie rushed to say.

"How long will you be staying?" her father asked.

"No time at all," Ellie answered for him.

Neither parent paid any attention to her.

"William, Max is Ellie's plus one. He'll be staying at least until after the wedding. Won't you, Max?"

"He's my what?" Ellie asked.

"Your plus one, dear."

"No, he's not —"

"I'll be leaving when Ellie leaves," Max said, and the look he shot her suggested she not argue.

"You'll be flying back with her?"

"That's right."

Ellie was shaking her head at Max. Her parents ignored her protest and so did he.

"Our daughter couldn't be in safer hands,

with her own FBI agent at her side," William said. "Have you checked into one of the motels or the hotel yet?" he asked Max.

"No, sir, I came directly here."

"Good," he replied. "You'll stay in the apartment over the garage. It's not as bad as it sounds. In fact, it's very comfortable, isn't it, Claire?"

"Oh yes, it is."

"*I'm* staying in the apartment," Ellie said.

"Yes, dear, you are," her mother agreed.

"There are two bedrooms," her father reminded her.

"And you're both adults," her mother added.

Ellie was speechless. It was so unlike her father to be lackadaisical about sleeping arrangements. Yes, she was an adult, but until this minute, her father had never treated her as such. And her mother's attitude was even more shocking. She was always so prim and proper, a true Southern lady, who tended to worry a little too much about what other people would say. She apparently didn't give a hoot about them now, though.

"I'll admit I'll sleep easier knowing you'll be watching out for her," William said. "Has Ellie mentioned Evan Patterson to you?"

Max nodded. "Yes, sir, I know all about him."

He sighed with relief. "My daughter keeps things inside. I wasn't sure whether she'd shared her past with you, but I'm very pleased she did. Now you understand why I'm happy you'll be staying with us."

"Dad, Max didn't say he could stay —"

"I'd love to stay here."

"Good," William said. "Do you think after dinner we might sit down and talk about Patterson for a minute?"

"Of course," he answered.

"I'd love to find out about you two," her mother said. "How long you've been seeing each other and how —"

"Later, Mom," Ellie interrupted. "After dinner you may ask all the questions you want. The paintbrushes are going to dry out. Come on, Max. You offered to paint. Let's go."

He followed her upstairs. She was muttering something, but Max couldn't make out what she was saying. From her tone, he knew she wasn't happy. Too bad, he thought. He had come all this way to protect her, and by God, that was exactly what he was going to do.

Concentrating solely on the job was going to take discipline. The first thought he'd had when he'd arrived at her house and saw her coming down the stairs toward him was that she was safe, and he'd felt a tremendous jolt of relief. The second thought was less professional. He'd wondered if her legs had gotten longer since he'd last seen her. By the time she'd reached him, he'd conjured up all sorts of fantasies about her.

Ellie led the way into Annie's bedroom. Max took a step back when he saw the color on the walls.

She waited until he had shut the door behind him and then said, "It's bad, isn't it? Of course, it's bad. You wouldn't have come here if it was good news. You would have called, right? So it's bad. Just tell me, Max. How bad?"

Max heard her father coming up the stairs. Now wasn't the time to explain. Ellie was bound to get upset, and from her father's response to seeing his gun, Max knew he wouldn't take the news well at all.

"Roller or brush?" Max said.

She blinked. "I'm sorry?"

He repeated the question just as her father opened the door and stepped inside, saying, "I'll use the roller. Why don't you two paint the trim. How much do you have left to do, Ellie?"

"Two windows," she answered.

The trim was white, the walls an iridescent shade of lavender. Max took one window, Ellie the other. She kept glancing over at him while she tried to think of a way to get her father to leave, but he wasn't going anywhere. He was in a cheerful and chatty mood, no doubt because her friend was armed.

Once again she felt a pang of guilt. Having her home was a burden for him. She shouldn't have given in to her mother's pleas. It would have been so much better for her father if she had stayed away.

"You'll have to see the falls while you're here. It's a short hike but worth it, isn't it, Ellie?" he asked as he poured paint into the roller pan.

"Yes, it is," she replied. "I don't know that Max will have time —"

"Sure he will," her father argued. "You did say you were going to be here until Ellie leaves, didn't you, Max?"

"I did," Max answered.

Ellie glared at him. He winked at her.

"How long have you two been seeing each other?" her father asked.

Determined to nip the personal questions in the bud, she said, "Awhile now, Dad. Max, did I tell you that my father has a Ph.D. in mathematics? He's a dean now at the university. Did I mention that to you?"

"Ellie, Max doesn't want to hear about my achievements. I'll bet he's curious about yours."

"I am," Max said. "What was she like as a child?"

"Difficult," he said, grinning.

"I'm not surprised," Max said.

"Hey . . . ," she began in protest.

"And challenging," her father added. "She kept . . . amazing us."

"How?"

Pausing in his task, William held the roller over the pan while he considered which story to tell.

"She was about seven or eight, and there was a visiting professor . . ."

"Oh, Daddy, don't tell the auditorium story."

"Ellie, it's one of my favorites," he protested.

She knew it was pointless to argue. When her father was set on something, no one could change his mind.

"I was much older," she muttered.

He ignored her correction. "There was this professor in mathematics from England. Dr. Nigel Goodrick was his name, and he was a real interesting fellow. He never would have lectured at such a small university, but he was visiting a relative who happened to live here, and so he agreed. Goodrick was a bit persnickety and quite arrogant. Wasn't he, Ellie?"

"I thought he was mean," she said. "And he smelled funny, like mothballs."

"Ellie was spending a couple of hours with me at the university that afternoon, and it just happened to be the time Dr. Goodrick had picked to give a lecture to our math students on the great nineteenth-century German mathematician Carl Friedrich Gauss. We anticipated a large gathering, so the lecture was moved to the main auditorium. He was down on the stage, and Ellie and I were sitting on the aisle about fifteen or twenty rows back. The kids, the students . . . were bored. I'll admit Professor Goodrick was a little dull."

"He was a snooze," Ellie interjected. She was working on the windowsill and stepped back to check her work.

"No one left the auditorium, though. The students were getting extra credit by attending, but instead of signing in, they had to sign out after the lecture was over. Otherwise, they would have left. Most of them zoned out the minute he began his dissertation on Gauss's life and his contributions to mathematics."

"Can't say that I would have been any different," Max admitted. "Afraid I've never heard of Gauss."

"If you're not in the field, it's unlikely that you would know much about him," William said. "You could have heard a pin drop in that auditorium, but it was because most of the audience was asleep — which made what Ellie did all the more conspicuous."

"What was that?" Max asked.

"Dr. Goodrick had just told one of the legends about Gauss. It's said that he was quite precocious as a youngster and was always getting in trouble in school. One day a teacher, for punishment, told him to add all the numbers between one and one hundred. Of course, the teacher assumed that this would keep young Friedrich busy for quite some time, but when Gauss completed it in just seconds, the teacher was astonished.

"Dr. Goodrick told this story, and then he asked if any of the students in his audience could tell him the answer that Gauss came up with or how he did it. The room was silent. Several moments passed, and then Ellie stood up and looked around the auditorium . . ."

"I was waiting for one of the big kids to raise a hand."

"But no one did," her father said. "And so my daughter raised her hand. I remember Goodrick had a smirk on his face as he berated the students for not having even a guess, and he accused them of not paying attention — which, if you think about it, was actually a criticism of his lecturing skills — but he finally noticed Ellie and pointed to her. 'A child has a question for me?' he asked."

Max smiled. He had a feeling he knew what was coming.

"Ellie looked embarrassed because now everyone was staring at her, but she said, 'No, sir. I know the answer — five thousand fifty.' Goodrick then saw me sitting beside her and, thinking I had fed the answer to her, wagged the marker at her and challenged her to show the audience how she arrived at the conclusion."

Ellie turned around and interrupted her father's account. "I'm finished with this window. Want me to help you finish yours?" she asked Max.

"And did she?" Max asked William, ignoring her.

"She certainly did," he answered. "She went up on the stage, took the marker from him, and showed that the problem could be broken down into fifty pairs of identical

208

sums of one hundred one. And fifty times one hundred one gives the answer: five thousand fifty. Goodrick looked thunderstruck, but to his credit, he did congratulate her on getting it right. He then asked if she could solve another problem. I realized he was trying his best to trick her with the second one, but she got that right, too."

Ellie waved her brush at her father. "Dad, Max doesn't want to hear —"

"Yes, I do," Max said.

Her father continued, "I put a stop to it after those two problems and took Ellie home."

"He made me promise not to tell Mom what happened," she said.

"How come?" Max asked.

"Claire and I had agreed to help our daughter lead as normal a life as possible," William said. "Getting up onstage and drawing attention to her capabilities at such a young age . . . her mother and I didn't want that, and . . ."

"And what?"

He looked sheepish. "And I knew I'd catch hell if my wife found out." He laughed and said, "I swear it was the only time I allowed her to perform in public. Ellie always loved math. She read all the books I brought home, and she and I would do problems

209

together every now and then at night when the twins were having their baths or doing their homework."

Fortunately, her father resisted the need to tell more stories about her, and Ellie was thankful. She finished the painting, and while her father took Max out to the garage to show him the apartment, she showered and changed into clean jeans and a blouse.

Her mother didn't approve of the outfit. "You should put on a skirt. We have company."

"Mom, he's just a friend."

"Set the table in the dining room."

"We have a huge, round kitchen table. Max will be just as comfortable here. Besides, you've already got it set for dinner."

"I just thought it should be a little more formal. When Ava and John come for dinner, she always insists we dine in the dining room."

*Of course she does,* Ellie thought. Ava was all about appearances.

"We don't need to impress him."

"Oh, all right. Go ahead and set a place for him at the kitchen table."

"Thanks, Mom." She kissed her mother on the cheek.

"Since you're in such a good mood . . . ,"

her mother began.

Ellie got a plate down from the cabinet. "The answer is still no."

She carried the silverware and linen napkin to the table and set a place for Max. Never in a million years would she have guessed she'd be doing this for him.

"You don't even know what I'm going to ask," her mother said as she began to gather vegetables from the refrigerator.

Ellie took them from her and put them on the counter next to the sink. Her mother handed her a chopping board.

"I was just saying that since you're in a good mood, you might want to reconsider . . ."

"I'm not going to be in the wedding."

"Now, Eleanor Kathleen . . . ," her mother said.

"You're wasting your time."

"You'll break your sister's heart."

Ellie shook her head slowly. "Guilt isn't going to work. The answer is no."

"No, what?" her father asked as he came in the back door with Max.

"Your daughter is being stubborn," her mother said.

Max was carrying tomatoes from the garden William had proudly shown him. He laid them in the sink and turned the water on to wash them. Next to him, Ellie was chopping vegetables. Her mother saw how fast she was working and immediately cautioned her.

"You be careful with that knife. It's sharp."

Ellie didn't look up. "Yes, ma'am."

"And slow down, for heaven's sake. You'll cut your finger off. Here, give that knife to me. I'll do it."

"I'll slow down," Ellie promised.

Her father had gone into the hearth room and was standing with his hands in his pockets, watching the news on television, and her mother had gone into the dining room to get one of her fancy salad bowls when Max leaned into Ellie's side. "Your mom knows you're a surgeon, right?"

She laughed. "Yes, she does."

"So she's got to know you use sharp knives."

"Both my mom and dad know what I have become, but neither one of them saw me get there. I was a child when I left home. They weren't there to see the progress from university to medical school to residency to fellowship. They didn't hear all the stories that happen during training."

William walked into the kitchen. "Max?"

"Yes, sir?"

"It appears it will be a while before dinner

is ready. Do you have a minute to step out in the backyard and have a talk?"

Uh-oh, Ellie didn't like the sound of that. "A talk about what?" she asked.

"Patterson," her father answered. "If Max is interested, I thought I would catch him up on what I've learned from my friends in the FBI."

"Sure," Max said. "I've got the time." Turning to Ellie, he whispered, "Don't you leave this house."

Ellie stood at the sink, staring out at the yard. She couldn't see the two men, but she could hear the low murmur of their voices. She was certain Max was asking all sorts of questions.

He knew just about everything about her; she knew absolutely nothing about him. Well, not exactly. She knew he lived in Honolulu but grew up in Montana. And that was it. Sisters? Brothers? She didn't have a clue. She needed a plan, she decided, to get through dinner. As soon as it was over, she'd get him alone and start demanding answers.

Dinner was a challenge.

"Where did you grow up, Max?" her father asked as Claire served the salads.

"Butte, Montana."

"Are your parents still living there?"

"No," he answered. "When I was a fresh-
man in college, they moved to Minneapolis,
Minnesota."

"Do they live in Minneapolis now?"

"Yes, sir, they do."

"It gets so cold there and so much snow,"
her mother interjected.

"I wouldn't think it would be too much
different from Montana. Gets real cold
there, too," her father said. "What does your
father do for a living, Max?"

"He's an attorney," he answered. "He
worked for the Department of the Interior
for twenty-five years, retired, and now works
as a children's advocate for the State of
Minnesota."

"Admirable," William said. "I imagine it's
a difficult job. Do you have any brothers or
sisters?" he asked without pausing.

Ellie listened to the interrogation with
mixed feelings. She wanted to hear more
about Max, but she was terrified by the possibilities of where the discussion would lead.

"Dad, stop with the questions please," she
said. "Max isn't interviewing for a job."

"We're just having a friendly conversation," her father protested.

Max, Ellie noticed, didn't seem the least
fazed by all the questions. She, on the other
hand, was sick to her stomach and could

214

barely get her salad down. She never should have lied to her father. As soon as she'd introduced him to Max, she should have told him the truth, but she didn't. She made the decision to keep quiet because her father hadn't looked well, and she'd put him through such heartache. How could she have burdened him with more?

"And your mother? Does she work outside the home?" her father asked.

"She teaches music."

"Any brothers or sisters?" he asked.

"Dad, enough already. Let Max eat."

"No sisters," he answered. "I have six brothers. Simon's the oldest, then me, then Bishop, Sebastian, Bradley, Tyler, and Adam."

"Your parents had their hands full with so many boys," Claire said.

"Simon Daniels," her father said. "That's the same name as the football player Ellie's so crazy about. He's always her number-one pick in her fantasy football leagues."

"When I get first choice," Ellie explained.

Max flashed a smile. "You know who Simon Daniels is?"

"Of course I know him. He's one of the best quarterbacks in the NFL. His stats last year were amazing: over forty-three hundred yards passing, a sixty-eight percent completion rate, lowest number of interceptions in the league. Don't you follow football?"

"Sure, I do," he replied. "How many fantasy leagues are you in?"

"I'm cutting back to two this year."

"Max, would you like more roast beef?" her mother asked.

"No, thank you."

"What does your brother do for a living?" William asked as he took the platter that Claire handed him.

"He's a football player."

Silence followed the statement. It didn't last long. Ellie dropped her fork.

"Are you telling me your brother is *the* Simon Daniels, the future Hall of Famer?"

"That's what I'm telling you."

Ellie's mother looked puzzled. "But he's African-American, and you're . . . not."

"Simon's parents adopted me," he explained. He smiled as he added, "Then they got on a roll and adopted the others. I was eight years old when my adoption was final."

"What happened to your biological parents?" William asked.

"Car accident."

"No more questions, Dad," Ellie pleaded.

She knew her face was flushed. She could feel the heat in her cheeks. Max had all but knocked her off her feet with his oh-so-casual announcement that Simon, the perfect quarterback, was his brother. She was flabbergasted and trying not to let it show.

"Ellie, I couldn't help but notice you looked thunderstruck by the news that Simon was Max's brother. You didn't know?" her father asked.

"Uh . . . no," she stammered. "Max never mentioned it." Her mind raced to find an excuse. "But I understand why," she said.

"Enlighten me," he persisted, frowning now.

"He wanted me to like him for him . . . not who he's related to," she explained and hoped to heaven she was making sense.

Her father nodded, and that gave Ellie hope that he was buying yet another lie.

"There are still lots of things about Max I don't know yet," she said. Was that ever an understatement! "We're getting to know each other."

She pushed her chair back, stood, and snatched Max's plate. She was on her way to the sink as she asked, "Finished, Max?"

She cleared the rest of the dishes while her father told an amusing story about one of the professors at the university. Then the topic moved to the wedding.

"The relatives will be pouring in here in two more days, and William and I have been frantically working on the house," her mother announced.

"Not frantically, Claire."

"Are there any other bedrooms that need painting?" Max asked.

"No, the lavender room was the last," William said.

"Who chose that color?"

Ellie was rinsing the salad bowl and putting it in the dishwasher. "You don't like the color?"

"I didn't say that. I just wondered who chose it."

Her parents glanced at each other before answering. The question seemed to surprise them.

"No one chose it," Ellie's mother said. "We purchased what was on sale, didn't we, dear?"

"That's right. That particular color had been discontinued."

Max could understand why. The color practically glowed.

"We got it for a song," William said proudly.

"Would you like some coffee, Max?" Claire asked.

"No, thank you."

By this time, most of the dishes had been cleared, rinsed, and placed in the dishwasher by Ellie. Her mother carried a pitcher to the counter, and Ellie practically wrenched it from her hands to begin washing it.

"Ellie," her mother said, "why don't you and Max get settled in your rooms for the night. It's been a long day, and I know you two would like some alone time to catch up. And just maybe, after a good night's rest, you'll reevaluate your position on the wedding."

"I assure you that won't happen," she said, and before her mother could start in again, Ellie rushed ahead, "Are you sure you don't want me to finish the dishes?" Without waiting for an answer, she grabbed Max's hand and headed for the back door.

Max made her wait while he thanked her parents for dinner, then followed her outside.

"I like your parents."

She didn't look over her shoulder as she crossed the yard at a fast clip to get to the steps.

"Uh-huh," she agreed. "You've probably got a hundred questions about my family, don't you?"

"No," he answered. "Okay, maybe a couple."

"Yes?"

She rushed up the stairs and waited for

Max to unlock the dead bolts. He leaned around her, wrapping her in his arms as he slipped the keys in the dead bolts and unlocked the door. If she moved at all, her lips would touch his warm skin. He swung the door open and pulled back so she could go inside.

She walked to the center of the living room, turned around, and folded her arms in front of her while she waited for him to lock the door and give her his full attention. As soon as he was facing her, she said, "Okay, start talking. Why are you here?"

He leaned against the door and grinned. "I thought it was my turn to ask questions."

She sighed in frustration. "Okay, I'll give you two. Then you start explaining. Go ahead. Ask away."

"What's a plus one?"

# SIXTEEN

They were on round three of the argument.

Max had taken a shower, put on a clean T-shirt and jeans, grabbed the channel changer, and now sat on the lumpy sofa with his bare feet up on an ottoman, trying to watch the late news on a television screen the size of a breadbox while he patiently waited for Ellie to calm down and be reasonable. He doubted it was going to happen anytime soon.

The remote kept falling apart in his hand. It had been duct taped together, but the tape was obviously old. He made the mental note to buy a universal remote tomorrow or another roll of tape. It was downright barbaric not to have a decent channel changer.

"Are you listening to me?" she demanded.

"Yes, I am," he lied.

God, she looked good. He watched her resume her pacing while she ranted. She had also showered and was now wearing a pale pink-and-white-striped nightgown that barely touched her knees, and a matching long cotton robe that tied at the waist. The robe was too big for her, and the hem dragged on the floor, but to him she looked sexier than if she had been wearing a flimsy negligee. She looked hot in everything she wore, even the baggy scrubs he'd first seen her in.

Unaware of where his thoughts were, Ellie continued her tirade. She had every reason to be upset. She hadn't said a word while he'd explained his reason for coming to Winston Falls and his intent to be her shadow until the two of them returned to her home, but when he'd finished explaining, she'd reacted. She hadn't flipped out on him, though. She'd become outraged, and he much preferred that reaction. Furious was better to work with than terrified or weepy.

"You are not telling my father or my mother." She was so irate her voice shook. She wasn't a screamer, and he appreciated that, too.

"Yes, I am," he calmly announced for the sixth or seventh time now. "They need to be aware of the danger."

"You aren't even certain the Landrys hired

anyone to kill Sean or me."

"Yes, I am certain. Ellie, we've been over this. I'm staying with you until you're safely back home."

"Then what?"

"If Willis Cogburn hasn't been captured or killed, another agent will take over."

"Killed?"

"If he tries to hurt you, damn right I'll kill him." Anger swelled up inside him at the thought of anyone hurting her.

"You have to capture him, not shoot him," she muttered. "Then you can make a deal with him for a lighter sentence so he'll testify against the Landrys."

"You're a physician, not an attorney," he countered.

"It makes sense, doesn't it? Ask a lawyer. He'll agree with me. Willis Cogburn should stay alive to testify."

"I am a lawyer," he said. "And I'm telling you, hit men don't usually testify. And if I have to shoot him, I'm shooting to kill."

Hands on hips, she glared at him. "When did you become a lawyer?"

The conversation was becoming ludicrous. She was acting as though he'd pulled a fast one on her by going to law school.

"Right after I graduated from Vanderbilt."

"Where?"

He smiled. "Vanderbilt University Law School in Nashville," he said.

"Then the FBI?"

"Yes."

"So you're smart, too."

He shrugged. Tired of pacing, Ellie went into the tiny kitchen. She got a Diet Coke out of the refrigerator, got another for Max, and went back to the living room. She sat down beside him, handed him his drink, and swung her feet up on the ottoman next to his.

"You saw the look on my father's face when you got out of your car and he noticed the gun at your side. In that instant, he went from happy to scared." She put her unopened can on the table, sat back, and said, "I've taught him to expect the worst."

Max put his arm around her and pulled her into his side. "Ellie, you know I'm right. Your dad needs to be aware, and I'm required to inform him of the possible danger. It's just the way it is."

"I've put him through enough."

"*You've* put him through enough? You haven't done anything wrong. You are not responsible for Evan Patterson's obsession."

"Intellectually, I know that's true, but in my heart, I feel as though I'm at fault somehow. I know it doesn't make any sense, but there it is all the same."

"How old were you when it started with Patterson?"

"I had just had my eleventh birthday." It was a full year of hell, she thought but didn't say.

"Reason it through. You were a little girl. You didn't do or say anything to encourage him."

"I wasn't the only one affected by his bizarre behavior. Some days, especially when my dad wasn't home, he would walk up and down our street, staring at our house as he passed by. He would do it for hours and hours," she said. "Annie was terrified. She had to have all the lights on in her bedroom at night, and I could hear her crying under the covers. That's why she's becoming a lawyer. She'll end up doing something in criminal justice. Ava went the other way. She lashed out. She was angry all the time — angry at me."

"Come on. You know none of this is your fault."

"That doesn't change how my family feels. My poor dad is quietly freaking out because no one can find Patterson, and now you want to tell him that there's a killer out there hunting me."

She stood, grabbed her can of soda, and

put it back in the refrigerator. There was a door at the end of the kitchen that led down into the garage. She made sure it was locked, then checked the other door to make absolutely certain both dead bolts were in place, and headed to the bedroom.

She hadn't even thought about the sleeping arrangements or a bed with Max in it until she opened the door to the room she'd slept in the night before. There was a queen-size bed her parents had gotten at a discount store. In the smaller bedroom was a double bed that used to belong to her aunt Eleanor, the woman she was named after. The bed had been in her aunt's guest room, but when the older woman downsized, she'd donated the bed to the apartment.

Ellie thought she should probably sleep there because Max was so much bigger than she was.

Or she could sleep with him. That thought sent her heart racing. No, that can't happen, she told herself. She wanted him to go away, not stay . . . didn't she?

Talk about conflicted. Back home, after their date, he'd kissed her senseless, and when he'd left, she had regretted not sleeping with him. And now? Max was just feet away from her, and right this minute she couldn't come up with a single reason why she shouldn't throw herself into his arms.

The apartment seemed to be closing in on her. The air conditioner had stopped, and the temperature was rising. Thinking about wrapping her arms around Max's hard body wasn't helping her cool off. Just one night. What would be the harm?

Ellie went into the bathroom and brushed her teeth again just to give herself time to come to her senses. Yes, she wanted him. Okay, nothing wrong with admitting it, and, yes, it would be amazing and electrifying, but it would also just be a brief physical release. A great, mind-blowing release, she qualified.

The fantasies were bombarding her, but she blocked them from her mind. She couldn't let her hormones or her animal instincts take control. Besides, Max would still be here in the morning, so she couldn't pretend she'd had a temporary lack of sanity.

She took a good long look in the mirror and shook her head at her reflection. She wanted more than casual sex. She wanted romance. She felt silly admitting it, even though it was true. She had worked so long and so hard on her career that it had all but consumed her, leaving no room for the fanciful or the impractical. But deep down, it had always been there. She was a romantic at heart. There wasn't anything practical or reasonable about it.

Okay, she'd made up her mind. She wasn't a rabbit, and she wasn't going to hop into bed with any man — no matter how hot he was — without first having an emotional connection.

As she was opening the door, it suddenly occurred to her that all her angst might have been for nothing. Max hadn't made any moves or given any indication that he'd like to go to bed with her. Still, the electricity was there between them. If she could feel it, so could he.

When she entered the living room, Max was sitting on the sofa, leaning forward with all the broken pieces of the channel changer spread out on the ottoman in front of him. The old tape hadn't held, and the plastic cover had broken in several places.

"Someone must have thrown this against a couple of walls," he remarked. "Is there any tape around?"

"I'll look," she said as she retied the belt on her robe. It dragged on the floor when she walked into the kitchen, and she really wanted to take the thing off because the air was becoming stifling.

She found some Scotch tape in one of the

kitchen drawers and two thick rubber bands.

Max quickly put the remote back together and reinforced it with the rubber bands, then he sat back and began to channel-surf. She sat down next to him.

"Men and their remotes," she said, shaking her head.

"Women and their hair stuff," he countered.

She laughed. "Hair stuff?"

He shrugged. "You know. That lacquer stuff they spray on their hair. You don't," he added, "but a lot of women do."

"What do you mean, I don't?"

He put his arm around her and his fingers slid through her hair. "It's soft, not stiff, and my fingers don't get caught."

"What kind of women have you been going out with?"

He didn't answer. He was rubbing the back of her neck, though, and it felt wonderful.

"Your hair's so soft. Smells good, too. Like strawberries."

"How do you know . . ."

He smiled. "I've got a good memory."

Whoa. So did she. She remembered his mouth on hers, the touch of his tongue rubbing against hers, the taste of him, the way he'd held her in his arms, his masculine scent . . . oh yes, she had a good memory, too.

She cleared her throat. "It's hot in here."

"Yes, it is," he said, turning back to the television. "Did you turn the air conditioner up?"

"I should explain how the thermostat works. It's right outside your bedroom door," she said. "You get the bigger bed because you're . . ."

Wow. All he had to do was look at her, and she lost her train of thought. There was a warm glint in his eyes that captivated her. The man just kept getting better and better.

"Because I'm what?"

She didn't have a clue. "What?"

He grinned. "You said I get the bigger bedroom . . ."

"Because you're bigger than I am. It's a queen, so your feet may still hang over."

"And the thermostat?"

"What about it?" She really needed to stop staring at him so she could concentrate.

"What is it I need to know?"

She forced herself to look at the television when she explained. "It only has two settings no matter where you turn the dial. Hot, like now — only it will get hotter — or cold — and not just cold, arctic cold. You choose," she said.

"Sweat or freeze are the choices?"

"Yes."

"Freeze."

She patted his knee. "Then that's what we'll hope for."

He laughed. "You don't have any control over it?"

"Sorry, no."

She'd found out the night before how faulty the air conditioner was. She had alternated between near heatstroke and frostbite all night long. It was miserable. She had intended to mention the problem to her father this morning, but she'd forgotten about it until now, and the heat index was rapidly rising.

She loosened the neck of her robe and fanned herself. "Do you mind if I watch *SportsCenter?* The roundup is coming on soon."

He handed her the remote as he asked, "How old is the air conditioner?"

"It's brand-new."

"Then why . . ."

She found the channel, muted the program that was ending, and turned to Max. "Daddy got a deal," she explained. "He doesn't buy anything unless he can get a great deal."

"I don't care if he got it for half price, if it

231

doesn't work —"

"Half price isn't a deal to my father. Eighty percent maybe, but not fifty."

He shook his head. "He should take it back."

"Yes, he should," she agreed. "But he won't. He'll get a repairman to fix it one of these days. I'll mention it to him tomorrow. Would you like a beer? You can't watch *SportsCenter* without a beer."

"Sweetheart, you're a dream come true. A beautiful woman who likes *SportsCenter* and drinks beer."

"We're not such a rare breed," she said.

She put his unopened can of Diet Coke back in the refrigerator, got out two bottles of Bud Light and a jar of mixed nuts, and went back to the sofa. She handed Max one bottle, twisted the cap off the other, then tapped his bottle and took a drink.

She put the jar of nuts on the table and sat down next to him. "It's getting hotter in here," she said as she placed the cold bottle against the side of her neck. She adjusted her position on the couch a couple of times and ended up leaning into him. "I'd move over and give you some room, but there's a lump, and it's very uncomfortable. I think a spring's about to pop through."

"I like you pressed against me."

232

"I'm not making you hot?" After asking the suggestive question, she put her bottle against his cheek. "Feel good?"

"You feel good. The roundup is on."

It was one of her favorite shows, and tonight the topic was once again the upcoming football season. Simon's name was mentioned about a dozen times. Max was answering texts, but she noticed he smiled whenever one of the commentators complimented his brother. He didn't show any reaction to the criticisms.

Halfway through the program, Ellie removed her robe. She didn't care whether it was appropriate or not. She was burning up.

"We could open the windows in the bedrooms, maybe get a crosswind. They're the only windows that open."

"What's it like outside now?"

She found her cell phone, looked up the weather, and groaned. "It's ninety and humid. I think we're going to have to sleep in the house tonight. This is worse than paint fumes."

"I don't think so," he said. "It's not so bad."

"I can suffer through it if you can," she said. "And it's only for one night. We're leaving tomorrow."

He nodded. "Good," he said. "I was going to bring it up if you didn't. We can't stay here. If there were a fire, we'd be trapped, and walking down the outside steps would give anyone a clear shot. We're going to have to find a better place to stay, one that isn't open —"

"We're not trapped here," she argued. "We could go down the stairs that lead into the garage or even go out one of the back windows. There's a rope in the garage, and it really isn't too much of a jump . . ." She stopped, realizing there was no need to protest. "You misunderstand. I want to leave Winston Falls and go back to St. Louis. If I stay here, I'm putting my family in danger."

Ellie stared at the television but she wasn't paying attention to the program. Frustration was building inside her again because she didn't have any control over what was happening. She put her beer down and went to check the thermostat. She hadn't even touched it when she felt a blast of cold air come through the vent in the hall.

"We now have air-conditioning," she announced.

"Good to hear." He turned off the television and stood. "Are you serious about going back home?"

He was walking toward her, and she was

234

feeling breathless again. "Yes, I'm serious."

"How will your dad feel about your leaving?"

She thought about it a few seconds and then said, "He'll be relieved, and that will make him feel guilty."

"When are you going to talk to him?"

"First thing in the morning," she said. She leaned against the wall, and he stopped in front of her.

"And your mother?"

"Oh God. She'll have a fit. She won't believe anything I say once I tell her I'm leaving. It's not going to be pretty," she added.

The dark look in his eyes made swallowing difficult. She wanted him to take her into his arms. She wanted him. She tried to block the thought but didn't have much success. Did he have to be so provocative and mesmerizing?

"There's no need to tell why we're leaving," she said. "Agreed? You are not going to tell my father about Willis Cogburn."

"Yeah, sweetheart, I am. I'm obligated to warn him of the possible danger."

"But I'll be gone —"

"Doesn't matter."

She poked him in the chest. "This is exactly why I'm not going to sleep with you.

You'd feel obligated to tell."

Max brushed her hair over her shoulder and trailed his fingers down the side of her cheek. Her skin was silky and soft, and he didn't think there was a single flaw in her complexion. "I don't remember asking . . ."

"Then you don't want . . ."

He leaned down. "I didn't say that."

She smiled sweetly. "I could have you in bed in less than ten minutes."

Max loved the way she smiled. Her eyes sparkled with such devilment. Damn, he wanted her. He leaned even closer until his mouth was just inches above hers and whispered, "Five minutes, sweetheart. That's all it would take me to get you in my bed."

Ellie could feel all her resolve melting away. She tilted her head and closed her eyes. His mouth brushed hers.

"This isn't a good idea," she said. Her voice was so faint, it was barely audible.

"I know," he said as he circled her mouth with gentle kisses.

"You're here because of your job, and we shouldn't let anything interfere," she whispered breathlessly.

"You're right." His lips moved to her earlobe.

"We've got to stop." She sighed.

"Uh-huh," he said as he nibbled on her ear.

It took every last ounce of willpower to slowly pull away, but Ellie gently pushed against his chest and stepped back.

"Good night," she said.

She walked into her room. Closing the door was the hardest thing she had ever done in her life.

# SEVENTEEN

Her bedroom felt like an inferno. She looked all over the room, even behind the bed and underneath it, but couldn't find any vents. Who had her father used to install the heating and cooling system in these rooms? she wondered. Whoever it was obviously gave him a deal he couldn't resist.

Ellie opened the door and felt a rush of cold air. She noticed Max's bedroom door was also open, and she wondered if the only vents in the apartment were the two in the tiny hallway.

She quietly got back in bed and was sound asleep in seconds. An hour later the cold awakened her. She was freezing, and the top sheet and thin blanket couldn't block the arctic blasts pouring into the room. My God, she could see her breath in the air. For some reason she thought that was hilarious and had to stifle her laughter with her pillow. Exactly what kind of a deal had her father gotten? It must have been a doozy.

She got out of bed to shut the door and remembered she had left her cell phone in the living room. She found it on the arm of the sofa, plugged it into her charger on the kitchen counter, and, shivering, headed back to bed.

She turned the corner and came to a quick stop. Max was leaning against the door frame to his bedroom watching her. His hair was tousled, his gaze intense.

It was impossible not to stare at him. He was so incredibly virile. A perfect specimen, she thought. She took a breath and forgot to let it out. No other man aroused her the way Max did. He was bare-chested and had pulled on a pair of jeans. He hadn't bothered to zip them, leaving the suggestion that he hadn't worn anything to bed. Picturing him naked made every nerve in her body tingle.

Another blast of frigid air blew across her face. Rubbing her arms to try to warm her skin, she whispered, "Did I wake you?"

He lazily moved away from the door and reached for her, gently pulling her into his warm arms. She could have easily stepped back if she had wanted to, but turning away from him was out of the question given her insane need to touch him.

Heat radiated from his chest, and she sighed against his shoulder as she put her arms around his neck. Even his scent aroused her. And his touch was making her warm all over. His strong hands caressed her back, then moved lower to firmly grasp her hips. His chin rubbed against the top of her head. She leaned back and looked into his eyes, saw the passion there, and knew he wanted her as much as she wanted him.

Her fingers spread upward into his hair as he lowered his head and kissed her. He wasn't in any hurry. The kiss was slow. His tongue penetrated and rubbed against hers, and when she imitated the action, he growled low in his throat and deepened the kiss.

Holding her in his arms, his mouth slanting over hers again and again, Max backed into the bedroom but stopped when he reached the bed. Her mouth was hot, wet, wild under his, and the way she stroked his neck made him crave more. She didn't resist when he pulled her gown over her head. Her hands got in his way as she tried to push his jeans down. In seconds they were both naked and fell into bed together. He rolled over, nudged her thighs apart, and stretched out on top of her.

Max let out a long, raspy breath. He

wanted to savor the moment. He could feel her heart under his as he lifted a strand of hair from the side of her neck and began to kiss her there.

She moved restlessly against him as he slowly moved down her body, gasping when he began to caress her breasts. His hands moved lower to span her waist then lower still. He kissed her navel, heard her indrawn breath, and knew he pleased her. There was a scar above her right hip. He kissed it, then moved lower to stroke and taste her until she was writhing in his arms and moaning with desire. He lifted up, kissed her again, a scorching kiss with no reservations.

Ellie pushed him onto his back and began to make love to him. She stroked his shoulders, his arms, marveling at the strength and heat she felt under her fingertips. She kissed every inch of his chest, loving the feel of his coarse hair against her breasts. She stroked his tight stomach with her tongue while her hands moved lower to caress his arousal. He sucked in his breath and shuddered.

He pulled her up, kissed her once more, then rolled away from her.

She tried to pull him back.

"I want to protect you," he whispered, his voice thick with desire.

Seconds later, he pressed her onto her back, and shaking with his need now, he spread her thighs, covered her mouth with his, and thrust inside her.

She cried out and raised her hips to take more of him. Max's head dropped to the crook of her shoulder and he took deep shuddering breaths to try to slow down. Hot liquid heat enveloped him. It was exquisite torture to stay still. She began to move under him, stroked his shoulders, and drove him wild with her uninhibited response. He moved, slowly at first, and then more forcefully until he was burning.

For the first time in his life, he lost control. He couldn't slow the pace. She wouldn't let him. He had absolutely no discipline as he drove into her, trying desperately to give her as much pleasure as she was giving him. Her nails scored his shoulders, and she began to tighten all around him, squeezing him, and as he pushed harder, she climaxed.

Ellie said his name in a whisper, then shouted it as sensations unlike anything she had ever experienced before rippled through her.

His climax followed and was as violent and satisfying. It consumed him, drained him, took every ounce of his strength. With a loud, lusty groan, he collapsed on top of her.

It took several minutes for both of them to recover. When he was finally able to take a normal breath, he lifted up and looked at her. Passion was still there in her eyes, and her cheeks were flushed from their lovemaking. She was so very beautiful, and he realized he was once again in awe of her.

He leaned down and kissed her. "Are you okay?"

She sighed. "Oh yes," she whispered. "It's all good."

He laughed. "Yeah?"

"Yes," she repeated.

He rolled onto his back. Their bodies were slick with perspiration, but blasts of freezing cold air cooled their skin.

"I'll be right back," he said gruffly as he swung his legs over the side of the bed. He glanced over his shoulder at her golden body and then laughed. Ellie was sound asleep.

He guessed she was right. It was all good.

# EIGHTEEN

Ellie was unlike any other woman Max had ever known. The women he had taken to his bed usually wanted pillow talk and sometimes praise after sex, or at the very least to be held. Ellie, on the other hand, wanted to sleep.

An hour later, he made love to her again. He woke her by trailing his fingers down the valley between her breasts and her navel. He watched her face. Her eyes didn't open, but she sucked in her breath. Smiling, he leaned down and kissed her.

"This time I'm setting the pace," he told her in a gruff whisper. He tugged on her earlobe with his teeth to get her attention. He was determined to teach her how to relax and take it slow even if it killed him, and it damn near did. If she hadn't been so responsive, he might have been able to get their lovemaking to last a little longer, but neither one of them could stop their release.

She ended up on top of him, and after the tremors left, she put her head on his shoulder and was sound asleep less than a minute later with his arms wrapped around her.

They woke up in a sauna. Ellie was sleeping on her side with her head on his shoulder and one leg draped over his. She opened her eyes as Max was trying to gently move her off of him so he could get up. She was instantly wide-awake. She rolled over him and tried to move off the bed. He caught her about her waist and pulled her down for a long kiss. The flash of embarrassment she'd felt waking up with him was gone, and she kissed him back just as thoroughly. Then she got up and went into the bathroom to shower.

Max went into the kitchen and drank a glass of orange juice while he tried to figure out how to turn the air conditioner down, but the dial on the thermostat wouldn't move.

Her dad definitely had been ripped off no matter how much of a discount he'd received. Max wondered how he would react the next time he opened his electric bill. If the wiring was faulty, the thing could be a fire hazard. Max decided, before he and Ellie left for the airport, he should talk to him about it.

The air came back on while Max was in the shower. Ellie went into the smaller bedroom to get ready. She applied a little makeup and lip gloss, and even put on a skirt to please her mother. It was short, pale blue, and barely wrinkled. Her crisp white blouse was fitted but not too tight.

Since she hadn't slept in the bed, she didn't change the sheets. She smoothed the covers and then went into Max's bedroom to strip the bed, but he'd already made it. She wasn't surprised. She'd noticed what a careful, disciplined man he was when he was working, and that spilled over into his personal habits. His shaving kit was organized, and his shirts were perfectly folded in his bag. Max controlled what he could in his environment. She surmised that the trauma of losing his parents at such an early age had a lot to do with his behavior. It was also probably what made him so good at his job.

She stared at the bed a long moment as pictures of what they had done the night before flashed before her. She actually blushed as she remembered how enthusiastic she'd been. Max most likely thought she was a sex fiend, and with him, she just might be.

With a sigh, she went back into the living

room. After they had their talk with her father, she'd change the sheets, she decided.

She drank a Diet Coke for breakfast and was leaning against the counter checking her phone when Max came into the kitchen. He was sliding his gun into his holster at his side. She watched him bring the leather strap over the gun and snap it in place.

She was suddenly feeling shy again. "I haven't changed my airline ticket yet," she said.

"Let's talk to your father first, then worry about getting back."

"Thank you for not fighting me on this."

"Protecting you will be easier if you're in the hospital all day and home the rest of the time. We'll have more manpower."

"I'm not going back to the hospital permanently," she replied. Then she added, "Maybe if they're shorthanded for a little while until . . ."

"Until you find out where Patterson is?"

She shook her head. "No, until I figure out where I want to live and work."

Ellie heard someone calling her name. She was pretty sure it was her father, and she went to the door to open it. She'd unlocked the dead bolt when Max put his hand on top of hers and said, "You don't open doors. I do. And I go out first. Understood?"

She turned around and found herself plastered against the door. His hands were on either side of her.

"Last night . . . ," he began.

He was frowning. Oh no, was he going to tell her it had been a mistake? Or worse, apologize for what happened? She thought she just might kick him if he did.

"It's okay," she said, trying to ease what she perceived to be guilt. "It's all good."

Then she noticed the amusement in his eyes and realized he wasn't feeling guilty about anything. He kissed her. It was a brief glad-to-see-you-again kind of kiss and definitely unsatisfying.

"Good? Sweetheart, it was a whole lot better than good."

"Yes, it was," she said, sighing.

Just standing this close to him made her weak. She had thought that after making love most of the night, she would have moved past this crazy reaction to him. It didn't happen. He still could turn her stomach into jelly.

Had she not been anxious to get the talk with her parents over and done with and be on their way, she would have kissed Max the way she wanted, but she had no intention of starting something she couldn't finish.

Her father bellowed her name. She took a deep breath and said, "Okay, let's do this," and stepped back to let him go outside first, then followed him.

He made himself a target. Whoever would try to hurt her would have to go through him first.

"I'm good at removing bullets," she whispered. She didn't know why she needed to give him that inconsequential information. Was she telling him this so he wouldn't worry? The possibility of him getting injured was too awful to think about.

"I know you are," he said. "One of the other surgeons at the hospital told Sean you hit the one hundred mark before your third year of residency."

"That's not something I want to be remembered for," she said. She poked him between his shoulder blades. "Don't you dare get shot."

"I won't," he promised as he looked around.

Ellie's parents' backyard was square, extremely large, perfectly manicured, and surrounded by trees and bushes on all sides, blocking the neighbors' view. Behind the greenery was a fence, but that, too, was hidden from view. It would be difficult for Cogburn to get a good shot, Max thought. Even if one of the neighbors didn't notice a stranger cutting through his yard, the fence and the bushes would be a deterrent. No, there were better places to wait for his target. Too many, in fact.

Her father held the door open for them. "I made waffles," he announced. "Your mother's starting the eggs, and the bacon is already on the table getting cold. Didn't you hear me calling?"

"Dad, Max and I need to talk to you and Mom. It's important," she said.

"Important can wait until after breakfast," he said.

"But this is —"

"Eleanor, you heard your father. No worrisome talk before breakfast," her mother said.

"Is that a new rule?"

"It's a Southern rule."

"Yes, all right," she said. "But directly after breakfast we need to talk."

Neither parent responded to her demand. "Mom?"

"All right, dear. Now eat your breakfast."

Ellie wanted only a PowerBar or a piece of toast, but she couldn't hurt her father's feelings, and so she ate a little of everything that was offered. Max ate like a man who'd been starving for a week.

"Want to know the secret to my waffles? Club soda," her father said proudly. "That's why they're so light and fluffy."

"Dad's an expert on waffles," she explained.

"And baking bread," he added. "It's therapeutic. But that's all. Waffles and bread."

"Did you sleep well last night?" Claire asked Max.

The question reminded him about the air conditioner, and he told William that he should call the store where he had purchased the unit and make them replace it.

"It was all sales final," William said. "But I'll have a repairman over here today. I know just who to call. In the meantime, would you mind helping me disconnect it?"

Max followed her father outside. "Don't forget to tell him about the thermostat," Ellie called.

He raised his hand to let her know he'd heard her just as the door closed.

Now that Claire had Ellie alone, she sat down at the table next to her.

"I see you still drink milk," she remarked with a smile as Ellie finished her glass.

She then began to talk about all the wedding arrangements, and in the midst of describing the wedding cake, she burst into tears.

Ellie was astonished and alarmed. She hadn't seen her mother cry in years, not since the day she had to leave her with the Wheatleys.

"Mother, stop that," Ellie demanded. She grabbed a tissue from the box on the shelf and handed it to her. "Please, stop crying."

"I know how hard this is for you," her mother began. She wiped the tears away as she continued. "I wish things were different. It breaks my heart to see you and Ava not getting along. I love all my girls, but I'll admit that Ava has been a trial for your father and me. She's so headstrong, and what she did to you was cruel and despicable."

Ellie was speechless. She knew her mother loved her, and she also knew she didn't favor one daughter over the others, but she had never expressed strong feelings about what happened between the two sisters until today.

"Ava knows how her father and I feel. After you left so abruptly — and who could blame you — we got into quite an argument. You were so devastated and destroyed by the betrayal."

No, she wasn't, Ellie admitted to herself.

She was neither devastated nor destroyed. She was furious and humiliated, but there hadn't been any heartbreak.

"Ava said it wasn't deliberate, that there was this instant attraction between the two of them. That does happen."

Yes, it does, Ellie agreed as she replayed her initial reaction to meeting Max. There had definitely been an instant attraction, and it seemed to be getting stronger.

"Then she should have come to me and told me instead of jumping into bed with him," Ellie said.

"Yes, she should have," her mother said. "I know you don't want excuses, and I understand that, but Eleanor, we have to find a way to get past this. Ava's going to marry John a week from Saturday, no matter how any of us feel. She loves him, and he loves her. Please try to be all right with it."

"Okay, Mom. I'll try. Now please, stop crying," she pleaded as she handed her mother another tissue.

"Do you want to hear about the preparations for the garden party?"

"What garden party?"

"You didn't get your invitation?"

Ellie shook her head. "Maybe," she said then. "There was a lot of mail piled up. I paid the bills, but I didn't have time to go through all the rest . . ."

"Annie's giving a garden party here Saturday evening for Ava. It's going to be lovely. Annie's taken care of all the preparations long distance, if you can imagine. Of course, Ava insisted that she approve every choice. There will be about eighty people here, maybe more."

Ellie continued to listen while her mother talked about all the difficulties with the planning and how nervous and demanding Ava had been to have everything just so.

"You're not paying for this wedding, are you, Mother?"

"No, no," she rushed. "Ava and John are paying for everything."

Ellie didn't think she was telling the full truth, but she didn't argue.

"Ava's done most of the work. It's just been very stressful. I'll be so thankful when this is over."

Max walked in with her father but stopped when he saw Ellie's mother dabbing at her eyes.

"You told her?" he asked.

Ellie was shaking her head. "Not a good time."

"Tell me what?" her mother asked, the worry already creeping back into her eyes.

Ellie braced herself for the battle ahead. "Something's happened, and we have to leave. I didn't think it was necessary for Max to tell you because we wouldn't be here, but he insisted, said it was important that you know and I . . ." She realized she was rambling and forced herself to stop.

"What's happened?" her father asked.

"Max, why don't you explain."

Max pulled out a chair next to Ellie, sat, and quickly told them about the Landry case and the shooting of Sean Goodman. The rest of the account took only fifteen minutes, but for the next hour Ellie tried to calm them down.

"But if you're not a witness and you can't identify these terrible people, why would they send someone to harm you?" her mother asked.

"They don't take chances," Max explained. "And they have their ways of finding out who potential witnesses are. She and Sean saw them."

"They were both wearing disguises, you said," William said.

"Yes, Dad, they were. I really couldn't identify them."

"What should we do, William? I don't want to let Ellie out of my sight. I want to keep her locked up in the house until they catch that man, but I know I can't."

"We'll figure something out."

Figure something out? "Dad, unless you want a plus two at the wedding, Max and I need to leave."

"What plus two?" her mother asked, not understanding.

Max understood. He put his arm around the back of Ellie's chair and gently tugged on her hair. Plus two would be Max and the hired killer. Not funny.

"I've been accused of ruining several of Ava's parties, and I don't think she'll appreciate someone shooting up the church during the ceremony."

"Oh my Lord, don't talk like that," her father said.

"I'm putting everyone in danger staying here. I do wish I could stay for a little while. I haven't seen Annie in over three years. And all the aunts and uncles will be here, some I haven't seen since I was a little girl."

"It's too dangerous for you," her mother said. "I so wanted you to attend the garden party, though. Annie's going to be disappointed. The whole family would be together, and that hasn't happened in years, has it, William?"

"Mom, please don't tell Annie or Ava the real reason I had to leave. Make up an excuse."

"How safe is my daughter going to be back in her apartment?" her father asked Max. "Strangers stick out here, but not in the big city." His face was getting red with anger, for it was all sinking in.

"There will be more agents and police to watch over her."

"What about you, Max? Are you going to keep my daughter safe?"

"Yes, sir, I am. I'm not going to let anyone hurt her." It was a promise he would die to keep.

"Then you aren't her friend, Max?" her mother asked. "You're here to protect her?"

He didn't hesitate. "I'm both."

"I know you care about Ellie. I can see it in your eyes," her father said. "Will that interfere with your ability to do your job?"

"No." His voice was emphatic.

"Did I mention that the garden party is in our backyard?" her mother asked.

Ellie could see how rattled she was. "Yes, you did mention it."

"By Saturday there will be large planters at each end of the yard and flowers galore all along the borders. The nursery will be here tomorrow morning to do the planting. There will be full-blown flowers in every imaginable color. Oh, and at the end of the yard will be a pristine white tent with tables covered in white linen cloths and covered chairs for those who don't want to stand. There will be music, too, a violin. I'll take lots of pictures to send you, Ellie, so you won't feel excluded." Tears welled up in her eyes.

None of this was her fault, but Ellie still felt guilty and responsible for her parents' pain. "I'm so sorry," she whispered.

Seeing the disappointment on his wife's face, Ellie's father turned to Max. "Couldn't you two stay until after the party Saturday? You could make it safe. If Ellie stayed in the house or in the tent during the party, and if we could get someone else to help with security, wouldn't it be possible?"

Her parents were looking eager and hopeful. Ellie knew how important it was to her mother that she stay, and she didn't want to disappoint her, but Ellie had to be realistic. Others could get hurt.

"It could be dangerous for you and your guests if I stay," she warned.

"I know we can make it safe," her father insisted. "Even if we have to hire security here. You've got that man's picture, so we'd know who we're looking for . . ."

"Landry could have hired someone else," Max said.

Claire looked hopeful. "But like William said, everyone knows everyone else around here. A stranger would stick out."

"Even a cable guy or a repairman? Would you look twice?" Max asked.

"I know the repairman I'm going to call to fix the air conditioner," William said. "And we won't let any other repairmen near here until the party's over."

"No one knows you're home, Ellie," her mother said. "Because none of us were certain you'd be able to get away. I only told the relatives that you were going to try to get home but that your schedule was difficult. We'll keep it a secret until the party. I'll tell Ava and Annie to keep it low-key, too, and not mention you."

The parents had a plan now and looked at Max for approval. When he didn't immediately agree, Claire asked, "What do you think?"

Ellie couldn't break their hearts. She made up her mind that if Max told her no, that she had to leave, she would pull rank and simply say that she was staying.

Max's cell phone vibrated, telling him he had a text. He pushed the chair back and stood. "Let me talk to some people and see what I can do."

Ellie's mother clasped her hands together,

and her father smiled. "Good, that's good."

Max put one hand up. "I'm not promising anything. If I don't get the people I want, then Ellie and I are leaving. You'll have to accept that. All right?"

"Yes, of course," her father said as her mother nodded.

"I really think I should stay for the party . . . ," Ellie began.

The look Max shot her suggested she not continue. If she thought she could show a little independence and throw her weight around with the I-can-do-whatever-I-want attitude, she was sadly mistaken.

Ellie stood up, thinking that she and Max should have their disagreement in another room so her parents wouldn't hear them, but Max didn't seem to care who heard what he had to say.

"Sweetheart, you don't make the decision. I do. And where I go, you go."

He excused himself and went into the living room to read his text and respond.

Ellie decided to clean the kitchen while her mother went in search of her good Irish linens. She'd packed them away in the attic when the hardwood floors were being refinished.

Ellie had just started the dishwasher when she got a call from Carlos Garcia's wife,

Jennifer. The woman was hesitant and sounded fearful over the phone.

"We met at the police station, and my husband, Carlos, had a mole on his neck . . ."

"I remember, Jennifer. How is everything?"

"We have a problem, and you told me to call."

"Yes, I did. What's the problem?"

"We're in the doctor's building next to the hospital, but the doctor's reception lady says we don't have insurance."

"Is the doctor in the office now?"

"Yes. I heard him talk to a patient."

"Okay, good. Could you give me the number for that office?"

A minute later Ellie had the number written down. "Sit tight for a few minutes, and I promise you Carlos will see the doctor today."

"Thank you, Dr. Sullivan."

"You're welcome, Jennifer, and please call me if there are any other problems."

Then Ellie dialed the doctor's office. Max walked into the kitchen just as she ripped into the receptionist, who had identified herself as Michelle.

"This is Dr. Sullivan. You knew that Carlos Garcia was scheduled to see Dr.

Shultz today. I set that up before I left town."

"But you didn't tell us he didn't have insurance." Michelle sounded snippy.

"Dr. Shultz is doing the surgery free of charge," she explained. "He must not have remembered."

"He doesn't do free surgeries."

Ellie's voice turned to steel. "You get him on the phone, and if he's too busy, tell him I'm going to get Dr. Westfield on the line, and Shultz can explain the little surgery he did on his girlfriend three months ago. Oh, wait. You're the girlfriend, aren't you, Michelle? Why don't we get Shultz's wife on the line, too. We'll do a nice little conference call."

"I'm getting him. I'm getting him."

Shultz was on the phone a minute later, and he was hopping mad. "I'm swamped today. I don't have time for any charity cases. You don't even know this man. Didn't you tell me you met him at the police station?"

"Yes, I did meet Carlos at the police station, and that's when I noticed the mole. You gave me your word you'd do the surgery."

"I don't have time . . ."

"Okay, that's it. I'm going to the hospital

board, and I swear to you your privileges will be revoked by the end of next week. That's when I get back."

"I didn't think you were coming back."

"Then I'm going to the state board and file a complaint," she continued. "And, of course, I'm going to have a nice chat with your wife —"

"Wait a minute. I know I promised . . ."

"You are required by the hospital to do a certain number of surgeries without compensation, and I know for a fact you haven't done any. I'll be sure to mention that to Westfield, too. When I'm done with you —"

"Okay, okay, you've made your point. I'll see your patient as soon as I get off the phone."

"Listen up," she said. "You treat him and his family like they're my closest friends. I better not hear you screwed up."

Max had heard the entire conversation. He remembered that Ben had told him how she had talked to a man at the police station but had refused to explain what it was all about. Now he knew what she was doing for him.

Ellie ended the call muttering, "Big jerk." Then she noticed Max watching her. He was smiling.

"What?"

He didn't answer. He walked over and lifted her chin to give her a kiss.

"What was that for?" she asked.

"Just because," he answered. He took a seat next to her. "I've got some news from Ben," he said.

"Yes?"

"Cal and Erika Landry just walked into the FBI office with their attorneys."

"Where?"

"Honolulu."

# NINETEEN

Ellie was going stir-crazy, desperate to get out of the house for a little while. Max had disappeared into William's home office and was making calls on his cell phone, so she tried to keep busy and not interrupt him. She came across her father, who was searching through the kitchen and hearth room for his car keys.

"Where are you going?" she asked.

"Lipton," he answered. "The only thermostat available for the new air conditioner is at Waid's Hardware Store."

"What about the Waid's Hardware Store here?"

"They're out, which is why I'm driving all the way to Lipton now. They won't be charging me for the new thermostat, since the first one was faulty, but if you and Max want air-conditioning tonight, I've got to get over there and back lickety-split."

"Max and I will go," she offered.

Shaking his head, he said, "I don't think it's a good idea for you to go out. Besides, Max has done enough. If he hadn't talked to the owner of the appliance store, I wouldn't have gotten a new air conditioner. I think he scared them into doing the right thing. Eighty percent off broken is still broken, right? It isn't legal to sell something you know doesn't work."

"Did he say that?"

"No, I did."

Ellie was pleased with Max. She hadn't known that he had done that for her father.

"It would be a big help if someone could go to Lipton for me," William admitted. He thought for a few seconds and said, "And I wouldn't need the thermostat until four. That would give us time to install it."

"But you said you had to get back lickety-split."

"Because the air conditioner is going to be delivered, and I've got to sign for the fountain and all the rest of the things your sister ordered for the garden party. Someone has to be here to direct where everything goes, and your mother is going to get her hair done and her nails and God knows what else. Pots today, more plantings tomorrow, and fresh flowers Saturday morning."

"Can't Ava and Annie help while Max and

I go pick up the thermostat?"

"Ava can't leave her store . . . oops, I mean her boutique. She hates it when I call it a store. And Annie won't get in until late afternoon. Besides, there's no reason for anyone to help me. All I have to do is sign and point to where I want the pots." He smiled as he added, "Ava drew me a diagram. And while I'm waiting, I'll get some paperwork done."

"All right. I'll go get Max now, and we'll leave right away."

"Eleanor, you're jumping the gun. Max agreed to let you stay here if he could get extra protection, remember? Are you sure he's going to let you remain in Winston Falls?"

"I'll go ask him now."

She went down the hall to her father's office. Max was sitting at the desk talking on the phone. She stood in the doorway waiting for him to notice her. When he motioned to her, she walked over and leaned against the desk facing him.

"Okay then, and thanks. I really appreciate this," he said and disconnected the call. He looked up at Ellie. "I've got two agents until Saturday. Both of them are coming from Columbia. They'll be here tomorrow."

"Who are they?"

"Agents Clark and Hershey."

"Aren't those candy bars?"

Grinning, he said, "Don't let them hear you say that."

"Then we can stay here."

"Until your yard-party thing is over."

"Garden party," she corrected.

He noticed a frown cross her face. "What's wrong?"

"I'm concerned about two agents showing up suddenly. Won't they be hard to explain? Everyone at the party will wonder who they are."

"They know how to blend in," Max assured her. "But I'll meet with them ahead of time, and we'll work out a game plan."

Her frown had eased a little, but Max could tell she was still thinking about possible problems. He tilted his head toward the desk. "See that new book?"

"Which one?"

"The big one. It's your dad's new math book. He can't wait for you to work the problems."

Her shoulders slumped. "I hate math," she whispered.

He laughed. "I know."

"How do you know?" she asked.

He grabbed her and pulled her onto his lap. "I saw how you grimaced when he was telling the story about the visiting professor. Why didn't you tell him?"

"He loved doing math with me, and I didn't want to hurt his feelings."

He slipped his arm around her waist. She pushed his hand away as she stood. "My father is in the next room," she whispered. "Tell me what Ben said."

"Ben is going to sit in on the interview with Cal Landry. When he's finished with him, he'll tackle his wife, Erika."

"Which one is the weak link?" she asked.

"Neither one," he answered. "They're both hard as" — he started to say a crude word but substituted — "nails."

"Have they said where they've been? Or did they admit they were there at the park?"

"No," he answered. "They insisted they've been on their yacht, cruising from island to island. They have several witnesses who will vouch for them."

"Do they know about the eyewitness? Greg . . ."

"Greg Roper," he reminded her. "And no, not yet. We're keeping quiet about him."

"Ellie, can you go?" Her father poked his head into the library.

"Go where?" Max asked.

She quickly explained she'd offered to pick up the new thermostat. "It's a beautiful day, and I really would like to get out."

Max didn't have any problem leaving as long as she didn't take any chances and listened to what he said.

They were on their way minutes later. Ellie grabbed a bottle of water from the refrigerator on the way out the door, tossed her purse on the floor of Max's SUV, and put her cell phone next to his in the cup holder.

Her father knocked on her window, and when she rolled it down, he said, "You remember how to get to 26, don't you? If you pass the exit for Mays Hill, you've gone too far. You might want to cut over on 223, then turn back on 168. That will take you right into the north side of Lipton. It shouldn't take you more than an hour to get there. Stop at the Goose for lunch," he added. "Great food."

Max drove down the street, turned left, and then said, "Did you get any of that?"

"Directions?"

"Yes, directions," he said.

"No. Did you?"

"I wouldn't have asked . . ."

"I know where Highway 26 is," she said cheerfully. "I can get you that far."

Max programmed the GPS to locate Lipton, and they were on their way. It was a pretty day, but the heat was rising. Ellie wished she could roll all the windows down, but she knew the humidity would make her miserable in no time at all.

She checked the weather app on her phone. "It's supposed to be in the mid-eighties," she said. "Seems hotter to me."

A half hour into the trip, the GPS indicated that they should turn off at the next exit and that Lipton was just twelve miles ahead. Max took the turn and said, "Why did your dad make it so complicated?"

"Maybe he didn't know about this exit."

They drove for a couple of miles on a two-lane road, and the GPS gave them another order to take a left at the next intersection. Fifteen minutes later, they were bumping along a dirt road with few signs of habitation in view. The GPS announced that it was recalculating the route, and Max looked as though he wanted to empty his gun into it.

"Maybe we should have paid attention to Dad," Ellie said. She could have sworn she saw Max's jaw flinch as he turned the SUV around on the narrow road and headed back in the direction from which they had just come.

Several miles and several turns later, they ended up on a road lined with construction signs but no construction equipment or workers.

"Is anyone following us?" she asked with a straight face.

They hadn't seen a single car or person in the past half hour.

Max was trying to turn the car around without sinking a tire in one of the multitude of holes.

"Not funny," he said. "We're out in the middle of nowhere."

He picked up her bottle of water, took a swig, and handed it over to her. He finally got the SUV turned around, and they backtracked to a somewhat decent two-lane road. It took another half hour before they found 168. Ellie wanted to laugh, but she didn't dare, so she rode in silence the rest of the way.

As they finally passed the sign proclaiming they had arrived in Lipton, Max grumbled, "Damn GPS."

Ellie couldn't help herself. She burst into peals of laughter.

Other than giving her a vexed look, Max didn't respond.

He slowed the car as they pulled into the town, which was tiny and quaint. There was a main street two blocks long with shops lined up on both sides. Cars were parked in front of most of them. Toward one end of the street was the hardware store, and at the other end was the Goose restaurant. Max noticed the first storefront they passed had SHERIFF'S DEPARTMENT etched on the glass above the door.

He stopped the car in front of Waid's Hardware Store, and they walked inside. Odors of leather and wood shavings and paint and engine oil greeted them. The old hardwood floors creaked when they stepped on them. A man wearing a carpenter's apron stood behind the counter waiting on two young men. As Max and Ellie entered, they all turned toward the door, raising their eyebrows when they saw the strangers.

Ellie assumed they had noticed the gun at Max's side. Max knew they were all noticing her.

After finishing his transaction with the two men, the clerk addressed them. "I know what you're here for," he said as he pulled the thermostat from a shelf behind the counter. He dropped it in a paper bag and handed it to Ellie.

Back outside, Max locked it in the car, and they headed down the street to the restaurant.

A cartoon caricature of a goose, who apparently was a close cousin to Donald

Duck, was painted on the large front window of the establishment. It was a narrow space with a cash register at the front door and red vinyl booths along the walls. The lunch crowd filled most of the seats. Max spotted an empty booth toward the back, and they were heading for it when Ellie stopped suddenly.

"I don't believe it," she said.

Max looked over at her. She was standing dead still and staring wide-eyed. When he turned back to see what had caught her attention, he saw a tall, burly man walking toward them. He wore a baseball cap with the word SHERIFF embroidered above the brim.

Ellie ran to him and threw herself into his arms.

Max was right behind her. He wanted to peel her off the sheriff but decided on diplomacy first.

"Let go of him," he snapped.

She ignored him. "Oh my God. I knew you'd either end up running from the law or becoming the law. I'm so happy to see you."

A huge smile spread across the man's face. "Ellie Sullivan. Where have you been?"

She finally let go of him and introduced him to Max. "This is Spike Bennett . . .

Sheriff Spike Bennett," she corrected.

"You sure grew up nice," Spike said.

They were standing in the aisle, and a waitress was patiently waiting to get past. Ellie slid into a booth, and Max sat beside her across from the sheriff.

If Spike hadn't been wearing any identification, Max would have thought there was a possibility he'd just been paroled from prison. Both his arms were covered with tattoos, and there were a couple of scars near his elbows. A larger scar ran from his hairline down to his right eyebrow. It made him look dangerous.

His affection for Ellie was apparent.

"How do you two know each other?" Max inquired.

"We were in school together," Spike said. "Are you married, Ellie?"

She shook her head. Max had the insane urge to put his arm around her shoulders and haul her into his side. Was he trying to mark his territory? Jeez, he was acting like a caveman.

"What about you? Are you married?" she asked.

"Yes, two years now," he answered. "I met my wife in college," he added. "You'd like her."

"I'm sure I would," she said. Turning to

275

Max, she said softly, "Spike saved me from Patterson. That's how he got the scar on his forehead."

"Tell me about it," Max said to Spike.

"It was a long time ago," Ellie said.

"Yes, it was," Spike agreed, "but I remember every minute of it as though it happened yesterday. It was lunch hour, and I was hiding behind that big oak tree by the chapel. Remember that tree, Ellie?"

She nodded. "Kenny Platte climbed it and fell. He broke his arm."

"Why were you hiding?" Max asked, curious.

Spike grinned. "I was trying to get the matches to work to light a cigarette I had stolen from my uncle. I had a plan. Once I got it lit, I was going to stroll past the principal's office puffing away. I figured smoking would get me kicked out of school no matter how much money my father had. The matches were wet, though, and I never did get the cigarette lit."

"Spike had a bad-boy image to keep up," Ellie explained.

"Yes, and it took work," he admitted. "So there I was behind that tree when I heard you screaming. I ran around the corner to see what was happening, and Patterson was trying to drag you away." Turning to Max, he said, "The guy was built like a bull, and was at least six feet. By the time I got to him, he was on top of Ellie, using his fists. She was curled up in a ball on her side, so her shoulders and her legs took most of the beating. Sister Mary Frances tried to pull him off, but he knocked her down and —"

"He hit Sister Mary Frances?" Ellie was appalled.

"You don't remember?"

She shook her head. "I just remember you jumping on top of him."

"That's right. I did get him off of you, and I shouted for you to run, but you wouldn't."

"I thought I could help you."

"It was crazy," Spike said. "Soaking wet, you probably weighed fifty pounds back then," he exaggerated. "And it all happened so fast. I got in a couple of good punches, but Patterson shook those hits off like a dog shaking water off, so I decided to choke him. I was squeezing his neck for all I was worth, but it didn't faze him. To this day, I'll never forget the look in his eyes. Not crazy eyes," he stressed. "Evil . . . mean."

"What did he cut you with?" Max asked.

Spike touched the scar on his forehead. "A penknife. It was on his key chain."

"You became my hero that day," Ellie said.

His neck turned pink. "I'm no hero. I just got to him before anyone else could. It took three big seniors to pull him off me and pin him down until the police arrived."

"We both went to the hospital," Ellie interjected. "Sister Mary Frances rode in the ambulance with you."

He nodded. "The nuns called me the town terror, and if it hadn't been for my dad's donations to the school, they would have thrown me out, but after that day, they all but sainted me." He laughed and said, "My bad-boy image was ruined."

He turned serious again, shaking his head. "I've seen Patterson's record, and I can't understand why he didn't end up in prison. Any one of his assaults should have been enough to lock him away, but it looks as though he had some pretty shrewd attorneys who convinced the court he needed treatment not incarceration." He looked at Ellie with genuine compassion. "I'm really sorry for what happened to you. Your dad did everything right with the restraining orders, but I know Patterson didn't stop. After he kidnapped you and nearly killed you, we heard you were in critical condition and they airlifted you to Harrisburg. My dad promised he'd take me to see you as soon as you were awake, but you disappeared.

No one knew where you were."

The waitress interrupted to give them menus, but talk of Patterson had soured Ellie's appetite. She ordered a salad. Max looked over the offerings and decided on the specialty of the house, the Paul Bunyan. The menu boasted it was the largest barbecue beef sandwich in the state. Ellie decided she didn't have to worry about Max's dangerous profession. Cholesterol would get him before any bullets did.

"There was talk that you'd moved in with a relative in Los Angeles and you had become an actress," Spike continued. "But years later I heard you were an attorney in Miami. There was even a rumor floating around not too long ago that you were working on the space shuttle in Houston."

The waitress smiled at Spike as she placed three iced teas on the table. He nodded to her and took a drink.

"Your dad was smart to hide you from that lunatic."

"Do you know where Patterson is now?" Max asked.

He shook his head. "I've got a couple of suspicions, but nothing concrete. He got out of the last institution about six months ago, and then he up and vanished. His parents swear they don't know where he is."

"You asked them?"

"Yes, I did. I wanted to know if I could expect more trouble. My concern was that he'd latch onto another girl or try to hurt someone else."

"His parents still live in Winston Falls?" Ellie asked.

"Yes, they do. In the same house."

Ellie got goose bumps and leaned into Max's side. "Four blocks over and three down from my house," she said. "That's how far away he was. Is he wanted for anything now? Was he supposed to report in to anyone?"

Spike shook his head. "He's not wanted for anything, and no one's looking for him — at least not officially. When he was released, it was recommended that he continue his therapy. That's all I know." He sighed as he added, "Everyone thinks he's crazy."

"From what I've read and heard, when it comes to Ellie, he's certifiable." Max made the comment.

"You're right about that. She'd been in the same school, but he hadn't paid any attention to her until they were at a science camp together. He saw her there, and he instantly wanted her. The fact that she was only eleven years old didn't matter to him.

He couldn't let her go. And he certainly couldn't accept rejection. I believe that, if he saw her today, he would attack her."

Max handed Spike one of his cards. "If you hear anything about him, please contact me. Day or night."

"If you'll do the same," Spike said, giving Max one of his cards. "I've been watching the Patterson house whenever I get over that way. It's a big Victorian house, and I swear one afternoon I saw the curtains move in the third-story attic dormer. I had seen Patterson's parents leave a few minutes before, so it couldn't have been them up there. A couple of kids were walking past his house, and I happened to be at a stop sign adjacent to the street. No one in the house could have seen me."

"You think he might be hiding in the attic?"

"Maybe," he allowed. "Keep in mind, Patterson's parents insist they haven't seen Evan, and the father threatened to bring harassment charges if I kept bothering them. I did a little experiment, though. Several times during the last month of school I made a point to watch the house just about three o'clock in the afternoon. Kids walk past the Pattersons' house every day. I saw the curtains move once more.

Just once more, though. So, yeah, it could be him hiding up there."

"Living in a house for six months and never going out, never being seen?" Ellie said. "I don't know about that."

"There's another problem you should know about," Max said, and for the next ten minutes he talked about the Landrys and the shooting Ellie had witnessed.

"I think it's going to be Willis Cogburn coming after her," Max said. "I have to consider the possibility that the Landrys could send someone else, but they like working with Cogburn."

"He's been in prison, so he's in the system. I'll pull up his photo when I get back to the office."

"What's your cell phone number?" Max asked. "I'll send the photo to you now."

Less than a minute later, Spike was looking at Cogburn's face. "Okay," he said. "What can I do to help?"

"I'd like to get Ellie out of here today, but there's this party . . ."

"My parents pleaded that I stay for Ava's garden party," Ellie explained. "If Max can make it safe."

"I can help you with that," Spike said. Turning to Ellie, he said, "You can't catch a break, can you?"

Trying to stay positive, she said, "Everyone has their ups and downs . . ." She stopped when she noticed their incredulous expressions. "I don't know," she said, shrugging.

"Let's talk strategy later," Max suggested after seeing how pale Ellie's face had become. He knew this had to be difficult for her, but she was handling it with courage.

"Good idea," she said. She didn't want to talk about the Landrys or Patterson any longer and asked Spike to catch her up on all the people she remembered. By the time their food arrived, her appetite was coming back.

"What about you, Ellie? What are you doing these days?" Spike asked.

"Looking for a job," she answered.

"Would you ever consider moving back here?"

She shook her head. "I don't think I could."

"Even if Patterson was living somewhere else?"

"Even then. All my memories revolve around him. I just don't think I could do it. What about you?" she asked. "What made you decide on law enforcement?"

"After I helped you, I kinda liked doing some good, I guess, and after college I decided this is what I wanted to do and this is where I wanted to live."

Spike asked a few personal questions about her life away from Winston Falls, but Max wouldn't let her answer. He was smooth about it. He skillfully deflected the questions or changed the subject. Ellie realized what he was doing when he put his hand on her knee.

When they were once again in the car and on their way back to Winston Falls, Ellie said, "I noticed you wouldn't let me tell Spike about where I live or what I'm doing. I do trust him."

"That's fine, but how much do you want to bet he'll go home and tell his wife about running into you, and she might tell a neighbor . . ."

"I understand," she said. "I wouldn't have been specific."

"Your dad went to a lot of trouble and expense to hide you until you were old enough to take care of yourself. None of the people here know where you live, do they?"

"No," she answered. "Not even the relatives know much about me, only that I was sent away to school after I got out of the hospital. They don't ask questions, though, which is good. At least that's what my mother told me."

"None of them know you're a surgeon?"

"I don't think so. My aunt Vivien thinks I'm a perpetual student. Her sister thinks I'm still in school because I'm slow."

He laughed. "You don't do anything slow."

"Is that a criticism?"

"No," he answered, glancing at her. She looked disgruntled, which amused him. "You just don't know how to relax."

"There hasn't been time."

"Now that your full-time work at St. Vincent's is over, you've got all the time in the world."

"Did I mention I owe around two hundred thousand dollars?"

"You could still take some time off."

She didn't disagree.

Her father was in the backyard with the repairman when they arrived home. The huge space had been transformed into a construction site while they were gone. Empty flowerpots lined the porch and were scattered around at strategic spots on the lawn. A large fountain was being erected in the center. Max handed William the thermostat and stood talking to the two men while Ellie went on into the house. She noticed that some of the flowers had been delivered early. There were bouquets on the kitchen table and more in the living room on the sofa table. The arrangements, white hydrangeas and white roses mixed with vivid green leaves, were simple but elegant.

The dining room table was set for dinner. Seven table settings. She knew what that meant, and she immediately tried to think of somewhere she and Max needed to be. She would go to any lengths not to have to sit next to Ava or John. The problem was, she couldn't think of anything.

Her stomach felt a little nauseous, so she poured herself a glass of milk and leaned against the kitchen sink drinking it.

Max walked in, took one look at her, and asked, "What's wrong?"

Was it that obvious that she was irritated?

"Nothing's wrong. Just wanted some milk."

When her mother entered the kitchen, Ellie noticed she was dressed for a special occasion, wearing a white sleeveless sheath and heels. "Is that a new dress?" she asked.

"No, I've had it a couple of years. You just haven't seen it."

"It's pretty," she said. "You look nice, Mom."

"Thank you, dear. Now, Ellie," she said, "there's something I want to discuss."

Ellie finished her milk. Putting her glass in the sink, she said, "Oh God, here we go."

"What did you say?"

"Whenever you start a sentence with 'Now, Ellie,' I know you're going to tell me something I don't want to hear."

"Your sister Ava and her fiancé are coming over for dinner."

"And I was right. I didn't want to hear that."

"They're picking up Annie at the airport and should be here around six thirty."

Ellie turned to Max. "You'll love Annie. Growing up, she had the nickname Candy Annie because she was so sweet."

Her father had come into the kitchen in time to hear Ellie's remarks. He shook his head. "Until you went away," he said. He took a handkerchief from his pocket and wiped his brow, then dropped into a chair to catch his breath before continuing. "Annie became withdrawn, and it took her a long time to recover, and that's when she decided she wanted to do something in law enforcement when she grew up. She couldn't understand why Patterson hadn't been locked up for life. Frankly, neither could we." He added, "She felt so helpless."

Max nodded. Helpless. He could identify with Annie's mind-set. When he was a young boy, he'd felt the same way after he'd run away from foster parents.

"Annie's still sweet," Ellie insisted. "We text each other all the time. She's still got a wicked sense of humor, too."

"And Ava?" Max asked. "Did she have a nickname?"

He mother tried to stop Ellie from answering. "They're twins, you know. Identical."

"There are times I still can't tell them apart," her father exaggerated.

"I can," Ellie said. "Ava's eyes glow red in the dark."

"Oh, for heaven's sake," her mother muttered.

Her father decided to ignore the comment. "The repairman installed a window unit because he said the replacement air conditioner was missing a few parts. He'll be back tomorrow to fix it and put in the new thermostat. I'm going to keep the window unit, though. I got a real deal on it."

The doorbell rang, and her mother hurried to answer. She crossed back through the kitchen saying, "William, tell the tent people where they can set it up."

Her father was slow to get up, and after the two of them had gone into the yard, Ellie said, "I'll be right back."

She ran into her parents' bathroom and went through the medicines in the cabinet.

Her father's color was much better than it had been, but she was concerned about him. Stress could be a killer. She was looking for heart medicine but didn't find any. The only prescribed medication she found was a bottle of sleeping pills. She read the label and unscrewed the cap. About half the pills were gone. She knew these were nothing to worry about, but she was troubled nonetheless.

"What were you doing?" Max asked when she returned. He was standing at the window in the living room looking out at the street.

"I was checking out the prescription bottles in the medicine cabinet to find out what they're taking. If something was wrong with either one of them, I would never know. They wouldn't tell me."

"Did you find anything?"

"Sleeping pills for my dad," she answered. "I think the anxiety I've caused him over the years — not to mention all the stress of Ava's wedding — has taken its toll."

"Are you going to tell me about Ava? I sense a little hostility."

She laughed. "No wonder you're an FBI agent. You're so perceptive."

"No reason for sarcasm."

She crossed the room and stood beside

him looking out at the street with her arms folded. "I'm here to attend Ava's wedding because my mother insisted. Really insisted," she stressed emphatically.

"Okay."

"She's marrying John Noble, my ex-fiancé."

He raised an eyebrow. "Yeah?"

"John had only just asked me to marry him a few days before I brought him home to meet the family."

"I see," he said when she hesitated.

"Everyone wanted to make him feel at home . . . especially Ava."

Max suspected where this was headed and waited to hear her tell him.

"The night after we arrived, I found him in bed with her."

"Ah . . ."

Frowning, she said, "Ah, what?"

"Do you blame him for what happened, or do you just blame your sister?"

"Ava knew what she was doing."

"And he didn't?"

"Of course, he did," she said. "But Ava and I always had a contentious relationship, and this was the last straw. I packed up and went back to St. Louis."

"What had made it so contentious?" he asked, curious.

"When we were young and anything went wrong, Ava blamed me. She and Annie each had her own birthday party, and Ava accused me of ruining one of hers. In a way, I guess I did."

"How did you ruin it?"

"I was beaten and unconscious," she said. "And my parents had to go to the hospital."

"That was when you were taken away from Winston Falls, wasn't it?"

"No, not that time."

"Jeez, Ellie, how many times did Patterson send you to the hospital? The court records didn't tell that."

"Just a couple."

She tried to act blasé about it, but he knew talking about the bastard made her anxious. He could hear it in her voice.

"Is it difficult to be here, even though it's just for a couple of days?"

She didn't see any reason to lie. "I get this stone in the pit of my stomach, and it doesn't go away until I'm out of here, all because of him. I used to think it was odd that he didn't try to find me."

"How do you know he didn't?"

"I don't think it would have been all that difficult to find out where I was. I took the Wheatley name for a long time, but I went back to my name for my M.D. A psychiatrist

291

suggested to me that Patterson's obsession was somehow tied to Winston Falls."

"Maybe," he allowed, though he wasn't convinced.

"The doctor said that part of Patterson's obsession or fantasy was that he had to kill me here. It's one theory," she added with a shrug.

Max had another theory. A man with a violent obsession would stop at nothing to get his victim, and the only reason he hadn't killed Ellie was because he couldn't find her. From what he'd read in the file, he also knew that Patterson would never stop until he was locked away for life.

"I'd rather not talk about him anymore."

"Okay, tell me about this Noble guy. Did you love him?"

"He looked good on paper."

Max laughed. "In other words, no," he said. "What exactly does looking good on paper mean?"

"John's a dermatologist, so there's very little chance of danger in his job. That made him safe." *And God knows, I'd love to find out what it's like to feel safe,* she thought to herself.

"What else?"

"We were both residents, so we had the hospital and medicine in common."

"What else?"

"He was extremely polite and easygoing."

Max noticed she hadn't mentioned an emotional or physical connection. "You wouldn't have married him."

"No, I wouldn't have," she admitted. "I realized after that fiasco that I can't marry anyone. My life's too unpredictable."

"And it wouldn't be safe for the man you married?"

Had he read her thoughts? "Yes, that's right. It wouldn't be."

"You're letting that bastard, Patterson, continue to run your life."

She didn't disagree. "Aren't you going to ask me if I slept with John?"

"No," he replied. "I already know you didn't."

She looked up at him. "How could you know?"

He didn't say what he was thinking, that any man who had gone to bed with Ellie would never want or need any other woman. Instead, he said, "I just know."

# TWENTY

Bridezilla arrived at the house at seven o'clock with her fiancé and her sister.

Max watched from the window as John carried Annie's suitcase and walked between the two striking women. The twins were identical, all right. Both were of medium height and had long blond hair a shade darker than Ellie's, and delicate features. In Max's opinion, the sisters were very pretty, but in no way could they compete with Ellie's beauty.

John Noble was something else. He looked as though he should be working on Wall Street or maybe as a mannequin in a department store window. He was tall, thin, and neatly dressed in a starched, light blue shirt and pressed khakis. Not a hair was out of place. There was something odd about him, though. Max couldn't figure out what it was until John got closer to the house. He realized then that John's forehead didn't move when he smiled. It was as though his skin had been frozen. Botox? Surely not.

Ellie came up behind Max. "The bad seed's the one on the left," she whispered.

He tried not to smile. "Try to get along," he whispered back.

"You sound like my mother."

"Just do it, sweetheart. Play nice."

Her father rushed past them and opened the front door.

Annie spotted Ellie. "I didn't think you would make it," she cried out. "I'm so happy you're here."

The sisters were talking a mile a minute as they hugged each other. Though they were speaking at the same time, they still seemed to understand what the other was saying.

Ava stood behind Annie, waiting. She clutched a notebook in her arms, and Max noticed she acted irritated that she was having to wait for Ellie's attention. When it was her turn, she gave Ellie an air kiss on her cheek.

"I'm glad you decided to behave like an adult and come home for the wedding," Ava said. She lowered her voice. "And, by the way, you are in the wedding."

"No, I'm not," Ellie replied.

She plastered a smile on her face and

introduced Max to her sisters. She didn't say anything negative about Ava, though there were a few choice words she would have liked to use. Then she introduced John.

He had been standing in the door with his head down. When she said his name, he looked up, but he didn't look at Ellie. His face was red, and his eyes darted back and forth as though they were afraid to meet hers. He nervously stepped forward and shook Max's hand, and the room fell silent. Finally, he glanced up at Ellie and said, "Congratulations."

"Congratulations for what?" she asked.

"The Chapman Award."

"The hospital won the Chapman?"

"No, you did."

She shook her head. "You must be mistaken, John. I would know if I'd won it."

"Oh, Dr. Westfield probably wants to tell you himself," he said. His embarrassment turned his complexion an even deeper shade of red. "I guess I ruined his surprise."

"How did you find out about this?" she asked, still believing he'd made a mistake.

"I was talking to Westfield's assistant about some papers I still hadn't received for the hospital here, and she mentioned the news to me. Everyone at St. Vincent's is so excited. It's such a huge honor, and it means they'll get additional grant money and other funding. You should be hearing from Westfield anytime now. You're going back there, aren't you?"

"Yes," she answered. "I'm not signing a contract, though. I promised Westfield I'd help out for a little while when they need me."

"You did win it, Ellie," he assured her.

Now that the initial awkward moments were out of the way, Ava had lost interest in the conversation and had gone into the kitchen to talk to her mother.

"What's a Chapman?" Annie asked.

John answered. "It's a prestigious award given for outstanding achievement in the field of medicine. This year it was awarded to Ellie and, therefore, to her department, too. It's a coveted prize," John stressed, "because it's so rarely given. The last Chapman Award was presented eleven years ago to a senior resident and his department in Memphis."

"Will there be a presentation?" Annie asked. "And will Ellie get a medal or something?"

John smiled at Annie, glad to have somewhere else to direct his attention. "She'll get a little more than a medal. The award comes with a large cash prize. Half goes to the department and half to Ellie. She won't even have to pay taxes. That's included in the award."

"That would certainly help with your loans, wouldn't it?" Annie said.

Ellie was still incredulous. "If I had won it, Dr. Westfield surely would have called me by now."

Her father kissed Ellie's forehead. "Even if you didn't win it, you know your mother and I are very proud of you, don't you? We may not be able to brag about you to the relatives and our friends the way we'd like, but you know how we feel."

"Yes, Daddy, I do."

"My chicken's going to be all dried up if we don't eat soon," her mother called. "John, would you mind taking Annie's suitcase upstairs to the lavender room? Annie, fill the water glasses please."

Max's cell phone rang. Ben was calling. He excused himself and headed to the office again for privacy. He was crossing the hallway when he heard Ava ask Ellie whether she had brought a long black dress to wear in the wedding, or whether she needed to buy one. Without breaking stride, Max turned around, grabbed Ellie's hand, and pulled her with him into the office.

Since he was on the phone, Ellie waited

to explode, but it took work. She wanted to grab Ava by the shoulders and shake some of the smug attitude out of her. Annie passed by the door saying she was going upstairs to get something out of her suitcase, and a minute later Ellie heard her laughing. She knew why. Annie had seen the color on the walls of her room. For some reason her sister's laughter took the edge off Ellie's anger. She had promised her mother she would try to get along with Ava, and by all that was holy, that was exactly what she was going to do. She would not allow her sister to provoke her.

While sitting on the window seat waiting for Max to finish his call, she got a text from Addison MacBride asking about prenatal vitamins and water retention. It took four texts for Ellie to answer all her questions, and then Addison asked if Ellie would consider coming to Honolulu for a visit. She responded that she would love to visit, but she couldn't commit to a date because her schedule was so screwy at the moment.

That was an understatement. She didn't know what she would be doing the next two months or even the next two weeks. Her future was dependent upon the FBI apprehending the man who was hired to kill her. That is, if there was only one. Had the

Landrys hired more than one hit man? And how exactly did one know where to go to hire a killer? You certainly couldn't place ads in the newspapers. Those were becoming antiquated anyway. The Internet, she decided. You could get anything on the Internet if you knew where to look. Maybe the Landrys Googled it, she considered. Perhaps they typed "Need hit man" and then clicked the search button.

Okay, her mind was wandering and her thoughts had become loopy. Max had walked to the other side of the office and was listening intently to what Ben was telling him. Ellie didn't particularly want to leave him to join the others, but she was about to get up and go into the kitchen to help when her cell phone rang.

Dr. Westfield was calling, announcing to her that she had, indeed, won the Chapman Award. She was shocked and humbled. She thanked him profusely, then she listened as he raved about what the award would mean to his department. She had never heard Westfield jubilant before and doubted that she ever would again.

Ellie decided to wait to tell the family. Tonight was all about Ava and the wedding, but she did want to tell Max right away.

After he finished his call, he turned to her.

She saw the grim look on his face and forgot all about her happy news.

"What happened?"

"Someone got to Greg Roper."

"What do you mean, got to him? Did he get hurt?"

He shook his head. "We don't know, he's missing."

Ellie's mother appeared in the doorway. "Dinner's on the table."

"We'll talk about this later," he said.

Dinner was a trial of endurance for Ellie. Her parents tried to keep the conversation light, but there was an undercurrent of tension waiting to erupt. After two glasses of wine, Ava was no longer even pretending to be interested in anything anyone else had to say. She wanted to talk about the wedding and all the work she had done to make it perfect. No one was going to ruin it, she declared more than once, and Ellie couldn't help but notice she stared at her each time she said it.

Ava made another snide remark, this time about Ellie's outfit, and that did it.

"John, you're right," Ellie said. "I just heard from Dr. Westfield. I did win the Chapman."

"I told you so," John said, beaming. "I really wasn't surprised when I heard. I always knew you were the best surgeon in the hospital. The residents were amazed at your skill. You should have heard them talking about you in the lounge. Westfield called you brilliant. Did you know that?"

She shook her head. "No, I didn't."

"And getting him to say anything positive about any of his surgeons would take a miracle. You were always special, Ellie."

Ava didn't utter a word, but the evil eye she gave John said it all. She was seething inside.

"Congratulations," Annie said. "I'm so proud of you."

"Honey, that's wonderful news," her father said.

"Yes, wonderful," her mother agreed.

"Does everything always have to be about you?" Ava demanded.

Ellie burst into laughter. "Oh, Ava, you just never change, do you?"

Ava's chin came up. "I'm taking that as a compliment," she said. "And by the way, you are going to be in my wedding."

"Are you asking?"

"No, I'm telling you."

Max was fascinated by the conversation among the sisters. He'd lived with brothers most of his life, and he now realized how unbelievably different sisters were. In his family, any major argument was settled with a couple of good punches, unless their parents were around, and then the problem was resolved and they moved on. There were no hard feelings. His brothers didn't hold grudges, but Ellie's sister Ava certainly did.

"My being in your wedding isn't going to stop any rumors, Ava," Ellie protested.

Annie nodded. "She's right, Ava. This wedding is making you a little paranoid."

Their father offered everyone at the table a glass of wine, but Ellie declined. After Ava's third or fourth argument on the subject of the wedding, Ellie excused herself from the table, went to the kitchen, and carried back a gallon of milk and a glass. She plopped both down in front of her plate.

"Put the milk in a pitcher," Ava instructed. "We aren't hillbillies."

Ellie ignored her, poured herself a glass, and took a sip.

"I don't think I want to listen to this," their father said. "Come on, Claire. You, too, Max and John. We'll let the girls hammer out their differences."

Her mother gave Ellie a slight shake of the head and a warning look before she left to sit on the porch with the others. Ellie wouldn't have been surprised if she had used two fingers to point to her eyes and then point to Ellie's to let her know she would be watching her.

As soon as the sisters were alone, Annie turned to Ellie. "Why didn't you tell me about Max? He's hot," she whispered. "Isn't he? A man with a gun and a badge. There's something sexy about it, don't you think?"

"He wears a gun and carries a badge because he works for the FBI, and he's also a friend, so I invited him to come along."

"Bet he didn't know what he was getting into," Annie said with a quick nod toward her twin.

"He's too tough looking for my liking," Ava said with a shrug. "John's so much more polished."

"Is he just a friend?" Annie asked.

"Yes, and, Ava, I'm not going to be in your wedding."

"Yes, you are. It's the only way."

"Please, let's not argue," Annie begged.

"Annie, are you feeling okay? You're so pale," Ellie asked.

"I'm tired," Annie said. "I've been up since five this morning, and I didn't get to bed until late."

Ellie turned back to Ava. "What do you mean, it's the only way?"

"Yes, the only way to what?" Annie asked.

Ava explained, "Being in the wedding is the only way to put those vicious rumors to rest."

"What vicious rumors?" Ellie asked. She poured another half glass of milk and took a sip. Being close to Ava was going to give her an ulcer. Fortunately, she wouldn't have to put up with her for long.

"You know."

"No, I don't know. Explain the vicious rumors."

Ava straightened in her chair and glared at Ellie. "Fine. People are saying I broke up your engagement."

"I don't understand how people in town would know that," Annie said. "Who would have told them?"

"No one had to tell them," Ava said. "Mom had spread the word about John before Ellie ever brought him home. All of her friends knew she was bringing him to meet the family. They had to wonder why he was suddenly marrying me and not her."

"But that's not so awful," Annie protested. "That wouldn't necessarily ruin your reputation."

Ava scoffed. "That's not all. Someone, and I don't know who it was but I'm guessing it was Mom's best friend, Mrs. Grimes — you know Mom had to confide in someone —

anyway, someone spread the rumor that John and I were found in a . . . compromising position the day after Ellie brought him home."

"Didn't that happen?" Annie asked. "I wasn't here, but Mom said —"

"Whose side are you on?" Ava demanded.

"I'm not on anyone's side. I'm simply asking if it really happened. Did it, or didn't it?"

"That isn't relevant," Ava snapped.

"I guess I'll have to ask John," Annie said.

"You keep him out of this. Yes, okay, I did have sex with John while he was engaged to Ellie, but I don't think anyone needs to know about it."

"So it's the truth, not a rumor. You do know the difference," Annie said.

"Look at you," Ava said. "Just finished law school, and you think you're a prosecutor. Quit interrogating me." Her voice reeked of sarcasm.

"I'm simply asking you how you can call the truth a rumor," Annie persisted.

"Because I want to." Ava raised her voice to a shout. "I am determined to quell these vicious rumors because I have to live in this town, and I don't want people talking about me behind my back, saying terrible things about my character."

Annie looked at Ellie and rolled her eyes. "Ava, are you sorry for what you did to Ellie?"

"No, of course not. Why should I be sorry? It was meant to be. John loves me, and I love him." She pushed away from the table and stood. "I'm going to check the backyard again before John and I leave. I probably won't get back here until the garden party, but if I need anything, I'll call you."

Annie and Ellie watched Ava until she'd disappeared into the kitchen. Annie was the first to start laughing, but Ellie quickly joined in. The two sisters began to clear the table.

"Should we ask Ava to help do the dishes?" Ellie asked innocently.

They shared another good laugh.

"Remember when we were kids? Ava always had something more important to do whenever it was time for chores," Annie said.

"I remember," Ellie said. "After I left, you got stuck with all the work. I don't understand why Mother didn't make Ava do her share."

"It was easier not to argue with her."

Ellie stacked the dinner plates and carried them into the kitchen. Annie followed with glasses.

"I haven't said congratulations to you for finishing law school," Ellie said.

"I'm not a lawyer yet, not until I know I've passed the bar. I told Mom and Dad we couldn't celebrate until then."

"Do you know what you want to do?"

"I liked the antitrust courses I took. That area interests me. I'm kind of at a cross-roads, I guess. I thought I had my future all mapped out, but now everything's changed."

Before Ellie could ask her to explain, Annie went back into the dining room to finish clearing the table. Ellie stood at the sink rinsing the dishes and putting them in the dishwasher.

"I couldn't do what you do," Annie said as she handed Ellie a platter. "Cutting into bodies. Just thinking about all that blood makes me sick."

"The coolest thing happened a couple of weeks ago." She told her sister about a case she found fascinating, but Annie appeared to be grossed out. "He swallowed coins? Why?"

"He couldn't explain why. Eleven dollars and fifteen cents."

"All change?"

"Yes," she said. She laughed at Annie's expression. "It weighed a lot, but he didn't rupture. Then there was this man who got into a knife fight. Those can be nasty," she explained as she continued to rinse salad plates. "His femoral artery was nicked and blood started spurting everywhere. I plugged the hole with my finger while . . ." She stopped when Annie gagged. "Queasy stomach?" she teased.

"I don't know how you do it. Don't you ever get sick?"

"Oh yes," she said. "I throw up on patients all the time." She thought what she'd said was funny, but Annie didn't laugh.

"Blood makes me gag," she said. "Where does Mom keep her plastic bags for leftovers?"

"Third drawer down," she answered.

Annie put the platter of leftover chicken on the table and searched the drawer. She held up a bread bag and smiled. "She still saves these. She used to put our sandwiches in them to take to school for lunch."

"Mom saves everything. There's a drawer with nothing but rubber bands, paper clips, and twist ties."

Annie put the chicken in the refrigerator and said, "Tell me about Max."

Ellie leaned back against the sink and wiped her hands on a dish towel. "What do you want to know? That I'm starting to

309

panic because I can feel myself getting more and more attached to him? Leaving him is going to be painful."

"Then don't leave him."

"He lives in Honolulu."

"Oh."

" 'Oh' is right," she said. "I've got to figure out a way to distance myself. You're so practical, Annie. Any ideas on how I can do that?"

"Let me think about it," she answered. She glanced out the window. "Here comes Ava," she whispered.

"We had twenty minutes without listening to wedding plans, and I'm thankful for that," Ellie said.

Ava didn't stop to talk to her sisters. She walked through the house and went to sit with the others on the front porch.

Annie and Ellie had just finished cleaning the kitchen when their mother joined them. She took one look at Annie and said, "Go up to bed. You're exhausted. Say good night to your father," she added.

"Where's Max?" Ellie asked.

"He's in your father's office. I think all the wedding talk spooked him. Now, Ellie . . ."

"Yes?" she asked suspiciously.

"I want you to go over the guest list for

the wedding with me. I'm worried sick I've left out a relative." She went to a cabinet drawer and pulled out a thick notebook.

Annie left the kitchen before Ellie could ask her to stay and help.

Sighing, Ellie pulled out a chair at the table and sat beside her mother. "Isn't it too late to add another guest?"

"I've got extra invitations. If I've missed someone, I'll simply tell them that their invitation was returned. A little lie is better than hurting someone's feelings."

What her mother was asking of her didn't make any sense. Ellie had left home when she was twelve. She didn't even remember half her relatives. She decided to humor her mother, though, because she knew the stress of having everything perfect for Ava's wedding was wearing on her.

It turned out to be a pleasant task. Ellie would read a name while her mother crossed it off the list. If she couldn't remember the people, her mother would tell her a story about them. It made Ellie feel more connected to her family, and when she did remember an aunt or an uncle or a cousin, her mother was so pleased.

They sat together until almost ten o'clock when Ava and John came in to say goodbye. Her mother and father were clearly worn-out and headed to bed. Ellie went into the living room and read a magazine while she waited for Max. Annie walked in a minute later.

"I thought you went to bed," Ellie said.

Max poked his head into the room and said, "Come find me when you're ready to leave the house."

"I will," Ellie promised.

"What was that all about?" Annie asked. She plopped down next to Ellie on the sofa, kicked her shoes off, and tucked them under her.

"It's a long story."

"I don't have anything to do but sleep."

"What about tomorrow?"

"Ava has me going ten different places with her. So tell me the long story now."

"Confidential."

"Confidential," Annie agreed.

"There was a shooting just outside my hospital," she began and told Annie everything that had happened since that day, and of course the real reason Max was with her. Annie asked a lot of questions, but she didn't seem worried.

"Mom and Dad know all about it, and they understand I'll have to leave after the garden party."

"Is it safe for you to stay that long?"

"I wanted to leave, but it's really important to Mom that I stay at least until the party's over. Max has other agents coming to help with security," she answered. "And I don't plan to stroll down the street alone. I'll stay close to the house during the party."

"You don't want Ava to know about this." Annie was making a statement not asking a question.

"Oh no."

Ellie kicked her shoes off and sat back. They talked a little more about the shooting, and then Annie changed the subject.

"Do you think Ava will sweeten up once she's married?"

"I don't know. Once you go to the dark side, it's tricky coming back."

Annie poked her arm. "You love her. You know you do. She's your sister. You have to."

Leave it to Annie to find the positive, Ellie thought. Whenever things were strained, she was the peacemaker. Ava and Ellie had caused their share of strife in the family over the years, but not Annie. She was the kind, gentle soul who brought everyone together. She had been the perfect daughter, the one who had never been a source of worry in the family.

Ellie finally relented. "Yes, I love her. I

don't like her, though."

"If she heard about a hit man, she'd flip out."

"No, she'd blame me," Ellie said. "Not many people have a stalker, and I've now got two."

"Actually, you've got a stalker and a hit man. There's a difference."

"They're both trying to kill me," she said. "Bet you can't top that."

"Bet I can," she said, nudging Ellie again. "Guess what."

"What?"

"I think I'm pregnant."

# TWENTY-ONE

Max made sure all the windows and doors were locked in the main house and then took Ellie up to their apartment. The air was stifling.

"I thought Dad had the repairman install a window unit," Ellie said.

"He did. He didn't turn it on, though. It must be ninety in here."

Ellie thought it was hotter. She followed Max into his bedroom but stopped when she saw the oversize window unit. "It's huge. Does it fit, or will it fall on the floor during the night?"

Max checked it out. "It barely fits," he said, smiling. "If it falls, it will go out the window, not in."

He looked at all the switches and dials and finally located the on and off button. He pushed it on and waited. The unit shuddered and began to make a low humming sound. Cool air immediately poured out of the vents.

"Okay, I think we're in business," Max said. "It's set for seventy degrees."

Ellie was feeling hot and sticky and took a quick shower. She put on an extra-large T-shirt for a nightgown, then went into the living room to see if *SportsCenter* was on while Max showered.

He walked into the living room wearing a pair of gray boxer shorts and nothing else. His hair was still wet, and he was drying it with a towel. Ellie felt that familiar stirring in her body just looking at him. He had a massive chest. It was all muscle. She knew that for a fact because she had kissed every inch of it. His dark, curly chest hair tapered to a V at his belly button. She'd kissed that, too, she remembered, and oh God, what hadn't she kissed? His legs and thighs were just as muscular. She remembered squeezing those thighs in the throes of passion.

Was it getting hotter in here?

Max put the towel on the rack in the bathroom, then went to the kitchen to get a beer. He noticed Ellie's face was flushed.

"Are you okay?"

"I need to buy a pregnancy test."

The announcement didn't faze him. "Okay," he said. "Can it wait until tomorrow?"

She smiled. "Yes."

Max opened the beer bottle, tossed the lid in the trash can, and sat down beside her, scooting her over to the end of the sofa so he wouldn't be near the lumpy springs. He took a drink and said, "Isn't it a little too soon to know if you're pregnant? It's only been one day," he added. "And I used protection."

"It's not for me," she said, exasperated.

She took a drink of his beer and handed it back to him. Max reached for the remote, but Ellie was quicker.

"It's for Annie, isn't it?"

Her eyes widened. "How did you know?"

"I'm an FBI agent. We're trained to be observant. Now give me the damned remote."

"Not until you explain."

"First of all, there's the process of elimination. Your mother is a little too old to get pregnant."

"True," she agreed.

"And Ava can barely stand to look at you, so she certainly wouldn't confide in you."

"And that left Annie."

"Yes," he said, reaching for the remote again.

She stretched her arm out to the side and held the remote in her fist.

317

"But there were other signs," Max continued. "And we agents are trained to pick up
on those signs."

She rolled her eyes heavenward. "Like?"

"Annie didn't drink any wine."

"Neither did we."

"Her complexion was gray."

"She was tired."

"She threw up." He halfheartedly tried to
grab the arm with the remote.

"Where did she throw up?"

"In the trash can in your father's office.
Fortunately, the can had a liner."

"What was she doing in his office?"

"Talking to me."

"About what?"

"She needed a favor."

"Are you going to tell me what the favor
was?"

"No."

She sighed in frustration. "Maybe she
threw up because she had eaten something
that disagreed with her. Were you there
when it happened?"

"I held her hair back for her."

"That was sweet." She kissed him on the
cheek and handed him the remote.

He immediately began to channel surf.
"But the number one reason I know why
she thinks she's pregnant . . ."

"Yes?"

"She told me."

Ellie thought about it for a minute and said, "Annie doesn't want anyone else to know. I wonder if she told Ava."

"No, she didn't. She doesn't want to take anything away from her focus on the wedding. Ellie, do all women get crazy about their weddings like Ava?"

"You mean act like a maniac?"

"Yeah."

"No, not all brides behave like Ava."

He nodded. "Where do you want to get the pregnancy test? I think I saw a drugstore when we were pulling into Winston Falls."

"Oh no, no, no. The entire town would think I was pregnant if I purchased a test here. My parents would hear about it before we got back home."

"I'll be meeting Agents Clark and Hershey before they get here tomorrow. I'll set it up in another town nearby. We could find a pharmacy there."

"There's a plan," she said, smiling. She took another drink from his bottle and handed it back to him. "You really won't tell me what favor Annie wanted?"

"I don't know what the favor is," he said. "We didn't get that far. But when I find out what she wants, no, I won't tell you. It's an

FBI agent and client confidentiality issue," he teased. "If she wants you to know —"

"Agent and client? That's a new one."

"That's right."

"Help me understand. She asked for a favor, but she wouldn't tell you what it was?"

"Couldn't tell me," he corrected.

"Why not?" She sounded disgruntled.

"Her face was in a trash can."

"I guess I'll have to ask her."

"I'd have a trash can handy when you do."

Yawning, she stretched her arms above her head and stood. "It's still beastly hot in here. Think we could turn the fan up a notch or two?"

Max turned the television off and followed Ellie. "Let's go to bed."

She noticed the door to the smaller bedroom where she planned to sleep tonight was closed. She opened it and felt a rush of hot air.

"You're going to have to keep your door wide open, or my room won't get any air." She walked into his room to feel the cooler temperature.

"Do you want to sleep with me?" he asked.

She didn't answer him. Max couldn't have heard her anyway. A scant second after asking the question, he flipped the switch up to high on the air conditioner and was nearly lifted off his feet by the noise.

Ellie fell back onto the bed. The entire floor seemed to vibrate, and the bed was doing a shimmy to the middle of the room. It sounded as though a Lear jet was landing in the apartment.

She couldn't stop laughing. She wiped the tears from her cheeks and tried to catch her breath. She was getting a stitch in her side watching Max. He was cursing the air conditioner while turning every possible lever and button to get it to stop. He finally unplugged it.

The unit didn't die easily. It shuddered again. Its last gasp was so forceful, the glass in the window above rattled . . . then blessed silence.

Max stood over Ellie watching her. She was on her back with her arms above her head, and her laughter was so joyful and uninhibited. He dropped down on top of her, careful to keep his weight off her, and pinned her with his pelvis on top of hers, and his hands holding hers. He looked down at the tears in her eyes. God, she was something else.

"Daddy got another deal, didn't he?" she asked.

He slowly nodded. Then he leaned down

and kissed her. She pulled her hands free and wrapped them around his back.

"It's going to get hot in here," she whispered.

"Yeah, I know."

He was nuzzling her neck, and she couldn't stop herself from stroking his back and his shoulders. "You probably shouldn't let me do this, Max."

She pushed his shoulders back and rolled on top of him. Her shirt had ridden up, and she could feel him pressed against her. She stretched her body over his, slid her fingers into his hair, and kissed him on the mouth, a hot, wet kiss that made her want much, much more.

Max tightened his grip on her hips. Her breath was warm and sweet.

"If you don't want to do this, stop messing with me," he said.

She kissed the pulse at the base of his neck. "I want to, but I worry about you," she whispered. "This could become habit-forming for you."

She was moving downward, kissing his chest as she moved erotically against his pelvis. Her hands were stroking him, driving him crazy. When she reached his stomach, she smiled at his indrawn breath.

"I don't want you to become attached to

me," she said.

She moved lower, and he couldn't think. Only when he knew he was about to lose control did he take over. He rolled off the bed, telling her he'd be right back, and he returned in seconds. He wasn't gentle as he took her shoulders. He saw the passion in her eyes and knew she was ready for him. He entered her forcefully, and she cried out as the sensations began to build. She dug her fingernails into his shoulders.

Neither one could talk then, for the mating ritual was consuming them.

Max made it last longer this time so that she would climax before he did. When she lifted her hips to take him deeper inside and cried his name, he buried his face in her shoulder and found his own release.

Later, as Max was coming out of the bathroom, he fully expected Ellie to be sound asleep, but she surprised him. She was resting on her side waiting for him. As soon as he got into bed, she curled up against him and said, "I'll have sex with you if you answer a question."

"What's that?" he asked suspiciously.

"Is Simon going to be traded to the Colts?"

He laughed. "We just had sex."

"I understand it's possible to do it more than once."

"We have done it more than once. At least a hundred times last night."

She kissed him. "You wish. It was four, not a hundred. Will you ask him?"

"Yes."

He rolled onto his back and pulled her close. She rested her cheek on his shoulder. "Tell me how you became a Daniels."

His sigh was long and drawn out.

"You don't want to tell me?" she asked.

"I don't like talking about it."

She didn't prod, and five minutes later Max said, "My parents died in a car accident. A semi ran into them. I was five years old at the time. I didn't have any relatives, and the lawyer the court appointed me in foster care pocketed all the insurance money. I didn't have good luck with the three families I was placed with. The last was the worst."

"How old were you then?"

"Seven," he answered. "I ran away. It was the dead of winter, and I was hiding behind a Dumpster. I remember being so cold and feeling helpless."

"What happened?"

"Simon happened. He was on his way home and saw me. He took off his coat and gave it to me and dragged me home with him. I was kicking and screaming, but I stopped when he vowed I would never have to go back to that foster home." There was a smile on his face as he continued. "Simon was just a year older than I was, but he was big for his age and sounded as though he could pull it off. I believed him, anyway. So I went along. I lived in his house for over a week before his parents found out about me. The bruises from my foster parents were still evident. Simon's dad was an attorney, and he, too, promised I'd never have to go back."

"What was his mother like?" she asked.

"Loving," he said. "And kind."

"Did they adopt you right away?"

"If you were to ask them, they would tell you I adopted them. It became final when I was eight, and by then two more had joined the family. Bishop and Sebastian. And that court-appointed attorney who pocketed the estate money . . ."

"Yes?"

"Sent to prison," he said. "And Dad was able to get most of the money back. He put it in a trust fund for me."

"When did Bradley and Tyler and Adam join the family?"

"You remembered their names."

"Of course."

"Bradley and Tyler came five years after I did, and Adam was the last to become a Daniels a year later."

"No girls?"

He laughed. "Mom and Dad said it would be cruel to inflict the seven of us boys on a sister. We were a rowdy bunch."

"They sound like wonderful people."

"The best." He yawned. "We've got to do something about the heat in here."

"I say we give the window unit another chance. You plug it in, and we'll keep it on low."

"Stay here. I'll take care of it."

The plan worked. It seemed that, on low, the air conditioner cooperated. Ellie begged him to push the lever up a notch to medium to see what would happen. And once again the Lear jet all but blew them out of the room. Luckily, when he flipped it back to low, the humming sound returned.

Ellie had another good laugh, rolled onto her stomach, and was sound asleep seconds later.

# TWENTY-TWO

Max was standing in the living room waiting for Ellie when Annie motioned to him from the hallway.

"Could I speak to you in private?" Annie asked.

Since he was the only one in the room, he thought the question odd. "Yeah, okay."

"In your office?"

He laughed. "My office. I guess I've been using it a lot, huh?"

Annie nodded. "Ellie and I know what you're doing. You're hiding from Ava and John. I like the man, but oh God, he's boring. I shouldn't have said that, I know, but he really is."

Max followed her to the office. She went in first and held the door. Once he was inside, she shut the door and leaned against it. Her complexion was green. Max reached under the desk for the trash can and held it out to her.

Annie noticed the leery look in his eyes. "I'm okay," she said.

"You don't look okay."

She patted her cheeks, trying to get some color back. "It's the smell of coffee. It makes me sick to my stomach."

Max set the trash can down but kept it close just in case.

"I'm sorry about throwing up last night. I hope that didn't gross you out."

"I've got six brothers. Nothing grosses me out."

"I'm also sorry I didn't finish our conversation. After I ran upstairs to brush my teeth, I was having second thoughts." She looked uneasy and tentative.

"Would you like some fresh air? We could go out on the porch to talk."

She shook her head. "Ava's waiting in the drive."

As if on cue, they heard a horn honk.

"She can be impatient," Annie said.

"Uh-huh."

"About the favor . . ." She hesitated.

"Yes?"

"Can you find someone for me?"

"I can try."

"I don't want him to know I'm looking for him. I just want to know where he is because . . . because . . ."

The tears started, and Max was at a loss as to what to do or say. "Oh, don't do that," he implored. "Come on, don't . . . Let me go get Ellie or your mom. Don't cry, Annie. I'll find him for you."

He didn't know how to comfort her. He went to her, thinking he could guide her to her sister, but as soon as he touched her shoulder, she leaned into his chest, and the tears turned into gut-wrenching sobs.

What the hell? Max put his arms around her and held her. "It'll be okay," he promised. "It'll be okay."

Ava was honking the horn nonstop, and Ellie went looking for Annie while her mother ran outside to tell Ava to stop making so much noise.

Ellie opened the office door and saw Max trying to console her sister. He was patting her back as she cried all over him. Ellie quietly pulled the door shut. Then tears came into her eyes. How could she not love this man?

Ava could damn well wait.

# TWENTY-THREE

The article about the garden party was in the local newspaper Friday morning. Ava was upset. She had requested that they run the piece on Saturday because more people read the *Winston Falls News* on weekends, not during the week.

The first line in the article gave Ellie chills. It stated that Ava's sisters — as in plural — were hosting the affair. And that meant that anyone who read the paper would know she was back in town.

Had Ava deliberately included her as a way of getting rid of what she called "vicious rumors"? Ellie hoped not because that would make Ava a colossal bitch.

She couldn't ask her because she and Annie had already left on a day full of spa treatments and errands.

Ellie was finishing her second glass of milk, watching the repairman and her father cross the backyard to get to the air conditioner. Her mother was sorting through mail at the table.

"Have you seen the article in the paper about the garden party?" Ellie asked.

"Yes, I did. It was quite nice, wasn't it?"

It was apparent she hadn't noticed the word *sisters,* and Ellie decided not to make an issue of it. She would just be adding to her mother's worries.

"The backyard looks beautiful," she said instead.

Claire beamed. "I thought the tent would make the yard look so much smaller, but I think it actually looks bigger now."

Max appeared in the doorway. "Are you ready to go?"

"Where are you going?" her mother asked, looking anxious. "You're not leaving Winston Falls, are you? You promised you'd stay, and Aunt Vivien and Aunt Cecilia will be so disappointed if they don't see you. They're arriving this afternoon."

"Mom, we're just doing some errands and meeting the agents Max has asked to help."

"Dressed like that?"

"What's wrong with the way I'm dressed?"

"Eleanor, you're wearing tattered jeans and a T-shirt, and those shoes . . ."

"I thought I'd show Max the falls. That's why I'm wearing my old tennis shoes."

"At least take a change of clothes. You don't want to embarrass Max in front of his friends."

"She could never embarrass me," Max said. He tilted his head toward the door.

Ellie kissed her mother on the cheek and whispered, "We'll be home in time to help with dinner."

Ellie assumed Max hadn't seen the article in the paper. She waited until they were on their way out of town to tell him.

He didn't take the news well. "Son of a . . ."

"Maybe no one will notice."

The look he shot her made her feel foolish. "Okay, but very few people read the local newspaper."

The muscle in his cheek twitched. That wasn't a good sign. Hoping to change the subject, she said, "Would you like to see the falls today? It's a little hike, but not too bad."

He shot her the look again. "What?" she demanded.

"We aren't on a vacation, sweetheart. I'm supposed to keep you alive, got that? And trampling through the woods with a picnic basket isn't part of my job description."

"I never said anything about a picnic basket," she snapped back. "And stop calling me 'sweetheart.' That's supposed to be a term of endearment. You growl the word."

His cell phone rang. She poked him in the arm. "If that's Simon, you'd better ask him."

"I will," he said.

Unfortunately, it wasn't Simon. It was Ben with more information about the missing eyewitness, Greg Roper.

Max finished the call and said, "Agent Hughes doesn't think Roper's been killed. He thinks he's running. Someone got to him and scared him."

"What happens now? Can they even hold the Landrys without witnesses?"

They discussed the possibilities for several minutes and ended up frustrated with no answers. "Ben said he'll call me later, after he's had a chance to talk to all the agents involved."

"Hughes will expect me to take the stand if the Landrys do go to trial someday. I'll have to tell what I saw, even though I can't point them out. Right?" Ellie asked.

He shook his head. "I don't know what the prosecutors will decide, but I'll do everything I can to keep you out of this. It's a wait-and-see game now."

Max was taking his time getting to his destination. He was on the highway for a little while, then took an exit and drove down a side road for several miles before getting back on the highway again. He watched the traffic ahead of them and in the rearview mirror as he drove. She knew he was making certain no one was following them.

He spotted a sign for a pharmacy at the next exit. "Want to stop there and get the pregnancy test?"

"Too close to home," she said.

He got the same response the next three times he asked. Finally, he said, "Are you going to buy this pregnancy test soon, or do you want me to drive to Miami?"

"You can stop at the next one," she said.

"What would you do if you found out you were pregnant?"

She didn't hesitate. "I'd have a baby."

"That's what Annie said."

"I'll help her any way I can."

"Would you tell the father?"

"Yes, of course I would. I would have the responsibility to tell him. Did you ask Annie that question?"

"No."

"She just took the bar exam."

He nodded, indicating that Annie had also mentioned that. How long had they talked? she wondered.

"Where are we meeting Agents Clark and

Hershey?"

"A restaurant called Hathaways. It's about a mile off the highway."

A sign for a national pharmacy chain appeared, and Max pulled into the parking lot. Ellie bought three pregnancy tests, each a different brand.

"Just to be sure," she told Max at checkout.

The clerk behind the counter, a stout woman with rosy cheeks and short, curly hair, gave Ellie her change and, looking at Max and then back at Ellie, said, "I'll be rooting for you."

Ellie smiled. "Thank you. I'm keeping my fingers crossed."

Once they were back in the car and on their way, Max said, "You're keeping your fingers crossed?"

"I didn't want to disappoint the woman."

He shook his head. "You're something else, you know that?"

"I bought dessert," she said and held up a Hershey bar and a Clark bar.

He laughed and shook his head again.

They reached the restaurant a few minutes later. They were early and had their pick of tables. Max chose one in the corner for more privacy. From where he sat, he could look out the window, and their backs were to the wall.

"Do you know Agents Clark and Hershey?" she asked.

"I've talked to them a couple of times, but I haven't worked with them. I've been told they're good," he added.

"How are they going to blend in?"

"You won't know they're there."

"Max, it's a small community. Every stranger sticks out."

"Stop worrying."

The waitress brought glasses of water and handed them menus.

His cell phone rang.

"If that's Simon . . ."

"It isn't," he said. "And stop obsessing about football."

She looked appalled. "That's un-American."

He answered the call on the fourth ring. "Agent Daniels."

He didn't say another word for several minutes but the look on his face told her the news wasn't good. When he put the phone back in his pocket, he turned to her.

"That was Spike," he began. "He said he got a call from a friend who runs a guns and ammo shop near Winston Falls. He told Spike that, about five minutes after he

opened the store, Evan Patterson walked in
and tried to buy a gun."

# TWENTY-FOUR

"This isn't bad news," Ellie insisted. "And don't give me that look. Now I know where Patterson is, and hopefully he'll come after me again, and you can arrest him."

"Ellie, he'll find a gun."

"Would he know how to get one from the street? Where to go? Who to talk to?" Agent Clark asked the questions. He and Agent Hershey had joined Ellie and Max just minutes after Max had talked to Spike.

Max had been right when he'd said the two agents could blend in. John Hershey was under six feet and slight of build, though muscular. Ellie guessed him to be a runner, maybe even a marathon runner. With his thick, wiry hair and glasses, he reminded her of a professor at her father's university. Pete Clark had a stocky physique and a balding head, and his jovial round face made him look like everyone's favorite cousin.

"This Patterson guy's mental, but that doesn't mean he's stupid," Hershey said.

Clark had a photo of Patterson and another of Willis Cogburn downloaded to his phone. Ellie looked at Cogburn's photo and thought he looked like a normal person. Certainly not a hired killer. But then, she thought, what do those men look like? What would be so different about them?

Her attention was drawn back to the conversation about Patterson when Max said, "He won't shoot to kill. He would try to kill anyone who is with her, but he likes using his fists. He'll want to wound her so she can't run. If he gets a chance, he'll try to beat her to death."

Ellie didn't disagree with Max's conclusions. Clark had read part of Patterson's file and so had Hershey. Both of them felt the same as Ellie. This was an opportunity to get him once and for all.

"If he has a gun and goes after her, we could put him away for years," Clark said.

"All right, we're looking for two men now. We've got their photos, and we all know what we need to do," Hershey said.

"Put them down," Clark answered. "Like rabid dogs. That's what I'd like to do."

"But you'll arrest them instead," Ellie said.

Max smiled at her. "You're the voice of

reason."

"It's my understanding you'll be leaving directly after the party, right?" Clark asked.

"I'm not leaving until Patterson is behind bars," Ellie vowed.

"Ellie . . . ," Max began.

She wouldn't let him finish his thought. "If I have to knock on his parents' door and taunt him to get him to attack me, I will. I want you to catch him and put him away. Please. I want this nightmare to end." Her voice shook with emotion, and she took a deep breath to calm down.

Hershey nodded. "Let's get this mother . . ."

"And Cogburn," Clark added.

Hershey agreed. "Maybe we'll get lucky and get him this weekend, too."

Ellie was quiet on the ride back to Winston Falls. Although it didn't show on her face, Max knew she was upset because she had ordered milk at the restaurant and downed it as though it were Pepto-Bismol.

"Do you have an ulcer?"

Ellie looked up with a quizzical expression. The question came out of the blue. "No."

"You drink a lot of milk."

"I like milk. It soothes my stomach."

"You ordered it right after you heard that Patterson tried to buy a gun."

"Yes, I did," she admitted.

Neither one of them said another word for a while, and then Max broke the silence. "Come on, Ellie. Tell me what's going on in your mind. I know you're worried."

Worried? That didn't even come close to describing the way she was feeling. "I want to stay in Winston Falls and catch Evan Patterson. You have no idea what it's like not knowing where he's been hiding, but now he's here, and I have an opportunity to draw him out. Hopefully, he'll do something that will get him arrested."

"That has to scare you."

"Seeing his face again will probably freak me out," she admitted. "But right now I'm not scared. You'll be there. You won't let him hurt me."

Her faith in him was humbling. "Damn right."

She crossed her legs and shifted in her seat as she turned toward him. "His parents have been enabling him and making excuses for him and blaming me for years," she said. "They're on record saying I'm the reason their son is tormented."

"I know, sweetheart. I read your file. I think it's time I had a little chat with Mr.

and Mrs. Patterson."

"Why would you go there? If Evan is hiding in their house, they'll lie and say he isn't. They'll do everything in their power to protect him."

"Probably," Max agreed.

"Then why would you go over there?"

"To put the parents on notice. They need to hear that their son is trying to buy a gun."

"I don't think it will make a difference."

The closer they got to Winston Falls, the more anxious she became. Her palms were sweaty and she was finding it difficult to breathe, signs of a post-traumatic disorder. Who could blame her? The name Patterson was synonymous with pain.

She wanted to drive him out of her thoughts, but each time she erased his name from her mind, the name Cogburn rushed in. Same game. Different player.

Seeing the distress in her eyes, Max reached over and took her hand.

His phone rang. It was Ben calling back. Max put the phone on speaker and set it on the console.

"Ellie's with me, Ben," Max said. "Tell us what's going on."

"Hughes thinks the Landrys are going to call off Cogburn," Ben said.

"Why?"

"Greg Roper," he answered. "No one knew about Greg Roper until he came forward. And now he's disappeared. The only logical explanation is that there's a leak. Someone's feeding the Landrys information about our investigation. We've already appointed a task force to find out who it is."

"And that means the Landrys know that Ellie couldn't identify them from the mug shots," Max concluded.

"That's right," Ben said. "According to Hughes, the Landrys now have no reason to get rid of Ellie. He thinks she'll be fine on her own."

"Has anyone found Cogburn yet?" Max asked.

"No."

"Then I'm not leaving her alone," he stated emphatically.

"I agree," Ben said. "I think Hughes is jumping the gun here."

After he'd ended the conversation, Ellie turned to Max. He was frowning.

"You think I'm still in danger from the Landrys?"

"I don't know," he admitted. "But I'm not letting you out of my sight until I know where Willis Cogburn is."

# Twenty-Five

The forecast for Saturday was gloomy. Rain showers were expected to develop in the early evening. The morning of the garden party, however, was sunny, and there wasn't a cloud in sight to mar the blue skies.

Ellie's parents were sitting at the kitchen table with William's aunts, Vivien and Cecilia, when she walked in with Max.

"I don't think it will rain tonight," William predicted.

"It wouldn't dare," Ellie said. "This is Ava's big night."

"No, dear, the wedding is her big night. This is her second big night," Claire said.

Ellie was about to laugh until she realized her mother was serious. "Does Ava have a list of big, bigger, and biggest?"

"Don't start, Eleanor."

William introduced Max to his aunts. He shook their hands and smiled while they talked over each other greeting him and telling him their plans for the day. He caught the words *museum* and *boutique,* nodded because they looked expectantly at him, and laughed out loud when Aunt Cecilia patted Ellie's hand and asked her how she was doing in school.

"You remind me of my late husband," Cecilia told Max.

"I was thinking he looks more like my late Edgar," Vivien said. "He was a handsome man."

Max wasn't sure how to respond, but Ellie saved him from having to say anything when she asked the aunts, "Did you have a restful evening? I hope you were comfortable upstairs."

"Oh yes," Vivien declared. "It was so nice of Annie to give up her room for us."

"It's such a lovely room," Cecilia interjected. "The new color is just beautiful."

Ellie shared a quick smile with Max, then said, "Where is Annie?"

"She left early this morning," her father said. "Poor thing looked exhausted. She was white as a ghost."

"She just took the bar," Ellie said. "She should be exhausted. She probably studied night and day for months."

"That's right. Of course, she's tired. She took that exam."

"Where did she go so early?" Ellie asked.

"Ava picked her up at eight, and Annie took her dress for the party with her."

"Why?"

"The hem was torn," her mother explained. "Ava has a seamstress on call for her boutique. She'll mend it for her."

"Shouldn't we get going, Claire?" Vivien asked.

The three women stood and headed to the door.

"We'll be back at four," her mother said. "We're deliberately going to be gone all day so that the cleaning people and the caterers Ava hired can get their work done. We'd only be in the way."

"Won't you come with us, Ellie?" Vivien asked. "We're going to have lunch at that new restaurant downtown. We'd love your company."

"I'm sorry. I can't," she said. "I've got too much to do," she lied.

"We'll bring you two a little treat," Cecilia promised.

Her aunt acted as though Ellie were still eleven years old, but she wasn't offended. "That would be nice."

"Do you have a dress to wear tonight?" her mother asked.

"Yes, I do." She actually had brought two

dresses, one that was periwinkle and a bit snug and another that was pink with a full skirt.

"Because we could take you to the boutique, and Ava could find something for you to wear."

"I have a dress, Mom," she repeated. "When will Annie be home?"

"Ava wants to make an entrance, and Annie will ride with her and John. They'll be here promptly at seven forty-five."

"The party starts at seven."

"Yes, that's right."

"Ava wants to be late?"

"Fashionably late," Claire explained. "That's what she told me."

"But it's her party."

"I mentioned that to her, dear."

"Shouldn't she be on time? And Annie's hosting the party. She certainly should be here to welcome guests."

"Ava has two sisters. You can welcome guests until Annie gets here."

"Aha," Ellie said. Of course. Now she could see the plan. Those vicious rumors would go away if Ellie greeted the guests and welcomed them to the party. Ellie would be letting everyone know that she approved of Ava and John. Oh yes, Ava had it all figured out.

"Aha, what?" her mother asked.

"Never mind."

Time to let it go, she decided. No more resentment. No more anger or embarrassment. Ava and John belonged together, and it was time for Ellie to be happy for them. She was never going to have a great relationship with her sister because they were so different, but she was okay with that. And she would try to get along.

"Tonight has to be perfect for Ava," Claire said.

Ellie knew her mother's comment was a warning. "Why are you frowning at me? I'm not going to do anything to ruin her perfect evening."

# TWENTY-SIX

The Pattersons weren't pleasant people.

After Hershey and Clark arrived at the Sullivan house late in the afternoon, Max gave them instructions and made Ellie promise she would stay with them, then walked the few blocks to the Patterson home.

The couple opened the door together, but neither invited Max to come inside. Resentment etched Mr. Patterson's face, and anger radiated from Mrs. Patterson.

Max showed them his badge and said, "My name is Agent Daniels, and I'm with the FBI."

"Why don't you people leave us alone?" Mr. Patterson demanded.

"I want to talk to you about your son."

The couple edged their way out onto the porch, and Mr. Patterson pulled the door closed behind him.

"What is it you want with him this time?"

he asked.

"First of all, I want to know where he is," Max said calmly.

"Why?" Mrs. Patterson asked in a gravelly voice. "So you can harass him again?"

"Or do you want to lock him away again?" Mr. Patterson asked. He folded his arms across his chest and glared at Max. "Evan hasn't done anything wrong, and I know the law. You can't touch him."

"He was a good boy until she came along," Mrs. Patterson said. Only the slightest hint of disappointment flashed across her face before the anger took over again. "We had such high hopes for him. He was going to make something of himself. He was so smart and clever. All the teachers told us so."

"She ruined his life, getting the police involved and all. He didn't mean any harm."

Max wanted to argue, to remind them that Ellie was eleven years old the first time their son attacked her, but he knew it was useless to point out the facts. They had already twisted them to fit their agenda, and nothing he could say would change their minds. They wanted to believe their son was a victim.

"I'm not here to talk about the past," Max said.

"We don't know where Evan is. We haven't seen him in months," Mr. Patterson insisted.

"If we did know, we wouldn't tell you," his wife muttered.

"Your son tried to purchase a gun yesterday," Max told them.

"I don't believe it," Mrs. Patterson scoffed. "You FBI agents always lie." She pulled a pack of cigarettes out of her pocket and elbowed her husband for his lighter.

"Did that woman call you and tell you the lie about a gun so you would come here and harass us?" Mr. Patterson demanded.

"We know she's back in town. We read it in the paper. She's behind this." Mrs. Patterson lit a cigarette and inhaled. "She won't rest until she's destroyed our boy." Smoke billowed out of her mouth as she spoke. "She ought to be the one locked up is what I think. I hope she gets what she deserves."

Max was through being diplomatic. "I'm putting both of you on notice. If your son gets hold of a gun, and you do nothing to stop him, you're as responsible as he is if someone gets hurt. I'll lock you up, too."

They gave no response to his threat, but as he was walking down their porch steps, he heard their front door slam.

# TWENTY-SEVEN

Clark and Hershey were in the apartment with Ellie. Max was unprepared for what he saw when he walked in. Hershey was shirtless and perched on the arm of the sofa while Ellie appeared to be rubbing his side. Clark was at the coffee table using Ellie's laptop.

"What the . . . ," Max began.

"You're back," Ellie said. She patted Hershey's shoulder. "Okay, you can put your shirt on. It's scar tissue."

"You're sure?" Hershey asked.

"I'm sure. It's all good."

Ellie went to Max and almost kissed him before she realized what she was doing. She took a step back and asked, "What were the Pattersons like?"

"They won't ever win parents of the year," he answered.

Clark closed the laptop. "I talked to your friend Sheriff Spike Bennett," he said.

"Strange name, but a nice guy," he continued. "He wanted you to know there's a gun shop close to a town called Lipton, and the owner isn't real reputable. Spike's been trying to shut him down, but so far no luck. He said that for the right amount of money Patterson could get anything he wanted. Bennett's on his way there now to talk to the owner, find out if Patterson came around yesterday."

"Do you think he'd tell him if he had?" Hershey asked the question.

"Patterson might not know about this gun store," Ellie suggested.

"Bennett wants to warn him, just the same. After he's finished in Lipton, Bennett will come here to help with surveillance."

"You won't have to worry about anything tonight, Ellie," Hershey assured. He buttoned his shirt and tucked it in his pants.

Ellie checked the time. "I need to get ready," she said. "Thanks for babysitting me."

Both agents, Max noticed, were smiling like idiots at her, but as long as they did their jobs, he didn't care if they were infatuated.

"Does it seem a little cold in here?" Clark asked.

Ellie's laughter followed her into the bath-room.

Thirty minutes later she was ready for the party. Max had put on a suit and tie and was tugging on it when she walked out. She looked stunning. She wore a pale pink dress and high-heeled sandals.

"Do I look all right?" she asked. "Max?"

He shook himself out of his stupor. "Yes, you look fine."

*Fine?* Ellie knew he wasn't one to embellish . . . but *fine?* "Thanks," she said. She'd spent a long time curling her hair just so, and she'd even put on makeup. All that for *fine?*

"You look nice," she said. "But your tie is crooked."

She crossed the room and stood in front of him while she adjusted the knot in his striped tie. Her perfume enveloped him, and all Max wanted to do was tear her dress off and make love to her.

"I hate ties," he said instead.

"I'd think you'd be used to them," she replied. "Don't you wear a suit and tie every day in Honolulu?"

"No, we wear khaki shorts, no shirts."

She laughed. "Where do you put your badge and gun?"

"Waistband of our shorts . . . or swim

trunks. We have to be prepared for anything."

"What do the female agents wear in Honolulu?"

"Bikinis," he answered with a straight face. "We don't get a whole lot of work done."

"I'm not nervous about tonight, so you can stop trying to put me at ease."

He looked at her skeptically.

She kissed his cheek. "Okay, I am a little nervous."

"Maybe I could think of something to take your mind off tonight."

"Like what?"

"Give me a few minutes."

Ellie's cell phone rang. She didn't recognize the number and almost didn't answer it.

"You need to find out who it is," Max insisted.

She answered the same way she had for years. "Dr. Sullivan."

The voice on the phone was deep. "No, I'm not going to the Colts."

Ellie's hands were still shaking from talking to Simon Daniels, the most spectacular quarterback of all time. Oh God, had she told him that? She couldn't remember what she'd said for the first minute or two, but she knew she'd gushed, then she had recovered and grilled him on the upcoming season.

It turned out that Simon was a bit of a hypochondriac, and for the next half hour it was quid pro quo. He answered a question she posed, and she then answered one of his. Some of his questions were hilarious, but she didn't laugh.

"No, that particular disease comes from a parasite found only in the waters of the Amazon, and, no, it isn't contagious."

She saw Max roll his eyes, and she shook her head at him.

Max finally took the phone from her when she held it out to him and said, "Simon wants to talk to his white brother."

"I carry a gun now," he reminded his brother. "So stop calling me that."

Ellie listened to the conversation and was shocked at the insults Max was hurling, but then she decided he was giving as good as he was getting. Brothers were so different from sisters. She doubted they whined the way Ava did.

Oh Lord, the party. She was supposed to be at the house fifteen minutes ago.

When she walked down the steps from the apartment, she was glad to see the weather was cooperating. Dark clouds hung overhead, and the air was stifling hot and muggy, but it wasn't raining. She thought it silly to plan a party outside this time of year, but she wouldn't share her opinion with Ava or her mother.

Clark and Hershey were checking the backyards on either side of the house and behind it. It was six o'clock when Ellie and Max walked into the kitchen. The house was dressed up with flowers everywhere and candles ready to be lit. Even the worn furniture in the living room looked brand-new because of the roses on the coffee table. Her parents and her aunts were upstairs getting dressed.

Max was being sweet. He gave her shoulder a supportive squeeze and went to the refrigerator to get her a glass of milk. The guests would be arriving soon, and she was ready. She took a couple of steps across the living room and stopped to look out the window.

And there he was . . . Evan Patterson . . . pacing on the sidewalk in front of her house. She froze, and so did he, and for at least two or three seconds they stared at each other.

Then he smiled, and she ran.

"He's here. He's here." She couldn't get her voice above a whisper, but Max understood what she was trying to tell him.

"Where?"

"Front," she whispered. "He's in front."

Max grabbed her and pulled her to the hall closet. He pushed her inside and said, "You stay here until I tell you it's okay to come out."

She saw him draw his gun as the door was slamming shut. Ellie was shaking violently now and couldn't catch her breath, hyperventilating even as she was sinking to the floor.

Anger came like a shot of adrenaline. She wanted to go after Patterson, to hit him and kick him, to hurt him the way he'd hurt her. She realized she was having crazy thoughts, but she didn't care. She would rather be furious than terrified.

She reached for the door handle and came to her senses. She strained to hear any noise, but the only sound was the running water from the showers upstairs.

*Be careful,* Max. *He's mean and dangerous and cunning.*

It seemed she waited an hour, but she knew her mind was playing tricks. It should be hot in the closet, she thought, but she was shivering.

Max finally opened the door. She threw herself into his arms. "Did you get him?"

"No," he answered. He could feel her trembling and hugged her. "Clark and Hershey are still looking, but Patterson vanished. Are you sure . . ."

She tried to push herself away from him. He wouldn't let her. "Okay, you're sure it was him."

"Yes. He was wearing black pants and a white shirt."

"Where were his hands?"

"I couldn't see them. Behind his back, I guess, or in his pockets. He smiled at me, Max."

"We'll get him," he promised.

"And then what? What can you do? It isn't illegal to walk in front of my house. I don't have a restraining order anymore, and that didn't help anyway. So far, Patterson hasn't done anything wrong."

"If he's gotten hold of a gun, I can take him in."

"You're going to have to find him first."

"Ellie, what are you doing in the closet?" Her father asked the question.

Max pulled her into the hall and draped his arm around her.

"Daddy, the thing is . . ." She was trying to think of a gentle way of telling him about Patterson.

Max was blunt. "Patterson was out front

359

on the sidewalk."

The smile on her father's face vanished, and anxiety took its place.

"Dad, this is a good thing. We have three agents here, and if Patterson will try something, they can get him and lock him up." She didn't mention the possibility that Patterson might have a gun. "They've got this covered. I saw him, but he left before I could tell Max. He'll come back."

"Maybe we should cancel the party," he said.

She tried to make light of the situation. "Are you kidding? I'm more afraid of Ava than Patterson."

"Should I tell your mother?" he asked, and before she could answer, he shook his head and said, "No, we won't worry her." He turned to Max. "If that maniac comes back, you'll get him. In the meantime, you watch out for my daughter."

Before long there were caterers and servers going in and out of the house. Max talked to the man in charge, found out how many employees were working for him, and made certain he saw each face and spoke to each one.

Approximately eighty guests were on their way to the house now. The backyard could easily handle the crowd, but there were places Patterson could hide if he got that far. Each entrance would be closely monitored. Spike had offered to watch the street in front of the house. He would arrive soon. Until then, Ellie's father stood by the front door. Clark and Hershey would monitor the backyard and both sides of the house, and Max would stay with Ellie.

The caterers' two vans were parked in the driveway, so the guests reached the backyard by following a brick pathway on the other side of the house. They passed under a trellised arch and entered the garden between two tall planters filled with fresh-cut flowers.

Some of the older guests didn't want to take the roundabout way to the back but instead cut through the house. William ended up being a doorman. He greeted them at the door and escorted them through the house and out to the party, sometimes stopping in the kitchen for a conversation before the doorbell rang again and he was interrupted. As worried as he was about Patterson crashing the party, he was able to relax a little knowing that Ellie was safe with Max. He had no doubt that Max would give his life to protect her, though he prayed to God Patterson would be captured and led away peacefully.

While her father greeted guests inside, Ellie stood outside on the lawn welcoming the new arrivals. She felt as though she had said, "So happy to see you" and "So pleased you could come" at least a hundred times. And her hand had been grabbed and patted more than that. She heard, "You poor thing" and "What a heartbreak this must be for you" from some of her mother's friends, and "What a trouper you are" and "You're so brave" from others. Apparently, everyone in town had heard that Ava had stolen Ellie's fiancé.

Max stood behind her. When one woman patted Ellie's hand and said, "Don't you give up on love," Ellie heard him cough, no doubt to cover his laughter.

Ellie's mother was having a wonderful time, mingling among friends. Ellie couldn't remember when she had seen her looking so radiant and happy. Her father walked out the back door with Mrs. Webster, their elderly neighbor, on his arm. He helped her down the steps and smiled across the lawn at his wife before turning around and going back inside. This was as it should be, Ellie thought. Their daughter was getting married. It was a happy time.

Minutes later, Max whispered in her ear, "Spike Bennett just arrived. He'll keep an eye on the front now. I'll tell your father he can come outside."

At seven thirty the violin began to play. Aunt Cecilia and Aunt Vivien were holding court inside the tent and having a fine time. It was much cooler there because the tent company had thought to bring two small air conditioners. Each had been strategically placed near the back of the tent.

Once the stream of new guests began to dwindle, Ellie walked around the lawn chatting with old acquaintances and checking on the caterers. Max was never far away. If the opportunity arose, she introduced him as a friend of the family. Clark and Hershey were barely noticeable. Every so often she would catch sight of them strolling around the perimeter of the lawn, watching for any signs of danger. They were so inconspicuous, no one would have guessed their reason for being there.

Aunt Cecilia motioned to Ellie and asked her if she would please fetch her wrap. She was feeling the chill from the air conditioner but was too comfortable to move.

"She just wants to show off her new shawl," Vivien said.

Cecilia nodded. "It is pretty, and I rarely get a chance to wear it. It's on the chair in our bedroom. Be a dear and get it for me. I hate to move."

"What time is it?" Vivien asked. "Shouldn't Ava and John be here? And where's Annie?"

Ellie checked the time. "Knowing Ava, she'll be here in five minutes on the dot."

"Hurry then. You don't want to miss her entrance."

Ellie was happy for a break. Max followed her into the house. While Ellie ran upstairs, he went to check the front door. He was pleased to find that her father had locked it. He stood at the bottom of the stairs waiting for her when he heard the scream.

Ellie didn't get as far as the bedroom. The linen closet door was wide-open. When she reached to pull it closed, Evan Patterson sprang at her from behind it. She saw the gun in his left hand and the loathing in his eyes. She screamed and shoved the door as hard as she could. It caught him in the side, and that gave her a second to get away.

He was strong, terribly strong. As she turned to run, he grabbed her arm and yanked her toward him. His hand felt like a vise, squeezing hard enough to make her think he could snap her bone. It was impossible to get free. She saw his fist coming toward her. She kicked him in the shin with the sharp heel of her sandal, then kicked him again in the thigh. It didn't stop him.

He aimed for her jaw and would have shattered it, but she lowered her head just as his fist struck. The side of her forehead took the blow, stunning her. The ring he was wearing cut into her. She flinched from the searing pain.

She was kicking and screaming when Max pulled him off of her. Her dress tore because Patterson wouldn't let go. As strong as Patterson was, Max easily lifted him and threw him into the wall, but fury gave Patterson new strength.

Max was trying to get the gun away from him and at the same time shield Ellie. Patterson rolled, then went flying down the stairs. Max pulled his gun and aimed, just as Patterson turned and fired one shot at them before ducking around the corner and disappearing. Max flew down the stairs after him, and Patterson shot again. The bullet went wild, hitting the ceiling as he was running out the back door.

With a diving leap, Max tackled him to the ground, but Patterson managed to get two more shots off. The bullets shattered one of the flowerpots, sending ceramic shards, like missiles, into the air. With his knee slammed into Patterson's spine, Max forced the gun away. Clark grabbed it and helped restrain him while Hershey ran forward, pulling handcuffs from his back pocket.

Screaming, the party guests ran for their lives.

In front of the house, Ava had just stepped out of her car, too impatient to wait for John to come around and open the door for her. She adjusted her skirt, fluffed her hair, and took a step toward the sidewalk.

The stampede all but knocked her off her feet.

# TWENTY-EIGHT

The aftermath wasn't pretty.

Ava stood in the center of the backyard surveying the damage. She didn't hear the thunder and was still standing there when the skies opened up and rain poured down on her. When she walked into the kitchen, she was soaked through.

John got a towel and tried to pat her arms dry, but she pushed his hand away. She was shaking with outrage.

"Where is she?" she demanded in a shout that vibrated through the house and could have registered at least a seven on the Richter scale.

Her mother sat at the table with her head in her hands as Ava ranted her accusations that Ellie had deliberately set out to ruin her party. After listening to the ridiculous outburst for several minutes, Claire raised up and said, "Ava, stop talking and go home. You're giving me a headache."

Ava's hand flew to her throat. "Mother, this was supposed to be my night. And John's," she added. "How could you take Ellie's side?"

"I haven't taken any side," her mother said. "You don't know what happened before you got out of your car," she pointed out. "You shouldn't blame anyone."

"Oh, I know who to blame. Ellie."

"Stop shouting. I know you're upset —"

"Upset does not begin to describe what I'm feeling."

"This wedding has turned you into a crazy woman."

"I just wanted it to be perfect. What's wrong with that?" She burst into tears and moved into John's arms to let him comfort her. "And the yard was so pretty after the flowers were delivered . . . and the tent was perfect and . . ." She suddenly pushed away from her fiancé. "Where is she?" she shouted.

"In the bathroom," her mother relented. "Max and your father are tending to the cut on her forehead."

Ava stormed out of the kitchen, rushed past her aunts, who were sitting on the sofa enjoying slices of cake, and ran down the hallway, leaving puddles in her wake. She tried to get past her father, who was inadvertently blocking the bathroom door.

Ellie had already cleaned the cut with disinfectant from her father's first-aid kit and was now sitting on the side of the tub holding her hair back while Max applied Steri-Strips. He wasn't doing a good job because his hands were shaking. He was still so damned angry that Patterson had touched her, he could barely speak. Thoughts of what could have happened were racing through his mind. What if he had stayed outside? Patterson could have killed her before Max heard her scream.

"Max . . . ," Ellie began.

"Hold still."

"I am holding still. I'm a physician. Let me —"

"No, I need to do this."

Ellie had been holding her hair back so long, her arm was going to sleep. She didn't complain, though. The look of anguish on Max's face made her want to comfort him, but she knew he would have none of it. He felt he had failed her.

"Daddy, could you give Max and me a moment alone?"

"You're still bleeding," Max told her.

Her father put the first-aid kit in Ellie's lap and pulled the door closed behind him. Ellie heard Ava shouting and quickly got up to lock the door. She ignored Ava's pounding on the door as she took the Steri-Strips from Max and applied them to the cut. It took her three seconds to close the wound. Then she turned to him.

"Thank you."

He glared back at her, still angry. "I messed up."

"Thank you."

"What the hell are you thanking me for? Stop that. Now isn't the time —"

Ellie kissed his cheek, then his jaw. "Thank you," she whispered, "for saving my life and for catching him." She rubbed her lips over his. "Now you say, 'You're welcome.' "

"Ellie, you could have been killed. I should have —"

"Thank you."

He realized they were back where they'd started. "You're gonna keep this up until I say, 'You're welcome.' "

"No, until you kiss me."

He gently wrapped his arms around her, whispered, "You've got blood in your hair," and kissed her. Her mouth opened under his.

All the while, Ava was banging on the door, threatening everything short of murder.

When Max finally lifted his head, he said,

"Want to borrow my gun?"

"You can't hide in there forever, Ellie," Ava shouted.

"Might as well get this over with," she said.

Max got in front of her and opened the door. He backed Ava up by simply walking into her. She didn't have a choice.

The aunts were horrified by Ellie's condition. Her torn dress was splattered with blood, and the hair around her wound was matted and bloody.

"Come sit with us," Aunt Cecilia said, patting the cushion between Vivien and her.

Ellie obeyed and smiled as each aunt tried to comfort her.

Their sympathy enraged Ava. "I'm the victim here," she cried out.

"I don't see any blood on you," her mother snapped. She sat down in the wingback chair next to the sofa.

"Claire, the cake is delicious," Cecilia said.

"Where's Annie?" Ava demanded. "She'll take my side."

"She's changing her clothes, and for heaven's sake, there isn't any side to take."

Hershey motioned to Max. A minute later, Ellie looked over her shoulder to see the two men standing in the kitchen. Max had his hands in his pockets and was nodding every now and then at what Hershey was telling him.

As soon as Max walked back into the living room, William blurted, "This is all my fault. I left the front door unlocked when I was showing guests through the house. That's how he got inside. Before Spike arrived, he hid upstairs and waited. That's what he did, and it's all my fault."

"Who hid upstairs?" Ava was trying to follow the conversation.

"Evan Patterson. He got into the house with a gun, and he waited upstairs."

Ava was stunned. "Why didn't anyone tell me? I heard someone say Ellie was in trouble, but I didn't know —"

"You've been ranting and raving in the backyard for the last half hour," Ellie said. "No one could get a word in edgewise."

Claire turned to her husband. "You can't blame yourself, William."

"That's right, Dad," Ellie agreed. "You need to focus on the good news. Evan Patterson is on his way to lockup, and Max told me that, because he had a gun and tried to kill me and a federal agent, he's not going to get out for a long, long time, if ever."

Her father's spirits lifted. "Yes, that's true. I'll admit not knowing where he was hiding was a constant worry."

Ava slumped down in a chair. John kissed

her forehead and announced that he was going to eat some dinner. The kitchen looked like a smorgasbord.

"Every time . . . ," Ava grumbled. "It always becomes about you, Ellie. Every time. I'm getting married, but tonight wasn't for me. I swear I think you planned it."

Always the drama queen, Ellie thought. She felt a burst of irritation and said, "That's right, Ava. I planned the entire thing. I called Evan Patterson, and I said, 'Listen, Evan honey, go get a gun, sneak into my parents' house, and hide upstairs. I'll let you punch me again and try to kill me so that Ava's party will be ruined.' "

"Sarcasm isn't appreciated, young lady," her mother said.

Ava looked defeated. Her head fell forward, and her shoulders drooped. "Every time . . ."

"Oh, for God's sake," Ellie said. "Okay, Ava. I'm sorry. I'm sorry I ruined your party. I really am. Everything was beautiful. You planned it perfectly."

Her sister perked up a little. "I did, didn't I?"

"Yes," Ellie said. Her head was starting to throb, her nerves were shot, and she was beginning to tremble in the aftershock of what she had been through. "Everything was gorgeous."

"Thank you for admitting you ruined it," Ava sniffed.

"Yes, I did, and I'm sorry," she said for the third time.

"I'll forgive you if you'll just promise me one thing," Ava said.

"Anything."

"Promise me you'll stay away from my wedding."

# TWENTY-NINE

Placated by Ellie's apology, Ava and John went home.

"You need to get some rest, Ellie," her mother said.

"I will," she promised. "But I want to go upstairs and say good night to Annie first."

She was surprised she got dizzy when she stood, but she was certain no one noticed. She didn't take the stairs two at a time as she usually did and even held on to the banister to keep her balance.

Annie was sitting in the middle of the bed with the unopened pregnancy kit.

"Shut the door," she whispered.

Ellie quickly did as she asked, then sat down across from her sister. "You haven't taken the test yet?"

Annie shook her head. "Once I do . . ."

"Yes?"

"I can't undo it. I'll know."

"You need to know."

375

She nodded. "But what if I am? I don't have a job, and I have student loans to repay. It's a little overwhelming."

"If you are pregnant, do you want the baby?"

No hesitation at all. "Of course I want the baby."

"You aren't alone, Annie. You know I'll help you. You can move in with me. And there's the father," she said. "You should tell him."

"I'm such a screwup."

"No, you're not."

"You don't understand. I don't know where he is. I went a little bonkers, I guess. If I tell you something, will you promise not to be shocked?"

"What?"

"I'd never . . . you know . . ."

"What?" she asked again.

"Patterson scared me, and I didn't want to have anything to do with any man. I wouldn't let myself . . ."

"I see. I'm not shocked," she said. "So the baby's father was the first man you've slept with?"

Annie nodded. "Four months. That's how long we were together. It was . . . raw animal magnetism at first, I guess. I can't explain it."

"I know what you mean. Trust me, I do."

"It wasn't just the sex, though," she explained. "He was perfect. He was kind and considerate. We had so much in common. He loved the same things I did, and we could sit for hours and hours talking."

"So what happened?" Ellie asked.

Tears streamed down Annie's cheeks. "I don't know. We'd spent a terrific weekend together at the beach. He left my apartment Monday morning, and I never heard from him again. No call . . . nothing."

"What do you know about him?"

"He's a Navy Seal," she said. "I thought maybe he got a call from his commander and had to leave on a mission or something, but if that was the case, why didn't he call, or leave a note, or at least text me? He made me feel like a whore," she whispered. Tears clouded her eyes as she added, "I really did screw up."

"No, you didn't."

"We used protection," she said. "But I guess it isn't always dependable."

"Have you tried to get hold of him?"

"Yes. I tried calling him, but he didn't answer. I even left messages for him, but he hasn't responded. Nobody will tell me anything." She wiped a tear away. "If he cared about me at all, he would have left some word."

"What are you going to do?"

"I talked to Max, and he's going to try to find him for me."

"And when he does?"

Annie straightened her shoulders. "If I'm pregnant, I'll tell him because he's the father, and he deserves to know, but I'll make it clear I want nothing from him."

"You're emotional now," Ellie said. "Take the test tomorrow morning and find out."

"I could take it now."

"Yes, but your hormone levels will be higher in the morning," she said. "Or do one test now and another tomorrow morning. Either way."

Ellie tried to get more information about the man, but Annie didn't want to talk about him.

"You'll take the test first thing in the morning, then?"

"Yes, I absolutely will," she promised.

The sisters spent the next hour catching up. They talked about work, the people they knew, even Ava's wedding.

Ellie stood. "I need a shower and a bed," she said with a yawn. "I'm beat. I'll see you in the morning."

"You're leaving Winston Falls?"

"Yes."

Annie nodded. She watched Ellie open the door and then said, "It's funny really."

"What is?" she said, turning back.

"I was always the good girl."

"You still are."

## THIRTY

Max was waiting for Ellie downstairs. They said good night to her parents and her aunts and went up to the apartment. Max had left the window unit on low, and the bedrooms and hall were quite pleasant. The kitchen and the living room, however, were sweltering.

Ellie tripped out of her clothes, tossed the bloody and torn dress into the trash can, and got into the shower. She stood under the cool water with her eyes closed and tried to get her muscles to relax. She washed her hair, being careful to scrub around the cut, but she didn't bother to blow it dry. She brushed it over her shoulders, put on her cotton nightgown, her moisturizer and body lotion, and was ready for bed.

The storm outside had picked up. Lightning lit up the bedroom, followed by loud claps of thunder. Rain pelted the windows.

Ellie didn't ask Max if she could sleep

with him. She pulled the sheet back and slid into bed beside him. He was on his stomach, one arm over the side of the bed, sound asleep. His gun, holster, and badge were on his bedside table. She rolled over to glance at the alarm clock and was shocked to see that it was after midnight. She closed her eyes. It had never taken her more than a minute or two to fall asleep, but tonight was different. Ten minutes passed, then ten more, and she was still wide-awake. This certainly was different for her.

Ellie replayed the day's events, but when she got to Patterson, she felt her heart pounding in her chest. She took several deep, calming breaths. The threat was over; he was locked up and couldn't bother anyone. This, too, was different. She could go anywhere and do anything now, couldn't she?

Not quite. There were the Landrys and the possibility that a man named Cogburn might come after her.

And then there was Max. He was going back to Honolulu, and she would probably never see him again. It was for the best, she decided. He'd be safer there where people like Patterson weren't shooting at him. Ellie knew she wasn't being rational, but she was so rattled inside, she couldn't think straight. Was she reacting to Patterson's attack or was it the realization that Max was leaving?

No-brainer, she decided. It was Max. Ellie wanted to cry. She'd told him not to get attached to her, and look what she'd done. She'd fallen in love with him. So not acceptable.

She had to distance herself, or she'd become a blubbering idiot when he left. If she continued to lie there thinking about him, she'd start weeping now. She swung her legs over the side of the bed and tried to get up. Max stopped her.

"Can't sleep?" he asked as he pulled her down beside him.

"No, I can't."

"Come here." His voice was warm and husky. He covered her with his body and began to nuzzle the side of her neck. He rubbed her arms, then moved to her sides. "Your skin's cold."

As he moved against her, his chest grazed her breasts, and the pleasure was so intense, she moaned. Ellie threaded her fingers through his hair and pulled him toward her. His mouth took absolute possession, their tongues wild as they mated.

Max wanted to savor the feel of her, and when she wrapped her legs around his and moved seductively against his arousal, his mouth covered hers again, and he thrust inside her. Their lovemaking was wild, both of them losing control. Ellie screamed his name when the sensations began to spiral. Her orgasm lasted longer than his, and he held her tight in his arms until she recovered.

The scent of their passion clung to them, and they were both soaked with perspiration. Max could feel her heart pounding under his. He kissed her chin and lifted up to ask her if she was okay. Words weren't necessary. Ellie was asleep.

# THIRTY-ONE

Annie wouldn't take the test until Ellie arrived.

"What took you so long?"

"It's nine o'clock," Ellie said. "And I had to pack and change the sheets and help get everything in the car."

"Are you riding with Max?" she asked.

"Yes."

"But didn't you have a rental car? Isn't that how you got here?"

"Agent Clark took it last night. He'll return it to the rental company. Now stop stalling."

Annie grabbed the pregnancy kits and went into the bathroom down the hall. Ellie waited in her bedroom. She could hear the aunts chatting downstairs. Even with all the commotion, they seemed to be having a good time.

Ellie kept checking the time. Five minutes passed, then five more. No pregnancy test took ten minutes. She knew Annie was getting up her nerve. Just when Ellie was about to go get her, the bedroom door opened, and Annie walked in. She quietly shut the door behind her.

As soon as Ellie saw the smile on her face, she said, "Okay, you're not pregnant. I know it's selfish of me, but a tiny part of me was hoping you were."

"I am pregnant," she said, and she was smiling about it.

"You're going to be a great mother," she whispered.

"And you'll be a wonderful aunt. Ellie, did you mean it when you said I could live with you? For a little while, anyway?"

"Of course, I meant it, and not just for a little while. I'd love to help raise my niece or nephew."

Ellie told her what prenatal pills to take and what she could do to help with morning sickness.

"Are you going to tell Mom and Dad?"

"Of course," Annie said. "But not until after the wedding."

"What about Ava?"

"After her honeymoon. She'll be there for me, too," Annie said.

Ellie wasn't so sure, but she kept her opinion to herself. The bond between twins was different from the bond between mere sisters. Ava used to boast that she and Annie were telepathic, which Ellie thought was ridiculous, but they did have a strange connection as children and could sometimes communicate with each other without speaking. But if they were so alike, how could Annie grow up to be so sweet and Ava such a viper?

"Max is waiting," Ellie said.

"What about Max? I really like him," Annie said.

Ellie understood what she wanted to know and decided not to mince words. "I do, too, but . . ."

"But what?"

"He's not looking for anything long-term."

Ellie was walking out the door when Annie said, "One last question and I won't nag you about him again."

"Yes?"

"Are you in love with him?"

She sighed. "Yes."

Her parents walked Ellie and Max to their car. Ellie had lipstick on both cheeks from her aunts' kisses. They thought they would be seeing her at the wedding, and she didn't tell them she wouldn't be back that soon.

Max backed out of the drive, and Ellie watched her parents' faces as they waved good-bye.

"They look relieved," she said.

Max had to agree. "They don't have to worry about Patterson any longer."

"That's true, but they also don't have to worry about me ruining Ava's wedding."

"Now that Patterson is out of the picture, how could you ruin it?" he asked. He turned the corner and headed for Highway 169.

"I don't know. Something would happen, and she'd blame me," she said. "Max, when we get to St. Louis, will you go back to Honolulu?"

"Yes. I have to get back right away. Are you going to miss me?"

"No, I'll be too busy."

Ellie thought she'd handled herself okay. Her voice hadn't quivered when she'd asked him if he would be leaving, and she thought she'd been very calm and collected after he'd answered. She was getting a little too good at not telling the truth.

# THIRTY-TWO

When Willis Cogburn had first arrived in Winston Falls he thought he'd found the perfect spot for the ambush. It took several days to convince him otherwise.

He'd come prepared with a high-powered rifle, a couple of his favorite guns, and his surveillance equipment in the trunk of his rental car. It hadn't taken much finesse to find out that Dr. Sullivan was going to Winston Falls for a wedding. As soon as he'd gotten the information, he'd rented a car under a fake name and started driving.

Once he reached the small town, he checked into the Rosewood Inn under another false name and slept ten hours. Then he got down to business. He located where Dr. Sullivan's parents lived and spent the better part of the day sitting in his car a block away watching the house. He didn't see any sign of her until a car pulled into her driveway, and she came running out.

She obviously knew the man who got out of the car. She threw her arms around him. At first, Cogburn thought he was her boyfriend, but then he saw the gun at his side. And when the man walked up the porch steps and turned slightly, Cogburn saw the badge clipped to his belt. He didn't need his binoculars to know that badge. It belonged to an FBI agent.

A text gave Cogburn answers a few minutes later. It told him that an FBI agent was on his way to Winston Falls to guard Ellie Sullivan.

Cogburn knew he had to find a way to get her alone, and that wasn't going to be easy with an FBI agent shadowing her. He needed time to think about it and to come up with a plan. He started his car and drove around the town for a little while, then stopped in a fast-food place for a hamburger.

He needed to get the lay of the land first, he realized. He started his car and drove back to her neighborhood, looking for possible places to hide, spots where he could get a good shot. Nothing satisfied him.

Baseball cap low on his forehead, he parked the car at the corner of the Sullivans' block and got his surveillance equipment out of the trunk. He wasn't worried he'd be spotted using it because it was just a small earpiece. Anyone walking by would think he was using a Bluetooth. It was the first time he'd used this new earpiece, and he was impressed. According to the literature, he should be able to hear whispers as far as two blocks away. The ad hadn't exaggerated. Willis adjusted the magnification, sat back, and sipped on a limeade while he listened. A woman carrying a grocery bag walked up the sidewalk toward him, so he dropped his head and pretended to be talking. She smiled as she continued on.

For the first hour, Willis was able to catch only snippets of the conversation inside the house. He was thinking about getting some dinner when he got lucky. An upstairs window in the Sullivan house was open, and the voices of the people inside began to come through loud and clear. He heard an older man's voice talking about the falls and how Ellie should take Max to them. Cogburn assumed Max was the FBI agent because he knew Sullivan's first name was Ellie.

All right, he was in business. He hadn't found a place to hide near the Sullivan house, but maybe he had discovered something even better. Now he just needed to find out where the falls were.

■ ■ ■ ■

The people of Winston Falls were proud of their town. Each time he stopped for gas and food, he was asked if he'd had time to visit the falls yet. "Everyone does," he was told. "Why, you can't come to Winston Falls and not go to the crystal clear water."

Willis promised all the friendly townspeople he met that, yes, he would go to the falls.

He made good on his promise. It turned out the natural wonder was everything he'd been told and much more, for it was at the falls that he found the perfect spot for the ambush.

He expected Dr. Sullivan and the FBI agent to appear at any moment. She'd want to show him the town's pride and joy, right?

Wrong. For two long days and nights Willis sat cross-legged in the brush with his high-powered rifle in his lap, waiting. He wasn't alone. Hundreds of gnats and mosquitoes kept him company. There were also hordes of teenagers taking turns having sex behind the waterfall. Willis guessed the kids believed the water hid them from view, and he wondered why they hadn't realized that, if they could see out, anyone walking by could see in. One teenage boy brought two different girls to the falls, at different times, of course.

Willis felt as though he were watching porn, bad porn, with lots of grunting and groaning. He would have left and formulated another plan if the spot he'd chosen hadn't been the perfect place to kill someone. The noise from the water crashing down into the pool below would mask the sound of the rifle. And he was well hidden. Three teenagers walked right past him and never saw him.

He had a lot of time to think while he waited, mostly about his little brother, George. He missed the stupid kid. He'd told the Landrys that George was too young and not to entice him into their dirty business. They'd ignored him, and George was so eager to impress and so foolishly impatient, he'd gone and gotten himself killed.

George and he had such grand plans. They'd wanted to start some kind of business together. Nothing big, maybe just a pack-and-ship kind of place, but something legit. A stint in prison had been hard on Willis, and he didn't think he could go back inside again. George would never have made it inside. He was too soft, too childlike.

Going straight proved to be impossible

now. Once the Landrys had their tentacles around him, he couldn't get away. They knew the day he was released and contacted him that evening. "Welcome back," Cal Landry had gushed.

The money was too good to pass up. A hundred thousand to pop the doctor. Who could turn that down?

He thought it would be so easy, but the second day of being eaten alive by bugs changed his plans. He had to find another way to get her. But where? He knew he could get the doctor in St. Louis, but why wait? Why not get her here in her hometown where there was less law enforcement? He'd come to the conclusion that he might have to kill the FBI agent assigned to her as well, and that thought gave him chills. He'd get the needle in his arm for sure if he got caught.

Prison had changed him. It hadn't hardened him; it had made him fearful.

Willis finally came up with a new plan. He went over it several times until he was satisfied it would work, then he got up, zipped the rifle in the duffel bag with his two guns, and headed for his car. It was time to get his audio surveillance equipment out again. He'd driven around the area enough times to know that there was only one road anyone could take from Winston Falls to the airport. Now he just needed to find out when they'd be on it.

His cell phone chirped indicating he had a text. "Number unknown," he read, and that meant the Landrys. It was a one-word text: "Cancel."

He sat in the car for several minutes while he considered his options. The Landrys had already put half the money in the secret account. They'd want it back, and that just wasn't fair. After all the preparation he'd done? Then there was George. Cal and Erika had gotten his brother killed. Hell, no. He wasn't going to give them any money back. As far as he was concerned, he hadn't seen the text. He'd do the job and keep the money.

# THIRTY-THREE

Ellie watched the scenery out of her side window as Max drove around the curves of the worn two-lane road.

"Do we have plane tickets? Clark told me he was taking care of it, but — ," Ellie began.

"Yes, we do. You'll be sleeping in your own bed tonight."

Max saw a glint of steel out of the corner of his eye when they rounded another curve.

"We're near the falls," she said. "If there were time —"

"Down! Get your head down!"

Max shouted the command as he swerved the SUV to get out of the line of fire. Cogburn leapt onto the road, lifted his rifle, and fired two shots. Max recognized the high-powered rifle as he swerved again. "The son of a bitch is trying to hit the gas tank. Must think he can blow us up."

Ellie was amazed at how calm he sounded.

The side of her face rested on his thigh. She was trying not to knock the gearshift.

The third shot hit the left back tire, and at the speed they were going, it was nearly impossible to control the vehicle.

"Hold on, sweetheart. We're going off-road."

The SUV was spinning, and Ellie thought they were going to roll, but Max knew what he was doing. Within seconds the SUV had righted itself, and they were headed into the woods.

He slammed on the brakes, got Ellie's seat belt off and his own, and said, "Let's go."

Max threw his door open and pulled her out behind him. They both ran flat out, ducking under branches and leaping over scrub. Max stopped suddenly, motioned for Ellie to get down, and then pushed her back so that the branches concealed her. He put his hand up to tell her to stay still. And then he waited, crouched in front of her, listening to every little sound.

Ellie tried not to make any noise and to control her breathing. If Cogburn followed their tracks, he would find them. She remained motionless and silent.

How long had they waited? She didn't have any idea, but her legs were going numb, and she was trying to ignore the knot in her calf. How could Max stay in this position without moving a muscle for so long?

A twig snapped. Where had the sound come from? She thought the left, but Max sprang up and fired to the right, three shots in rapid succession as he moved forward, running toward his target.

He got Cogburn with the third shot. The hit man tried to get back to his car, but he had only made it to Max's SUV when he collapsed and began to scream. He wasn't given any sympathy. Max grabbed the rifle and tossed it into the back of the car, then squatted down next to Cogburn. "You're in a hell of a fix here," he said.

"I need a doctor," Willis cried. "I'm bleeding bad."

"You just tried to shoot a doctor."

Ellie ran to the car and got gloves out of her purse, nudged Max out of her way, and knelt down beside the man who had wanted to kill her. Willis's eyes were wide with terror as Ellie pushed his hands away to check the damage.

"The bullet went through," she said.

She got up and went back to the SUV to find something she could wrap around the wound until Willis could get to a hospital. She ended up using an old T-shirt and the only dress she had left. She wadded the shirt into a ball to apply pressure, then tore the dress into strips to hold it in place.

"There isn't any more I can do for him."

"I'm dying?" Cogburn began to wail.

Ellie knelt behind him now and was about to answer him when Max said, "You'd better hope you're dying because, if you're not, you're going away for life."

"No, I can't go back to prison. I can't."

"How about a deathbed confession?" Max asked. He was still so angry, he wanted to kill the bastard with his bare hands. He doubted Ellie would let him get away with that.

"This is all the Landrys' fault. It's because of them my brother's dead, and now I'm gonna be dead, too."

"The Landrys didn't fire that rifle. You did."

Ellie pulled off her gloves and reached for her cell phone. She was going to call 911, but Max gave her another number.

"Hershey should still be in Winston Falls. Tell him to send an ambulance."

The agent answered on the first ring. He told her he was at the hospital with the sheriff's deputy and Evan Patterson, and that he would send the ambulance right away.

"Did you know he was at the hospital?"

Ellie asked. She bent over Willis and checked his pulse. She didn't try to comfort him.

"Patterson was complaining of chest pain."

"What . . . ?"

"And they're required to provide treatment."

Ellie's shoulders sagged. "So I'll have to see him again."

"You're not going near him."

"Has he been there all night?"

Max nodded. "Handcuffed to a bed in ICU."

Willis started crying again. "I can't go back to prison. I just can't."

"Will you testify in court, tell the judge the Landrys hired you to kill Dr. Sullivan and Agent Goodman?"

"No. They hired my brother to kill Goodman. I was supposed to kill the doctor." He looked up at Ellie. "It's nothing personal."

"Yes, it is," she snapped. "It's very personal."

"I can't testify against them. I wouldn't last a day."

"Then you're going to prison."

Willis started screaming again. "This hurts bad."

Max got up and pulled Ellie to her feet.

He had to raise his voice to be heard over Willis's sobs. "I'm going to change the tire. You're coming with me."

"The SUV is ten feet away."

"You're still coming with me. I don't want you close to him."

"I want to make a deal. I want a deal," Willis pleaded.

Max looked down at him with disgust in his eyes. "What can you give me?"

"There's a shipment coming in from Singapore. Over a thousand guns with enough ammo to cover Iowa. Grenades, too. All sorts of crap. Cal had me on speakerphone, and I heard him tell Erika how big the buy was going to be. Cal likes to brag. I think he forgot I was still on the line. Maybe, anyway. But I know where it's going down. Get me a deal. I want witness protection."

Max kept his reaction contained. Son of a bitch, he thought. Maybe they could get the Landrys once and for all. If Cogburn was telling the truth.

"You don't talk to anyone about this," Max ordered. "You understand?"

"Okay, I won't," he groaned. "You better not talk to your people either. There's a leak, and if the guy running the investigation hears about me, someone in his office will tell the Landrys, and I'm a dead man."

He started crying again. "I want something for pain. Can I get a deal?"

"I'll see what I can do."

Willis was curled up in a fetal position. His gasps were pathetic as he moaned, "You don't have to worry about the doctor. Landrys called off the hit. I was going to act like I didn't get the text because I knew they'd want their money back, and I could never get away from them. I was going to use the money to run. Honest."

"They paid up front?"

"Half," he said. His voice was getting weaker. "I can't take this pain. It's hurting bad."

A few seconds later, Willis passed out.

Ellie had just pulled the jack from the back of the SUV but dropped it on the ground and ran back. "What did you do to him?"

Max shook his head. "I didn't do anything. He passed out."

"The wound isn't bad," she said. "He'll be in and out of surgery in under an hour."

"If he was in a trauma center, maybe, but this is Winston Falls."

"I'm sure the surgeons here know what they're doing. There's probably one on the way to the hospital now."

As it turned out, the small hospital had

several surgeons on staff, and one was waiting for Willis. It did take longer than an hour to repair the damage, but not by much.

Max had signed Willis in under another name. As soon as Clark got word of the shooting, he had turned around and come back to Winston Falls. He and Hershey stood guard outside recovery while Max explained what Cogburn had told him.

"Are you sure he was telling the truth?" Hershey asked.

Max handed him Willis's cell phone. "See for yourself."

All of them were concerned about the leak. "Do you think it could be Hughes?" Clark asked.

"Wouldn't that be something? He's been acting like a maniac going after the Landrys," Hershey said.

"I think it's someone in his office. He checks in all the time to update them." Clark made the comment.

"We'll let Hughes find out who the leak is after we trap the Landrys. Until then, we can't take any chances. No one in Hughes's office can know about the shipment," Max cautioned.

"Not even Hughes," Hershey added, nodding.

"Speaking of maniacs, where's Evan Patterson?" Clark asked.

Ellie had been sitting in the surgical waiting room for the past hour. Max had ordered her not to move while he went to check on Cogburn, but she couldn't wait any longer. She had to find out what was going on. Max saw her looking out and motioned for her to join them.

Hershey knew she'd heard their conversation about Patterson. He looked concerned when he said, "Being in the same hospital with him has to make you nervous."

"A little," she admitted.

"One of Sheriff Bennett's deputies is keeping Patterson company."

"Where?"

"Patterson's having a CAT scan," Clark told her. "He's been screaming about pain in his head, so they're scanning him. The sheriff wants to do everything by the book, which means Patterson has to be treated."

"There's not a damn thing wrong with him," Max said.

"Except he's frickin' crazy when it comes to Ellie," Hershey interjected.

"He already tried the chest pain route. There was nothing wrong with his heart. He knows his rights, and he's playing it for all it's worth. He's just looking for a way out, that's all," Clark said. The agent then turned the subject back to the Landrys. "How do we get Cogburn a deal so he'll cooperate?"

"Ben," Max answered. "I'll talk to my partner and let him take it to our superior. He'll decide what kind of deal Cogburn gets."

"Does your boss have the clout?" Clark asked. "Or does he have to go higher up? The more people who know about this . . ."

"He has the clout," Max assured him. "He . . ."

Max didn't finish. Two loud pops echoed up the stairwell. The agents knew the sound. Gunshots. A second later an alarm sounded. It was a low, pulsating noise.

"I'll take the south staircase," Clark shouted as he pulled his gun free.

Hershey yelled that he had the other staircase and sprinted down the long hallway.

A nurse poked her head out of a patient's room as Max grabbed Ellie. The woman shouted, "The hospital is in lockdown. Get out of the hall," and then pulled the door closed.

Max pushed Ellie into a room at the end of the hall. "Keep the door shut."

Déjà vu, she thought. Max was once again pushing her and telling her to hide.

She didn't give a second thought to who was firing the gun. It was Patterson. Had to be. People didn't realize how strong and cunning he was, and that gave him the advantage. It was Patterson, all right. And he was on a rampage.

Her heart sank, but it wasn't because of her own danger. Her concern was for Max. He had followed Clark down the stairs. How could she hide in a room if there was a possibility he could get hurt?

She leaned into the door and strained to hear. She opened it a crack. It was deathly still. Then laughter . . . eerie laughter. Patterson had gotten upstairs. How close was he? She opened the door just enough to peek down the hall. She nearly fell to her knees. At the end of the hall just outside the door to the stairs lay Hershey. He was facedown on the floor, and Patterson was standing over him, laughing. He must have surprised Hershey when he opened the door to the stairwell.

Patterson held a gun in his hand. He raised it and pointed it at Hershey's head. Ellie had to act. She opened the door wide and stepped out. He was at the opposite end of the long hallway, and his back was to her.

Her voice was strong. "Evan. Come get

me. Come on, Evan. Turn around."

He cocked his head and slowly turned. The grin on his face when he saw her sent chills down her spine.

Ellie had a split-second plan. If he raised his gun, she was going to dive around the corner, and if he came running at her, she would try to fend him off until help came. One thing was certain. She couldn't let him kill Agent Hershey.

His freaky grin terrified her when he said, "It's you. It's really you."

He stared at her for what seemed an eternity, and then he raised the gun.

Before she had time to react, Max was in front of her, firing his gun. Patterson fired a scant half second later. His bullet struck a light fixture as he dropped backward. He went down hard, but he still had the gun in his hand. He was bringing it up when Max fired again. He ran toward Patterson, his gaze locked on the weapon Patterson still clutched in his hand. Patterson wasn't moving. Max reached him, ripped the gun away, and checked his pulse. He was dead. Max pushed him off Hershey and shouted for assistance.

Ellie ran forward, slid to her knees, and took over. She saw the welt on Hershey's head, but fortunately he hadn't been shot.

She gently rolled him onto his back as he groaned and slowly opened his eyes.

"He might have a concussion," she said.

Max was astounded by how calm she was. "Why, in God's name, didn't you stay in that room?" He was so angry, he could barely keep himself from shouting at her. "You could have been killed. Do you understand? I could have lost you."

"I didn't have a choice. I saw that Patterson was about to shoot Agent Hershey in the back of the head. He was bringing his gun around and laughing, so I tried to distract him."

"Distract him?" He nearly choked on the words.

"Yes," she said. "I stepped into the hall and called to him."

"Son of a . . ." He threaded his fingers through his hair. "Son of a . . . You deliberately made yourself a target."

Ellie had never seen Max so out of control. She didn't think it was a good idea to try to explain her spontaneous plan. She knew he wouldn't respond well if she told him she intended to call Patterson's name and then run.

Fortunately, she didn't have to suffer his wrath long. The hallway filled with doctors and nurses. Aides rolled two gurneys toward them. Forgetting where she was, she rattled off orders to two nurses who were staring at her as though she'd lost her mind.

One of the nurses looked at her with a puzzled expression, and Ellie recognized her. Her name was Natalie, and Ellie had gone to school with her for a short time.

"Why is she giving us orders?" another nurse asked.

"I don't know," Natalie answered. "She's Ellie Sullivan. She does modeling in New York."

Ellie began to laugh. Oh God, now she was a model.

A doctor stepped forward and gave the same orders. He put his hand out to Ellie to help her stand. Max blocked him and pulled her to her feet.

Clark ran up the stairs, panting. "The deputy's out cold," he said. "They're taking care of him downstairs. The technician said the deputy was taking the handcuffs off. You can't wear them while you're getting a scan."

"Which Patterson knew," Max said.

Clark nodded. "He overpowered the deputy, got his gun, and started shooting. The technician dived under his desk and stayed there while Patterson shot out the glass. What happened to Hershey?"

One of the nurses pointed to the camera mounted at the ceiling. "Everything was recorded. You can watch it and find out."

The last thing Ellie wanted to do was replay what had happened. She looked down at Patterson and felt sick to her stomach. In death, the maniacal expression was gone. He looked almost peaceful.

The nightmare really was over.

## THIRTY-FOUR

Max and Ellie spent the night in a hotel close to the airport. They didn't check into their room until late that evening because of all the commotion at the hospital. Hershey and Clark had insisted on watching the surveillance tape. Then there were hours of questions, and papers to be filled out, and by the time Max and Ellie got back on the road, it was too late to catch their scheduled flight. At the hotel, Ellie showered and fell into the king-size bed exhausted.

Max was on the phone with Ben until after midnight. They were brainstorming, wanting to make certain they had a concrete plan in place to take down the Landrys. They couldn't afford any screwups or leaks. When he finally got into bed, Max's mind was racing, yet, once he took Ellie into his arms, he relaxed and fell into a deep sleep. Sometime during the night Ellie woke up and reached for Max. They made love and fell back asleep with their legs entwined.

They were able to get an early flight back to St. Louis. Clark's office had arranged the tickets and had notified the carrier that an FBI agent with a loaded weapon would be going through security. Max carried the necessary papers and badge with him.

Clark reported that Agent Hershey had a bad headache, but other than that, he was good to go. He and Clark were responsible for keeping Willis Cogburn alive and calm until the deal was done. Once his anesthetic had worn off, Cogburn had given them the time and place for what Hershey was calling the deal of the century. Since the Landrys had been in such a hurry to sneak back to Hawaii, everyone had bet that Honolulu was where the meeting would take place, and they were right. The Landrys were going to meet with the gun smugglers in a warehouse smack in the middle of the city.

Max barely said a word to Ellie the entire morning. She knew he was still upset about what she'd done in the hospital, but she wasn't in the mood to placate him.

Both of them remained quiet on the ride to the airport, but once they had boarded the plane and had fastened their seat belts, Max decided to let her have it. He closed his eyes for a minute to gather his thoughts, and then in a low voice said, "It's my job to protect you, not the other way around. Do you realize what could have happened in that hallway? If I had been two seconds late, you'd be dead. Patterson would have killed you. What if I had decided to go up the north staircase? I would have been too damn late, wouldn't I? And I would have found you on the floor, bleeding out. Son of a bitch, Ellie, you scared the hell out of me." He finally turned to look at her to see her reaction. Then he shook his head and whispered, "Son of a bitch."

Her deep breathing and closed eyes said it all. She hadn't heard a word.

# THIRTY-FIVE

Max said good-bye to Ellie at the airport, and because he was in such a hurry to catch another flight to Honolulu, he didn't have time to do more than give her a quick see-you-around kiss.

He was in a hurry, she reminded herself. Otherwise, he surely would have said something sweet in parting, wouldn't he? Come to think of it, Max had never said anything sweet to her in the past, so why would she think he would start now?

Since she had left her car in the Wheatleys' garage, she took a cab to their house and then decided she might as well spend the night. Millie and Oliver wanted to hear all about her visit home. Ellie glossed over the horror that had taken place inside the Winston Falls hospital. She told them that Patterson was dead and that she hoped he was finally at peace.

Then she told them about Ava's garden

party, and by the time she finished, they were laughing so hard, tears streamed down their cheeks.

Millie kept saying, "Poor Ava," and then she'd go into fits of laughter again.

After dinner, Ellie went up to her room and called Ava. Her sister, as cranky as she was, deserved a little sympathy.

Ava answered with, "What do you want?"

"Don't be rude, Ava. Patterson's dead."

"I heard."

"It would have been a wonderful garden party."

Ava agreed and began to talk about the details for the wedding. "I didn't mean what I said about staying away. I still expect you to be in the wedding."

Ellie didn't make any promises. She listened as Ava described the flowers and the music and even the table settings for the reception. Ellie knew what she was going to have to do, spend a fortune on another airline ticket, put on a black dress, and walk down the aisle for her sister. It didn't matter whether Ellie wanted to or not; it was the right thing to do.

She was glad she went. It was a quick and expensive weekend by Ellie's standards, but she was happy she got to spend more time with Annie and her parents. Her mother was thrilled that Ellie had stopped being stubborn and had finally agreed to be in Ava's wedding. Ava did make a beautiful bride. She was still obnoxious, but beautiful, all the same.

Once Ellie was back in her apartment, she became restless and out of sorts. She could go anywhere and do anything now that she wasn't hiding from Patterson. There was only one little problem — she didn't have the faintest idea where she belonged. And oh God, how she missed Max.

She went back to the familiar. Dr. Westfield patted her on her shoulder, which was an effusive gesture for him, and said, "Well done, Prod, well done."

"Sir, now that I've won the Chapman, will you please stop calling me Prod."

Because he was so happy about the money his department would receive, in a weak moment, he agreed. He also accepted the fact that she wasn't going to sign a contract but would fill in for a little while.

"We'll do week by week until you come to your senses and sign a contract," Westfield said, always wanting to have the last word.

One week passed and then another, and still no word from Max. Ellie went though all the emotions: anger, frustration, misery, and anger again.

Addison texted her on a regular basis — they were becoming good friends — but the only comment she'd made about Max was that he and Ben were doing undercover work for what Ben had told her was a special project.

At least once a day, Ellie told herself she was over him, and she desperately wanted to believe that, someday, it would be true.

She threw herself into her work. It was late on a Thursday afternoon, and she had just finished removing a ruptured gallbladder from a knife attack. She was heading to her locker to change when she saw Carlos Garcia's wife in the waiting room. She went in to say hello. The news was good, but Carlos had to go through a round of chemo before he could be released from the hospital. Ellie walked into his private room just as he was waking up. She was pleased to hear that his doctors were treating him so well. Amazing what a little blackmail could do.

Ellie was able to get through the days without thinking about Max, but as soon as she got home, he jumped into her thoughts. Sleep became difficult, a problem she had never had before. Misery. The word was synonymous with Max Daniels.

# THIRTY-SIX

Max was having a hell of a great day. Seeing Cal and Erika Landry down on their knees with their hands cuffed behind their backs was a thing of beauty.

Seven federal agents and twelve policemen surrounded the couple. The dealers, eight of them, were facedown on the cement floor with their hands behind their backs, but without a doubt, the Landrys were the stars of the show.

"Are you going to try to put hits out on all of us?" Ben asked. He was so happy, he couldn't stop smiling.

"I think they've run out of hit men," Max said.

Five crates filled with weapons and explosives — some he and Max had never seen before — were being opened and inspected. None of them would reach the streets now, and he was confident Cal and Erika Landry were going away for a long, long time.

Using his phone, Max took a photo of the unhappy couple as they screamed obscenities and claimed entrapment. He sent the photo to Agent Sean Goodman and Agent Rob Hughes.

Exactly one minute after receiving the picture, Agent Hughes was on the line. Max explained to the flabbergasted agent that he had been kept out of the loop because there was a leak in his office. At first, Hughes didn't take the news well, denying any possibility that there could be a traitor among his ranks. Max told him what the investigation by the special task force had turned up, that one of the assistants in Hughes's office was selling information to the Landrys for sizable amounts of money, but Hughes was still skeptical. However, when Max named the assistant and the number of cash payments that had been traced to a hidden account, Hughes relented. He was sickened that he hadn't been more astute. Max told Hughes that special agents from the task force would appear in his office momentarily to make the arrest, and Hughes agreed to assist.

The next day Hughes was on a plane to Honolulu. Since he had been chasing the Landrys for years and had the longest history with the facts, he was needed to help prepare the case. The FBI and the federal prosecutors were determined to leave no stone unturned. After looking at all the new evidence, Hughes strongly urged they add other counts to the weapons charges. With the testimony of Willis Cogburn, he insisted, they should be able to add on convictions for the attempted murder of Sean Goodman and also for ordering the murder of Dr. Ellie Sullivan.

"I want to get them for all of it," he said.

The prosecuting attorney agreed.

"Willis Cogburn testifies and then goes into witness protection," he suggested.

"I don't think that's going to be necessary," the prosecutor said. "There's no way a judge will allow these two to get out on bail to do their dirty work this time. We'll watch them closely. Potential witnesses won't have to be afraid. Dr. Eleanor Sullivan will have to testify, and I want Agent Goodman on call. Get all of them over here as soon as possible. The preliminary trial date has been moved up. Landrys' gaggle of attorneys isn't objecting."

"Why aren't they?" Max asked.

The attorney shook her head. "I guess we'll have to find out."

Max and Ben celebrated the arrest of the

Landrys over a couple of beers at their favorite bar, and Max showed him the picture he'd taken of the angry couple as they knelt in front of the agents and policemen with drawn guns.

"I wish you'd gotten one of their faces when the agents first rushed into that warehouse," Ben said. "Their expressions were priceless."

"They looked shocked, all right," Max said. "I especially liked the way Erika tried to feign innocence at first. I fully expected her to say she had no idea how those guns got there."

Ben raised his mug. "Here's to the Landrys. May their punishment fit their crimes."

"I'll drink to that," Max said.

Ben downed the rest of his beer and stood. "I've got to get home. I promised Addison we could have a quiet dinner with just the two of us tonight. I've been away so much lately."

"How is she feeling?" Max asked.

"The baby is kicking a lot. She's convinced he's going to come out carrying a soccer ball. Ellie's been terrific, texting Addison whenever she has concerns. Speaking of Ellie . . . have you talked to her?"

"No."

"She's one in a million. If I were you, I

wouldn't let her get away," Ben said as he headed for the door.

Max sat for a while, sipping his beer and mulling over Ben's words. In truth, every minute he wasn't focusing on the Landry case, he was thinking of her. It had been just a few weeks since he'd seen Ellie, but it seemed like months. He missed her.

What the hell had happened to him? The woman had blindsided him. She got right into his heart before he knew what was happening. He'd never felt this way before, and he didn't like it one damned bit. It made him vulnerable.

Don't get attached. That's what she'd told him, and she was right. There were hundreds of reasons they couldn't be together. The most obvious, they lived four thousand miles apart. Her life was centered on her career, and so was his. Their jobs were stressful and consuming. He couldn't ask her to live with the danger that surrounded him, nor could he ask her to rearrange her life to fit his. No, it would never work.

# THIRTY-SEVEN

Ellie wasn't given the choice to go to Honolulu or to stay home. Agent Goodman called her and explained that he and she were taking a flight out in four days. He believed that should give Ellie plenty of time to notify the hospital that she would be away for at least one week but probably two.

"What happens if I refuse to go?" she asked.

"Why would you refuse to go to one of the most beautiful cities in the world?" Sean asked.

"But if I did refuse?" she pressed.

"The prosecuting attorney would make it legal and force you. You don't want to make her do all that paperwork, do you?"

She really didn't have a choice. Getting away from the hospital turned out not to be such a big deal, but figuring out what to pack was a colossal pain. Ellie didn't have enough clothes in her closet to wear for one week, let alone two on an island. Her bathing suit — providing she could find it — was at least ten years old. She lived in scrubs, not sarongs and little island print dresses.

Swallowing her pride, she called Ava and explained her dilemma. Her sister had just gotten back from her honeymoon, so she was somewhat pleasant, and she loved having Ellie at her mercy. After complaining about Ellie's odd figure — she was a perfect size six except for her chest — she took the opportunity to give advice. Ava told her she was overendowed and should consider a breast reduction.

"You're joking, right?"

"You'd be a size four if you did," Ava said.

"I'd be built like a mannequin."

"Clothes drape beautifully on mannequins."

"I'm hanging up now."

"No, no, don't do that. I can't help it if you won't take constructive criticism. I'll go through the boutique and send everything you need, everything but undies and nightgowns, so spend a little money and buy some. I know you have it. Mom told me you paid off most of your loans with the money from that award and that you put twenty thousand dollars in their household account. There was a huge fight because Dad didn't want to take it, but Mom won and said the money would help with their grandchild."

"How did they take the news that they were going to be grandparents?" she asked.

"Oh, you know. Shocked at first because it was the good twin."

Ellie laughed. "But now?"

"Very excited," she said. "Dad's looking for a crib."

"Oh God, don't let him find a deal. Make him buy retail."

They talked about Annie and the help she was going to need to get through the pregnancy, and then Ellie said, "I appreciate your help with the clothes. Send me the bill."

"Don't forget to buy shoes, Ellie. And for God's sake, accessorize. Little strappy sandals and flats will work with what I'm going to send. I'll toss in some cool hoop earrings and bracelets. And, Ellie, promise me you'll wear the short royal blue dress I'm sending. I'm looking at it right now. You'll be stunning. Promise."

"Okay," she said. "I promise . . . unless it's lewd."

"Too late. You already promised."

"Which means it's lewd?"

"No, no, just a little low-cut. I'm sending everything overnight, so let me hang up and start packing what you'll need. I'm betting you won't have to have any alterations."

After she ended the call, Ellie checked the time and decided to drive over to Frontenac shopping center. Traffic was backed up on the highway, so she took side streets through Clayton and got there in twenty minutes. She parked in front of Neiman Marcus, ran in and purchased the undies and gowns she needed. She even splurged on a short silk robe. The store was having a shoe sale, and Ellie was able to get the sandals, flats, and a gorgeous pair of red stiletto heels she doubted she would ever wear. But she just had to have them because they were 70 percent off and looked great on her feet.

Was she turning into her dad? If it's a deal, get it regardless?

She told herself she wasn't getting new clothes to impress or entice Max. No, of course not. She needed the clothes because she had decided to start dating again, to get a social life outside the hospital. She would learn to have fun even if it killed her. When was the last time she had gone out to a club? A year ago? More like three years, she realized. Even then, she'd gone home before

425

the party really got started. She'd preferred her bed to jumping up and down to shrieking music.

Thursday morning she returned to Neiman Marcus to pick up her alterations. She had found a beautiful Armani summer fitted jacket and a pair of slacks and a skirt to wear with it. If she had to go into court, either outfit would be more than appropriate. She asked the alterations lady to pack the clothes in tissue so that all Ellie would have to do would be to unzip her suitcase and put everything inside.

Millie insisted on driving her to the airport, and she kept up the conversation most of the way.

"You haven't mentioned Max," she remarked.

"I'm over him."

"I see," Millie said. Ellie could hear the smile in her voice.

"Almost three weeks, Millie, and not one word. He just walked away, and I'm doing the same. I told him not to get attached."

"And he didn't."

"Exactly."

"But your reasons for trying to keep your distance have changed, haven't they?" Millie asked. "Your life isn't out of control any longer. Patterson is dead. Doesn't that change things?"

She didn't answer the question but said, "He lives in Honolulu, and I live here."

Fortunately for Ellie, they had reached the airport, and Millie couldn't prod her any longer to be reasonable.

Sean was waiting for her at the boarding gate. Ellie was surprised their seats were in first class and wondered what that had cost. She certainly didn't balk at the expense, though. The seats were much wider than in coach, and there was more leg room. She had carried her laptop with her and planned to read a couple of medical journals on the flight and maybe even watch a replay of the 2000 Super Bowl that she'd downloaded. She'd thought it would be fun to watch Kurt Warner lead St. Louis to victory again.

"We'll get to Honolulu at eight tonight, which is midnight our time," Sean said.

"Will Max and Ben be at the airport?" She couldn't stop herself from asking.

He shook his head. "They're in Maui. I don't think they'll be back until tomorrow."

"What have they been doing for the past three weeks?" she asked casually. It had actually been two weeks and five days, but she thought, if she gave the exact amount of time, Sean would know how much she missed Max.

"They've been undercover in the warehouse most of the time. Long hours wearing dirty clothes." He added, "It was worth it, though. They got the Landrys in the middle of making a weapons buy."

"Yes, I heard. Ben's wife texted me the news."

"Tomorrow afternoon is the evidentiary hearing. Landrys' attorneys are going to try to chip away at the charges. They requested the preliminary."

"Were the Landrys given bail?"

"No," Sean answered. "Their attorneys will tackle that, too. They'll try to get them out."

Ellie thought about how hard Max and the others had worked to get the Landrys behind bars. Now their well-paid attorneys would attempt to get all the charges thrown out. There was little chance a judge would toss out the weapons charges because the Landrys were caught red-handed. The attempted-murder charges weren't as clearcut. She assumed that part of Willis Cogburn's deal was that he would testify against the Landrys in return for leniency. It would be a new beginning for him, and she wondered if he would take advantage of his second chance and try to become a decent, law-abiding citizen. She had her doubts.

From hit man to what? Store clerk? That would take some adjustment.

Her thoughts moved to Carlos Garcia. He, too, had been given a second chance, and she hoped he would make good choices and grow old with his wife and child.

Ellie decided to take her mind off all her worries and watch the Super Bowl replay. Sean leaned over the armrest and watched it with her.

By the time they reached Honolulu, she was ready to stretch her legs. A driver was waiting for them and drove them to their hotel. Ellie's room was lovely. It had a balcony, and she could see the ocean from it if she leaned out and looked to the left. She could hear the waves from her room, though, and she fell asleep to the soothing sounds of the surf.

# THIRTY-EIGHT

Max was pacing in the lobby while he waited for Ellie. Sean had told her to be downstairs at one o'clock, and it was now fifteen minutes to one.

This was going to be the most difficult thing he had ever done in his life. He was trying to figure out what he was going to say to her. Using cell phones had been out of the question while he and Ben had been undercover, and he didn't want to talk to her on the phone anyway. He wanted a face-to-face for what he believed was going to be a miserable confrontation.

Ellie wasn't going to like what he was going to tell her and, in fact, would probably be furious with him, but it didn't matter. Even if she didn't understand, he knew what was best for her — as arrogant as that was.

He hated upsetting her. God knows, she'd been through enough, but he needed to explain what was on his mind because it was the right thing to do.

Max turned around and walked to the steps leading down to the pool. His mind raced.

Ellie stepped off the elevator and was walking across the marble floor of the lobby when she suddenly stopped. Max was standing in front of her. His hands were crammed in the pockets of his suit pants and his back was to her, but it was Max, all right, because her heart was doing that stupid, crazy beating, like a possessed drum.

Oh God, how was she going to get through this?

*Nice to see you again.* Yes, she remembered that's what she had decided to say. It was dorky, but it was the best she could come up with. *Nice to see you.* Forget the *again,* she decided.

"Max."

He slowly turned around. "Ellie."

They stood five feet apart staring at each other. She thought he looked tired; he thought she looked beautiful. Neither one of them said a word for what seemed a very long time.

It dawned on her that he was glaring. She retaliated by doing the same. The only thing missing was a pair of dueling pistols.

"You need to listen to what I have to say," he said.

Oh no, had he chosen a public place so she wouldn't make a scene when he told her he was moving on. She braced herself for heartache. "Go ahead."

He took a step toward her. "I love you. We're getting married, and that's the way it is. Get used to it."

"Wait . . . what?"

He grabbed her hand and tried to pull her along. "Come on, we're going to be late."

"Wait . . . what did you . . . wait."

He led her into an alcove and repeated word for word what he had just said. Her back was against the marble wall, and he'd braced his hands on either side of her. She wasn't going anywhere until he let her. She looked shell-shocked.

"I said, I love you. We're getting married, and that's the way it is."

"You love me." It wasn't a question. She was having trouble understanding.

"Yes, I do, and you love me. I don't want to hear any of your 'Don't get attached' and 'Don't fall in love with me' nonsense. I'm marrying you, Ellie Sullivan."

Tears welled in her eyes. "I don't hear a word from you for a month," she said, "and now you think you can —"

"Yeah, I do think." He leaned down and kissed her. "Your lips are so soft. You love me. I've missed holding you in my arms."

She tried to push him away. He was like a boulder that wouldn't budge. "You don't tell someone you're going to marry her. You ask."

He tried to kiss her again, but she turned her cheek, and he kissed her earlobe instead. "I asked your dad."

"You did?" She sounded breathless. "What did he say?"

"His exact words? 'Oh God, not another wedding.' "

The palms of her hands were pressed against his chest. "Did he approve?"

"Yeah, he did. I offered him a deal he couldn't refuse."

"What kind of a deal?" she whispered, dazed by what was happening. Max loved her. How could such a wonderful thing be happening to her? What had she done to deserve this?

"I promised to love you and protect you and do my best to make you happy."

"Max, it's too soon to know if you love me. We haven't known each other —"

"I love you."

"We should think about —"

"I love you. Get used to it."

"Such a romantic," she whispered.

His lips brushed over hers. "I need to hear you tell me you love me."

She could see his vulnerability. She put her arms around his neck. "I've loved you from the moment I met you."

"I know I can be gruff and abrupt at times," he confessed. "And I admit I'm a little opinionated. And I'm not always sensitive . . ."

She put her finger on his lips to stop his litany. "You're also caring, honest, kind, gentle . . ."

His arrogance was firmly back in place.

"So, I'm irresistible, huh?" he said with a grin.

She laughed. "You're the ideal man."

# THIRTY-NINE

Max wished he had been allowed to bring a camera into the courtroom to film Ellie on the witness stand. She made mincemeat out of the two-thousand-dollar-an-hour lawyers and did it with such grace.

The judge explained that this was an evidentiary hearing to determine which charges would be permitted and which would be thrown out for lack of evidence.

Ellie sat in the witness box with her hands folded in her lap, a serene expression on her face while she waited for the defense attorneys to try to discredit anything and everything she said.

Christopher Hammond, the lead attorney, had the most insincere smile she'd ever seen. He was a tall, distinguished-looking man, who, in his designer suit and perfectly knotted silk tie, was elegantly dressed . . . except for one little flaw.

The Landrys sat at the defense table,

stone-faced. Mrs. Landry in her conservative white blouse and cardigan sweater and Mr. Landry in his navy blue business suit looked the picture of propriety. Ellie had not been in the courtroom during Willis Cogburn's testimony, but Max had told her how Willis had described in great detail his relationship with the Landrys and then recounted the actions he'd taken under their orders. The slick attorneys did their best to discredit him, but Willis held up under the pressure. After an hour of testimony, he had actually become brave enough to make eye contact with the Landrys.

Hammond, his hands behind his back and staring at the floor, paced in front of the witness box for a few seconds, weighing his words before addressing Ellie.

"You have an impressive résumé, Dr. Sullivan," he began. "Someone as young as you a trauma surgeon . . . and to have received the recognition that you have . . . very impressive indeed."

If he expected her to chitchat, he was mistaken. She simply stared at him and waited. Once Hammond realized he couldn't charm her, he got down to business. He asked her to tell him what Willis Cogburn had said while she was attending to his injury on the roadside.

She answered his question but didn't embellish.

"Did you believe Mr. Cogburn when he told you he had been hired to kill you?"

"Yes, I did believe him."

"It's been established through testimony in this court that Mr. Cogburn has lied on numerous occasions to avoid prosecution. Your reasons for believing a habitual liar?"

The prosecutor started to object but sat back down as Ellie responded.

"He shot at me. So, yes, I believe he was trying to kill me."

"We are not here to determine Mr. Cogburn's actions," he reminded. "We are here to determine whether or not Mr. Cogburn was acting under the instructions of Mr. and Mrs. Landry. Do you consider yourself to be observant, Dr. Sullivan?"

"I do."

"You were in a terrifying situation," he said. "Willis Cogburn has admitted firing several shots at your vehicle in an attempt to blow up the fuel tank. Fortunately, he missed, but he did shoot out a tire."

"Is there a question, or are you just reminiscing?" the prosecutor asked.

Hammond continued, "Do you remember how many shots were fired?"

"I believe three shots were fired."

"But you're not certain."

"No."

"Yet you claim to be observant."

"I do."

"Under gunfire, I would think your perceptions would be greatly compromised. You were running for your life."

"Again," the prosecutor said, "is there a question in Mr. Hammond's ramblings?"

"Your ability to assess would be affected, wouldn't it?"

Ellie looked at the judge, then turned to Hammond. "If you'll recall, I'm a trauma surgeon. I'm trained for crisis situations."

"Yes, of course you are, but you have to admit this was different. You were being hunted by a crazed man who believed he had been hired to kill you. A delusional gunman."

Ellie didn't respond but waited for another question.

"Mr. Cogburn was in a great deal of pain at the time, was he not?"

"Yes. He'd been shot."

"Tell us exactly what you think you heard Mr. Cogburn say while you were treating him."

She repeated the conversation again word for word.

When she was finished, Hammond said,

438

"Even if he had said those words, you do accept that Mr. Cogburn could have been delusional and you could have made an inaccurate assessment as to his state of mind. After all, you'd just gone through a traumatic event yourself."

"His eyes were clear, and he was lucid," she said.

"These were your observations?"

"Yes. Willis Cogburn wasn't delusional and he wasn't lying," she insisted.

"So you believe your observations are that accurate?" he asked in a mocking tone.

Ellie was becoming irritated. Why was the attorney continuing with these inane questions?

"Yes, I do. I think I'm very observant," she said. She should have stopped there, but she couldn't resist. "I observe that the rash on your left hand isn't going to get better if you continue to use the same ointment. You're allergic to it. I observe that the gentleman in the third row on the left has a bad case of conjunctivitis — pinkeye, in layman's terms. And the woman in the second row has a bag of candies in her purse, and she's trying to figure out a way to eat them without making noise. They're M&M's. I also observe that your associate attorney at the defense table keeps looking at his watch and is very anxious to get out of here because he appears to have something going on with the court reporter."

The associate gave a look of panic and then dropped his head, staring at the desk.

Ellie paused, looked Hammond in the eye, and said, "And I observe you're unzipped."

The attorney turned crimson with embarrassment. He hastily zipped his fly.

"No more questions."

# FORTY

Max and Ellie planned to be married in Minneapolis, eleven months after he proposed. He wasn't happy about waiting, but as long as she told him she loved him every day and slept in his arms every night, he didn't complain too much.

Ellie didn't want to rush. It was important to her that her family be able to attend. She asked Annie to be her maid of honor. She was the older of the twins by two minutes, so Ellie figured Ava couldn't throw a fit.

The wedding was simple but joyful. Annie's baby girl, Meghan, was almost four months old and smiling all the time. She could usually be found in the crook of her grandfather's arm. He doted on her. Since Patterson's death and the birth of his first grandchild, Ellie's father looked twenty years younger. He'd even started exercising, walking a couple of miles every morning. He was determined to stay fit so that he would be around to watch his granddaughter grow up.

As a temporary solution, Annie had moved in with her parents until after the baby was born and she could decide what she was going to do with her life. She had passed the bar in California and knew that she would eventually move back to San Diego, but she didn't have any idea where she wanted to work. Her parents were helping her pay off her student loans, though she vowed she was going to repay every penny.

Max had kept his promise to her. Through his connections, he discovered the whereabouts of Lucas Ryan, Annie's lover. An old buddy from the FBI academy linked Max with Michael Buchanan, a Navy Seal, who was currently stationed in San Diego. Buchanan explained that he couldn't give out any sensitive information, but he'd see what he could do. Within the week, Max got his call. Lucas Ryan had been sent to Afghanistan, and that was all the information Buchanan could give. Max was told nothing about what Ryan was doing there or when he would be home.

# FORTY-ONE

One summer morning, with Meghan in her arms, Annie opened the front door, and there he stood, the man who had broken her heart. His left leg was in a cast, and he was using a cane. She wasn't sympathetic. She wanted to grab the cane and hit him over the head with it. But she also wanted to hug him. She stood there staring up at him and didn't have the faintest idea what to say. He looked wonderful. Dark hair, dark eyes, tanned face, great body — he was an extremely attractive man. No wonder she had fallen for him. He was tall, dark, and handsome.

And a snake in the grass who had left her when she needed him most, she reminded herself.

Lucas seemed as tongue-tied as she was, but he was first to recover.

"I've missed you."

She shook her head. "I don't believe you."

443

"May I come in?"

"No." She stepped back so he could come inside.

He smiled at the baby as he walked past. "She's cute," he remarked. "Are you babysitting?"

"Sort of."

"Annie . . ."

"You left me, Lucas. You never called; you never . . ."

She stopped because she knew, if she continued, she would start crying. Meghan started to squirm in her arms, and Annie realized she'd raised her voice. She shifted the baby to her other arm and quietly said, "I needed you."

"I love you," he said. "You know that. I couldn't tell you I was leaving, and I couldn't contact you. It was a special operation."

She didn't acknowledge his explanation. "What happened to your leg?"

"Shrapnel."

"Sit down and put your foot up," she ordered. She pushed the ottoman in front of the sofa. "Would you like something to drink before you leave?"

"I'm not leaving. I know you're upset, and you have every right, but . . ."

She poked him in the chest and, in a soft

voice so her daughter wouldn't become frightened, said, "I don't want to love you."

Tears came into her eyes, and she wanted to curse. The last thing she needed now was to become weepy. There would be plenty of time for that after he left.

"But you do."

"I did," she corrected.

He sat down on the sofa and pulled her onto his lap. She didn't fight him because she held the baby. Her back was ramrod straight.

His hand moved to the back of her neck. "How come you keep getting prettier?"

A compliment wouldn't soften her heart, she decided, but the baby was smiling at him and gurgling. He reached out and stroked Meghan's cheek. She was quick. She grabbed his finger and began to gnaw on it.

"She's teething," Annie explained.

Lucas looked around the room with a puzzled expression. "Does your mom run a day care or something?"

"Or something," she answered. "Are you still a Navy Seal?"

"Yes," he said. "Marry me, Annie."

"You're out of your mind. Shrapnel hit your head, too, didn't it?"

He pulled her toward him and kissed her.

His mouth was warm and coaxing. She couldn't stop herself from responding.

"I love you," he said again.

"And I love you," she admitted. "But that doesn't mean —"

He kissed her again, and she didn't resist. She wrapped her arm around his neck and leaned into him. Oh, how she had missed him.

And shed buckets of tears. No, she wasn't going to go through that again.

"I've got a surprise for you," he said as he reached into his pocket. "I've been carrying this around for a year now."

It was an engagement ring. Annie stared into his eyes and saw the torment there.

"Annie, I'm so sorry I couldn't tell you. Will you marry me?"

"I have to think about it," she whispered. "And I've got a surprise for you, too."

She stood, then placed Meghan in his lap. "Meet your daughter."

# FORTY-TWO

Yet another wedding.

Ellie was thrilled with Annie's news and hoped that Lucas's family was as wonderful as Max's. Simon had been Max's best man at the wedding, and his other brothers had been groomsmen. She loved all of them, but she had a special bond with their parents. They were such kind, loving people. Simon had saved Max's life, and his parents had nurtured him.

Max's two-bedroom apartment overlooking the ocean was her home now. Once she was licensed to practice medicine in Hawaii, she went to work at one of the hospitals in the city. Ellie loved watching the weather channel in the dead of winter and laughing every time she heard about another snowstorm in the Midwest. Max remarked that her laughter sounded absolutely ghoulish.

The Wheatleys, like Max's parents, had already visited. Everyone who came hated to go home. Who could blame them?

"We live in paradise," she whispered to Max late one night. They were in bed and had just made love.

"You're still awake?"

She laughed. "Yes," she said. "I've been thinking about the Landrys. Ben told me they were appealing the verdict."

"On what grounds?" he asked, rolling onto his back. He stacked his hands behind his head and yawned. "That they don't like life in prison?"

"The judge really gave it to them, didn't he?"

"They gave the order to kill you. Life in prison isn't long enough, as far as I'm concerned."

"What do you think happened to Greg Roper? After he pointed to those photos of Cal and Erika Landry, he vanished. Do you think he's still alive? Or did they get to him and kill him? I hope he ran and hid from them."

"There's a good chance he's still alive," he said. "Cogburn told us he went to Roper and threatened to kill him and his family if he ever showed his face in St. Louis again. The police still have a missing person's file active on him, but there's hope he'll show up sometime."

"I hope so." Ellie yawned. She trailed her fingers down Max's chest and cuddled up against him. "Simon called."

"What's wrong with him now?"

"He thought he found a lump, but by the time he finished describing it to me, he decided it might be a callus."

"He loves having a doctor in the family."

She adjusted her pillow and closed her eyes. "Don't forget we're having dinner with Ben and Addison and little Benjamin this weekend."

"I won't."

Ellie laid her head on Max's chest, and he stroked her hair. Since they had just made passionate love, he thought she needed to hear how much she pleased him. "Our marriage . . ." He paused while he searched for the right words to tell her how happy she made him. "Our marriage . . ."

Her deep breathing stopped him.

Smiling to himself, he pulled the sheet up over her and whispered, "It's all good."

# ABOUT THE AUTHOR

**Julie Garwood** is the bestselling author of historical and contemporary romance. More than 35 million copies of her books are in print, in dozens of languages, around the world. One of her most popular novels, *For the Roses*, was adapted for a *Hallmark Hall of Fame* production on CBS. Julie lives in Leawood, Kansas.

The employees of Thorndike Press hope you have enjoyed this Large Print book. All our Thorndike, Wheeler, and Kennebec Large Print titles are designed for easy reading, and all our books are made to last. Other Thorndike Press Large Print books are available at your library, through selected bookstores, or directly from us.

For information about titles, please call:
  (800) 223-1244

or visit our Web site at:
  http://gale.cengage.com/thorndike

To share your comments, please write:
  Publisher
  Thorndike Press
  10 Water St., Suite 310
  Waterville, ME 04901